*Ernest,
Enjoy Amsterdam ♡
Cassandra*

Going Dutch

CASSANDRA DALLAS

ProPress Books
Massapequa, New York

The opinions expressed in this manuscript are solely the opinions of the author and do not represent the opinions and thoughts of the publisher. The author has represented and warranted full ownership and/or legal right to publish all the materials in this book.

Going Dutch
All Rights Reserved
Copyright 2017© Cassandra Dallas

Cover Photo used with permission © Kuz'min Pavel\shutterstockinc

This book may not be reproduced, transmitted or stored in whole or in part by any means, including graphic, electronic, or mechanical without the express written consent of the publisher except in the case of brief quotations embodied in critical articles and reviews.

This is a work of fiction. Names, characters, places and incidents either are the product of the author's imagination or are used fictitiously, and any resemblances to any actual persons, living or dead, events, or locales are entirely coincidental.

ProPress Books, Inc.
Massapequa, New York
http://www.propressbooks.net

ISBN 978-0996994606

PRINTED IN THE UNITED STATES OF AMERICA

To Robert
  Day and night
  You are the man of my dreams

This is a work of fiction.
Resemblances to any persons or events are
almost entirely coincidental.
And no men were harmed
in the writing of this novel —
that I know of, anyway.

— *Cassandra Dallas*

ACKNOWLEDGMENT

To the Long Beach, Long Island Writers' Circle —
thank you all for welcoming me.
Your high standards of excellence
are what I work towards each time I put pen to paper.

Chapter 1
First Impressions

Did you have to wear your low cut black sweater and tight jeans? I thought as I ran through the KLM Dutch Airline terminal at New York's John F. Kennedy International Airport.

The TSA agent winked at me as I passed through the metal detector and pulled me over for a "random" search. "Just have to pat you down, honey, it will only take a second," he said. He ordered me to take off my belt, then he squeezed my rear and breasts. More like a strip search if you ask me. By the time he was done, I felt like I had been turned inside out. Plus I was really upset I'd be late for the last flight out of New York to Amsterdam.

By the time I reached the gate, the entrance to the plane from the terminal was closed. I pleaded with the KLM guy and told him what had happened at security. He sympathized with me and allowed me to board the plane.

I ran down the aisle to Row 10, and opened the overhead compartment to store my carry on suitcase. It was full so I tried the one in the row in back of me. I started to push my bag in when a female flight attendant grabbed it from me and threw it on the floor.

"You cannot put your things over someone else's seat. Only use yours."

"But mine is full, miss," I said. "Where would you like me to stick it?"

"Stick it…what do you mean by that? This bag is too large for the overhead anyway. You should have checked it before boarding. You are delaying the flight."

"This is the first time I haven't be able to use the storage space over another row. Boy, you at KLM are difficult, aren't you?"

"I am going to call security. I will have you removed from the aircraft!" she said and turned to walk to the front of the plane.

A tall dark-haired man blocked the flight attendant's path. "Wait just a minute, Christina, let's see if we can work this out," he said. I hadn't noticed him before. He was well over six feet, and looked down at the flight attendant with royal blue eyes. "I apologize to both of you. I travel on KLM regularly as you know, Christina, and so I've taken some liberties and have three carry-on bags stowed in the overhead. I am in the same row as this passenger. So all this is my fault. Please allow the young lady to put her bag in the space behind us. We all want to get underway as soon as possible, I am sure." He continued to stare down at the flight attendant, raising one thick eyebrow.

"Well," Christina said, "I suppose it would be all right to put your bag in this compartment," and she pointed to the one over row 11.

"Wonderful, and I will help you if you'd like," the man said to me.

I breathed a sigh of relief. "Yes, that would be great."

The flight attendant walked swiftly to the front of the plane and grabbed the microphone. "Please fasten your seat belts. KLM apologizes for the delay," she announced.

My savior put the bag in the overhead, and closed the compartment door.

"After you, miss," he said and gestured to the window seat.

I sat down and he did the same. Finally, I could relax.

"So, you just made the flight?"

"Yes, I got delayed at security, but I'm here now," I said, and smiled at him. "I don't know how to thank you. She was really going to have me thrown off the plane."

"Oh, don't pay any attention to Christina. She is always anxious to get home to her boyfriend in Amsterdam."

I looked him over more closely than I had before. Eyes. Blue. Hair. Black. Mouth. Full. Wide. Sexy.

I was so entranced by the man that I didn't notice Christina standing next to him. "Sorry Paul," she said, bending at the waist to show off her cleavage, "I know you usually fly first class but this was the only seat available at the last minute." She then stood at attention and pointed her right forefinger at me. "Miss, you MUST buckle your seat belt now! Hurry up, you are delaying the flight!" Then she turned to Mr. Red Hot and said something in what I assumed was Dutch. I caught the intent of her remark when I heard her say "Amerikaans!" as she rolled her eyes upward.

I smoothed my low cut short-sleeved black sweater, fluffed up my shoulder length strawberry blonde hair, and reached into my purse for a book to read. I crossed my legs to better show off my new black ankle boots and buckled my seat belt.

"My seat belt is buckled and I am ready for take off, Madam, whenever y'all are!"

I tried to read my book, but heard Mr. Blue Eyes say something in a foreign language to the flight attendant. He then kissed her three times on her cheeks, European style. She left to attend to preflight procedures.

"Please excuse Christina's behavior. She was rude just now, again. Getting to be a habit with her I'm afraid."

"No apologies necessary. So the flight attendant is a friend of yours? I'm afraid my dinner will be served to me on my lap!"

"She is upset with me for being late, too. By the way, I'm Paul Vermeer."

"Nice to meet you, Paul. I'm Deena Green. Y'all are Dutch?" I asked as his large royal blue eyes looked straight into my green almond shaped ones.

"Well, mostly Dutch. You are American, yes?"

"Yes, I am. I call New York City my home now," I said with pride. I glanced out of the window and saw we were in the clouds. I hadn't realized we had taken off already.

"I can tell you are a New Yorker, you gave Christina a definite New York attitude. Not all Dutch people are like her."

I looked at Paul and decided I liked what I saw. His thick tousled black hair fell on his forehead appealingly. He was probably in his mid thirties. I glanced at him from his neck down - his black dress shirt fit tight across his chest, around his shoulders and his upper arms.

I was usually very talkative. Now I seemed to be at a loss for words. "That's nice to hear," I finally said. "I've been looking forward to my first trip to Amsterdam."

"First trip, yes ? I can't wait to get back home."

"Then we have something in common. I can't wait to get to Amsterdam too!" I was beginning to relax sitting next to this attractive man.

"Yes, my German girlfriend is waiting there for me. She is tall and broad, as most German women are. A brunette with soulful brown eyes. Would you like to see a picture of her?" Paul said, grinning.

Bad news, a girlfriend! He reached under the seat in front of him, took out his cell phone from a sleek black briefcase and proudly displayed a picture of a huge dog, a Rottweiler. "Here is my girlfriend - Pandora! She's from Rheinberg, Germany. In that country, they don't crop a dog's tail. Much better! I brought her home from the breeder there four years ago on my 30th birthday," he said and laughed. "She is very loyal and protective of me. She has my heart."

"So dog yes, girlfriend no?" I said, and smiled.

"Correct, Deena. A woman as lovely as you must have several boyfriends, yes?" I liked the way he spoke. His voice was low, with a throaty quality to it. When he said my name, the accent was on the Dee, drawing out the ee sound. I liked that a lot.

"Well, I'm in between boyfriends now." The truth was my last boyfriend left me for a tall, slim brunette. I had vowed not to get so attached anytime soon.

"Then I'm lucky to have caught this flight, yes," he said. "Very lucky. Business or pleasure in Amsterdam?" His pronunciation of "pleasure" sounded French to me.

"Mostly business, but I'd like to relax and sightsee as well. You have a French accent."

"Good guess, yes. My mother was from Brussels. My first language was French. Jean-Paul is my real name. My close friends and family call me that. I'm Dutch on my father's side and was brought up in Amsterdam."

Jean-Paul. The name suited him – he did have a French look to him – his big blue eyes, his thick dark hair and his curved lips, which were just full enough for my taste. His square jaw, solid build and height were definitely Dutch.

"What about you? Are you one hundred percent American?"

"Yes, I'm originally from Baltimore, Maryland. I went to college in New York City and never left."

"So you are a southern belle! Your eyes, what an unusual color green. Your way of speaking is so interesting. You look very familiar to me. We've met before, yes, maybe in New York?"

Quite a charming pick-up line. "Thank you for the compliments. I don't think we've met before," I said, and laughed.

He turned to look at me face to face. "Then we must get to know each other better. I apologize but I'm busy Friday evening after we land. How about Saturday morning? I can pick you up at your hotel and show you the city. We can have breakfast together if you'd like."

"If I say yes, we'll be going Dutch, won't we? " "Going Dutch? Oh, you mean that we each pay for our own meal? Not on the first date, it would be rude of me to treat a guest in our country that way," Paul said and grinned at me.

"No Dutch treat then? In the interest of furthering Dutch-American relations, I will agree to your terms for one day only. After that, we'll see, won't we?"

I was thinking any terms, Dutch or not, would be fine as long as this handsome man was with me. I noticed his face was perfect, except for a scar on the right side which started under his cheekbone and ended at the corner of his mouth. It was darker than his light complexion and looked like the result of a wound. The scar made him all the more interesting.

"Good, I'll pick you up at your hotel. How does ten o'clock Saturday morning sound?"

Before I had a chance to answer, the pilot made an announcement: "All passengers and crew members please return to your seats at once and fasten your seat belts. We will be experiencing unexpected turbulence."

I am a coward when it comes to anything other than smooth sailing in an airplane. The pilot was not underestimating conditions either as the aircraft immediately dropped in altitude. Without thinking I squeezed Paul's right wrist with my left hand.

"Sorry," I apologized. "Bumpy airplane flights scare me."

"That's quite alright. Don't worry – we should be out of this fairly soon," he reassured me.

I was so nervous that I started shaking. Paul pushed the armrest between us out of the way, put his arm around my shoulders and drew me close to him. I leaned against him – I felt his hard, muscular body, strong and reassuring.

In a few minutes, the turbulence subsided. "See, Deena, I told you. It's over. I can still hold you if you want me to. By the way, is breakfast on Saturday morning at ten OK with you?" He took out a pad of graph paper and a pen from his briefcase. "Let me give you my cell phone number just in case you need to reach me."

He wrote his name and number

Jean-Paul Vermeer 020 607 2211

His handwriting looked like calligraphy, it was so beautiful and ornate. There was an old world quality to it. I wondered where he had learned to write like that.

I carefully placed the paper he had written his name and phone number on in an inside compartment of my purse, next to my passport. He put his arm around me again. I really liked being held by him. "Breakfast at ten would be lovely," I said. I yawned and realized I was very tired. Comforted by being so close to him, I fell asleep.

When I woke up sometime later, Paul still had his arm around me. He was napping. I wanted to stand up and stretch a bit, and then go to the restroom. As gently as I could I took his arm from around my shoulders and put it by his side. There was a light on over the seat behind me so I was able to get another good look at him. Strong square chin. Long legs. Large hands. His nose was crooked, as if it had been broken in a fight and hadn't healed quite right. His mouth was soooo unfairly tempting. I decided then and there I wanted those lips on mine.

Before I stood up I noticed on each of the fingers of his right hand a tattoo in dark blue letters spelling the initials

J P D V

in the same ornate script he had written his name and phone number. Paul was so handsome, despite his scar and imperfect nose. I was tempted to run my fingers through his hair, to smooth the unkempt but appealing look.

Instead, I carefully stood up, stepped over his long legs, walked down the aisle to the tiny bathroom cubicle and wedged myself inside.

There's just too damn much of you Deena, I thought as I examined myself in the small mirror. *Too much hair. Too much mouth. Too much boobs for your sweater and too much butt for your jeans. And not enough height.*

Maybe European men are different than American men. Maybe they will appreciate my extra curves. American guys all seemed to want women that are pencil thin. Just isn't ever going to be me, I concluded. I quickly did what I had to in the bathroom, reapplied my light pink lipstick, brushed my hair and went back to my seat.

Paul woke up as I sat down next to him. "Hi Deena," he said, his voice sounding deeper than it had before. "Feeling better? Let me get you a glass of wine. Red or white?"

"Red is fine. Thank you." He came back in a few minutes with two glasses. He gave me one, sat down and said, "Proost – cheers!"

"The wine is very good. I guess you know most of the crew members on board."

"Yes, I travel to New York often. My brother and I have an architectural firm in Amsterdam, but I confer with colleagues in Manhattan. I went to school at Pratt Institute in Brooklyn. And what do you do?"

I told him I became a gemologist after having first attended New York University, and then studying at The Gemological Institute of America while working for a diamond dealer. We drank the wine and talked about our college experiences in New York.

Before I fell asleep again, I thought my fortune had changed for the year 2013. Thursday, July 11, 2013 was turning out to be a great day for one lucky witch, me!

Chapter 2
Welcome to Amsterdam

"We've landed, Deena. Welcome to Amsterdam!" Paul was trying to wake me, not an easy task. I was having such a lovely dream, too. But the wonderful feeling continued as I woke up, because sitting right next to me was the man dreams are made of – tall, dark-haired and too handsome Paul Vermeer.

"Can I get your bag from the overhead? What color is it?"

"Red, my favorite color," I replied. While I struggled to wake up, he had already taken my carryon from the overhead and put it in the aisle, then sat back down next to me.

"We'll share a taxi to your hotel. Where are you staying?"

"The City Lights Hotel, right near the Leidseplein."

"Great, I live only a short walk from there. We can't go through customs together, but I'll meet you at baggage claim."

"Thank you. Are you sure about the taxi? I don't want to hold you up. I've got a couple of suitcases to wait for, plus I'll be longer going through customs than you." I wasn't used to this gentlemanly treatment. I always took care of my own travel details.

"I insist. Two suitcases, how could you manage them without me?"

I unbuckled my seatbelt, and stood up to stretch out a bit. *It'll feel good to get to the hotel and take a shower*, I thought.

I looked down at Paul. He was staring at my bare midsection. My sweater must have pulled up when I stretched.

"Thanks for the view. You have lovely skin….."

"Let's go!" I said, embarrassed. Lovely or not, I thought that I had much too much of everything.

Except height. He was probably a foot taller than me, about six foot two. I was only five foot two.

We walked side by side until we had to separate at customs. "See you at baggage claim," he said as he went to the European Union citizens' section, and I went to the foreigners' side.

I had to wait on line about thirty minutes. *He probably has changed his mind. What could he see in me?* I thought. *For sure, he has the pick of any actress or model he wants.*

I found the baggage claim area, and started to look for my luggage. "Deena, over here, I've got your suitcases." It was Paul! He had waited for me.

"How did you know they were mine?"

"Red suitcases, what else would you have?"

"Thank you!"

He called over a porter to help bring the luggage to the taxi stand.

We were in a taxi in no time. "City Lights Hotel, please," he said to the driver.

"Yes, Mr. Vermeer, right away," the driver replied.

"Wait a minute. The flight attendant knows you. And now the taxi driver…….?"

"Amsterdam is a small city. Everyone knows everyone here," he said, grinning.

I wasn't so sure about that. There was more to Mr. Paul Vermeer than met the eye. Even though that was quite enough.

Paul pointed out several famous places on our way to the hotel. We passed the Rijksmuseum which was newly renovated. I was overwhelmed by the beauty of the city. Charming old buildings resembling large dollhouses lined the streets. It seemed at almost every corner we turned there was a canal. Tour boats, pleasure boats, water taxis and houseboats created morning rush hour traffic. We passed several lush parks, and every street had beautiful trees and flowers. Outdoor cafes were plentiful.

Too soon we arrived at the hotel. "I love your city Paul, it's wonderful!"

"When I show you my favorite places you will love it even more. Are you looking forward to tomorrow, yes? I'll pick you up here at 10:00," he said as we got out of the taxi and walked into the hotel lobby. "Wait a moment Deena and I'll see about your room. I know the front desk staff here quite well."

I sat down on a comfortable sofa and waited for him. I was too tired to protest. In a few minutes, Paul was back with the key card to my room. "Number 510, can I help you bring your things up, yes?"

"No Paul y'all have done too much for me already. I'll just ask the bellhop to help me."

"Well, …OK. See you tomorrow morning."

"See you then. What shall I wear?"

"Something…..hmmm…..pretty, yes. Like you, Deena, pretty."

"Try my best." I waved goodbye to Paul, and he waved back at me. I followed the bellhop and my luggage into the elevator. I realized I was very hungry. I asked the young man if he could bring some fruit to the room.

"Mr. Vermeer has already ordered breakfast for you. It will be delivered to you very soon," he said.

We arrived at my room. I thanked and tipped the bellhop, closed the door and started to unpack. *I must be careful as Mr. Very Handsome Paul Vermeer could distract me from my purpose in coming to Amsterdam. It was more than just business, it was a mission.*

I thought about how important it all was to my Uncle Alan and to me as well. Alan Rosen was not really my uncle, but a dear friend of my parents. Uncle Alan's father and grandfather were Dutch Jews who could trace their ancestry back to the 1600s in Amsterdam. In the decades before the Second World War, Amsterdam was the center of the world's diamond industry. The city had a large community of Jewish diamond cutters and polishers. Uncle Alan's grandfather was among the most talented and respected in the industry.

Most of the Dutch Jewish artisans and their families were killed at the hands of the Nazis. Uncle Alan's immediate family survived by being hidden by brave Amsterdam citizens and moved to America after the war. His father started a diamond finishing business in New York and Uncle Alan worked in the business as well, taking it over when his father retired.

Uncle Alan wanted to bring Jewish diamond artisans and their skills back to Amsterdam. He felt the Jewish community would be revitalized by the new arrivals. Amsterdam was unique among European cities in that from the early 1600s up until the time of the Second World War it had provided a safe home to its Jewish residents. Uncle Alan hoped that long and successful partnership could be rekindled. Plus conditions would improve for the artisans, who worked in virtual sweatshops in Manhattan. He had already enlisted several young men who, with their families, wanted to relocate to Amsterdam.

My job was to make contact with lawyers and industry people in The Netherlands and find out how to go about obtaining government approvals for the project.

Working for Uncle Alan in his diamond finishing business, I had proved myself to be a very successful salesperson. He believed in me, and my powers of persuasion. He thought I was the right person to find out how to establish ourselves in Amsterdam.

Uncle Alan's idea was a good one. I believed, as he did, that

Amsterdam's Jewish community would grow and strengthen if we were successful. Serious business, and I was not about to be side tracked by anyone, not even the all too attractive Paul Vermeer.

There was a knock at the door. Brunch was served. I ate the delicious fruit and a croissant. I was grateful to Paul for being so attentive to my needs. Before lying down for a nap, I telephoned the operator for a wake-up call at two o'clock. I wanted to do some sightseeing, with my last stop being the Grand Canal and its famous swans.

Sleep came easily to me. I dreamt a fairy tale like dream – a handsome prince had chosen me from all the beautiful women in his kingdom to be his princess.

I woke up before the call. I looked in the mirror in the large bathroom, expecting to see a droopy-eyed me. Instead I was wide awake! I did sleep soundly, so perhaps I was well rested.

I took a leisurely shower. I got dressed in a new light blue tee shirt, matching shorts and navy blue running shoes. I brushed my hair and put on some lipstick. I packed a small jogging purse with the hotel key card, my cell phone, sunglasses and twenty Euros and fastened it around my waist.

As I was leaving the hotel room, I glanced in the mirror. The shirt and shorts were extra snug in my breasts and butt, and part of my bare midsection was showing. *Oh well, this is Europe, where people sunbathe in the nude. No one will even take note of your extras.*

I headed to the concierge desk to get a tourist map of Amsterdam.

"How are y'all today?" I said to the man behind the concierge desk. He glanced up at me. He appeared to be in his mid fifties, with reddish brown hair and dark brown eyes. He was of medium height and build. "I'd like directions to the Grand Canal, please."

"That depends where on the Canal you would like to go, miss…"

"Deena, Deena Green. Pleased to meet you," I said and stretched my arm across the desk to shake his hand. I could see from his badge his name was Mark. When we shook hands, he smiled at me. I was probably being overly friendly. Couldn't help myself, just being me.

"Yes, well, hello Deena, I'm Mark. Nice to meet you, too. Here's a map you can use to guide you to the Grand Canal. As you can see, it traverses the city," he explained as he showed me the details on a tourist map.

"I'm interested in seeing the famous swans."

"Hmmm. That part of the canal is in the Red Light District. It is lovely there in the daytime. Just be careful. You should be all right, but don't stay there by yourself after dark. And don't bring any valuables or take pictures in the District."

"Thank you Mark. Could you suggest some sightseeing along the way to the Grand Canal? I have the whole afternoon and evening free."

"I would have recommended you start at the Rijksmuseum. But it is undergoing extensive renovations, and not yet open to the public. But the Hermitage Amsterdam is great too and not as overwhelming as the Rijksmuseum. Here, I'll show you how to get there."

Mark circled the museum on the map and showed me the shortest route from the hotel. He then drew a line with a red pen from the museum to the Grand Canal.

"Enjoy your day and evening, Deena, but be careful."

"Thank you for your help, Mark, I will!"

I left the hotel by the nearest exit and started jogging towards the museum. It was a beautiful day, and getting warmer. I stopped briefly to put my hair up in a ponytail.

I had just turned thirty in February and noticed recently if I didn't jog for a few days, it was harder to get back in shape. I was so busy the week before I left New York I hadn't had time to exercise. I knew the run today would be tiring.

The streets were crowded with people walking their dogs. I had to be careful not to be run over by the herds of bicyclists. They seemed not to take notice of anything or anyone. After running for about ten minutes, I realized I wasn't tired one bit! I didn't feel sore either, as I expected to be. I was breathing easily, and felt like I could go on for hours!

I arrived at the museum. I stood on line to purchase an admissions ticket, and was ready to explore the sister museum to The Hermitage in Russia.

Everywhere I turned there was wonderful artwork. I was drawn to the paintings of Johannes Vermeer, two of which were on loan from the Rijksmuseum. *I could spend a whole day just admiring these. Vermeer? Isn't that Paul's last name? Are they somehow related?*

I got lost in the world of the beautiful Hermitage collection. A security guard tapped me on the shoulder. "Miss," he said, "the museum is closing now. It's five o'clock. Please hurry! Follow me to the exit."

Where did the time go? I wondered.

"Thank you sir," I said as I tried to keep up with him. "Could you show me the fastest way to the Grand Canal?"

"Yes Miss, but that's in the Red Light District. Are you sure you want to go there by yourself?"

"Well of course! I'm a city girl from New York. I'm used to traveling solo."

"OK, here's a map. Follow this route," he said, and pointed it out to me.

I left the museum and started jogging, but soon slowed down. Wonderful scents were coming from the open door of a bakery I had just passed. My appetite needed to be satisfied! I retraced my steps and hurried in. I tried to find the famous Dutch stroopwafels in the glass enclosed pastry case.

Ah, there they are!

"May I have two?" I said to the young blonde woman behind the counter as I pointed to the delicious looking confections.

"But of course. You have come to the best place in all of The Netherlands for our famous Dutch treat."

I paid for my treats, and took one out of its bakery bag as I waved goodbye to the clerk.

Oh how delicious! Two thin waffles with a caramel filling! There goes my resolve to lose weight in Amsterdam!

After finishing off one stroopwafel, and clutching the bag with the other one in it, I started jogging towards the Grand Canal.

Soon I had to slow down and walk so I could concentrate on finding my way. I also wanted to enjoy the details of the beautiful architecture.

I noticed flags emblazoned with yellow lions on a blue background adorning many of the buildings. I asked an older man what the lions signified and he explained to me, in impeccable English, that they were the personal coat of arms of the new Dutch monarch, King Willem-Alexander. He said that the King was the first male monarch of The Netherlands since 1890. His mother, beloved Queen Beatrix, abdicated the throne in April of this year.

Most of the people were tall, much taller than Americans. Men and women alike were slim too, probably from bicycling everywhere.

The map had been easy to follow, but now it was more difficult, as the streets became narrow and winding. Many did not have street signs, and I had to ask directions a few times. I had no problem finding people to help me as everyone spoke English. Finally, the Grand Canal was before me at the end of yet another picturesque pathway.

Dozens of swans were in full regalia in the waterway they claimed as their own. Their long, graceful necks and the brilliant white of their feathers were perfect. I loved their pure innocence.

I decided to jog alongside the canal, but first I bent down to tighten my shoelaces. I picked up my head and realized I was nose to nose with a black canine snout. The snout was attached to a huge dog with a wide, black head, thick coated black body, big brown eyes, and reddish brown markings on its massive chest, neck, front legs and above its eyebrows. The dog wagged its long tail. It was definitely a friendly Rottweiler. I couldn't resist petting its smooth ears and head. The Rottie responded by growling with pleasure, and giving me a doggie lick on my mouth. I wondered who the dog belonged to. I noticed two tags on its collar. Maybe there was a name or phone number or other form of identification on them.

I heard someone shouting, "Wait, girl, wait!" I stood up, turned around and saw a man running towards me.

I waved to him, and shouted back, "Here sir, here is your dog!!"

The man slowed from a run to an easy jog. When he reached us, he looked at me and laughed. "Deena!" he said. "What a nice surprise!" It was Paul Vermeer, and the dog was without a doubt his German girlfriend Pandora. "My clever dog found you for me. She is trained to track people. She must have picked up your scent from the clothes I wore on the plane. Good girl!"

"She's smart, and friendly. She gave me a wet kiss," I said as we both bent down to pet the big dog at the same moment. We smiled at each other and then laughed. Paul and I sat on a nearby bench, and Pandora lay submissively at Paul's feet.

"Dora," Paul said as he hugged her around her thick neck, "don't run away from me anymore! Deena, what are you doing here? You are a little out of the way from your hotel, yes?"

"I wanted to see the famous swans on the Grand Canal. They were at the top of my sightseeing list in Amsterdam." I couldn't help noticing his tight black tee shirt and black shorts. I looked him over and thought his clothes served as a backdrop to incredibly powerful looking legs, which were longer than possible in a mere mortal. I stared at his lower limbs. "You must bike a lot."

Paul took my chin in his right hand and looked into my eyes. "Since my Pandora gave you a kiss, it's only fair I do the same...." He moved closer to me and kissed me. I expected a quick preview but instead was treated to a full length x-rated movie. I was spellbound by his full, moist lips which sought and found mine. I was sure I would melt from the heat wave which had nothing to do with the weather.

"Mmm, very nice, Deena. Very," he said, and kissed me once more. "Would you like to have dinner with me tonight, yes? I have had a change of plans."

I didn't have to think twice. "Sure, sounds great! What time?"

Before he had a chance to respond, his cell phone rang. He answered it and listened for a moment. "Excuse me, Deena," he said as he stood up and walked several feet behind me.

He spoke into the phone in Dutch. He said something I could not fully understand, *"ik kom definitief niet naar De Wallen deze nacht."* And he repeated it, louder the second time, *"ik kom definitief niet naar De Wallen deze nacht."*

What did all that mean? He was definite he was not going somewhere tonight. I got the gist of most of what he had said from my knowledge of Yiddish, similar in many ways to Dutch and German. But what or where was De Wallen? That was where he definitely was not going.

As I was trying to make some sense out of it, he startled me by pulling me up by my hand. "I apologize for the interruption. A business call. Ah yes, dinner, how about nine o'clock? I'll pick you up and take you to my favorite restaurant. How does that sound? Are you thirsty?" he said as he jogged over to a nearby water fountain.

Pandora and I followed him at a slower pace. I drank from one spout as Paul drank from another one next to me. He turned the children's spout on for Pandora. I was grateful for the cool water, and splashed some on my face and my neck. My hair had come undone and fell into the fountain. I was soaking wet.

    Paul looked at me, his blue eyes widening and then narrowing. "Nice. You look great. What's in the bag?"

"Oh, a stroopwafel. Want to have some?" I said, trying to distract him from staring at my wet tee shirt.

"Yes, I'll have some." I opened the bag and offered him a piece. "Not only that Deena, I'll have some of you. Later," he said as he munched on the pastry.

Oh no, I'm blushing! I can feel my cheeks getting red hot! Can't you keep your cool Deena? What's he saying? I better pay attention!

    "My new club is just around the corner from here. I planned all the renovations, and it's on schedule to open next Saturday night. I would love to show you the outside at least. Workmen are busy completing the interior. Let's walk past there on the way back to your hotel. OK?"

"Lovely!" If he had asked me to swim the canal with the swans, I would have acquiesced willingly. I walked alongside Paul and Pandora through the narrow streets. The old buildings were ornately decorated on their facades. At night, many of them would be crammed with customers of the prostitutes the Red Light District is famous for. On display in the large first floor windows would be women selling sexual favors.

    Paul pointed out a building wider than most, the entranceway a few steps down from the sidewalk. As we stopped in front of it, I could hear the buzzing of saws and the clanging of hammers.

"Here it is, my club! I've named it 'The Flying Fox'. I hope you'll join me for the opening as my guest, Deena."

"I'd love to!" I replied.

"The building dates from the early 1700s," Paul explained. "It was a brothel from the very beginning until it was closed last year by order of the City Council, in an effort to clean up the Red Light District. My brother and I bought the property soon after."

We crossed the narrow street so we could admire the intricate details of the architecture.

"Up for a jog back to the hotel?" Paul challenged me. "Pandora can use the exercise!"

"Sure!" I had a feeling I would need lots of energy to keep up with the Dutch Superman I had a date with later that evening.

Too soon, we arrived at the hotel. Paul and Pandora walked me into the lobby.

"Can we escort you up to your room?"

"No thanks. I want to check out the gift shop in the hotel lobby. Bye Pandora." I bent down and gave her a hug.

"OK. See you here later tonight, Deena, at nine o'clock! I can not wait!" he said, and gave me a quick good-bye kiss on my mouth.

I knew I had to find out the exact meaning of what Paul had said in Dutch in his phone conversation. *Where was he planning to go tonight, and then changed his mind?*

I thought my best chance was to ask for a translation at the concierge desk. I was so impatient that instead of going up to my room to change, I went into the gift shop, bought a souvenir towel and draped it around my neck. At least it covered some of my chest which was still wet.

As I approached the concierge desk, I was happy to see Mark was there. "Hi Deena, so nice to see you again. Get caught in the rain?" he said as he looked at my hair and then my tee shirt.

"No, just careless at the water fountain. May I please have a piece of paper and a pen, Mark? I would like a translation of some Dutch words, but first I need to write them down."

"At your service." He found paper and pen and handed them to me.

I wrote down the words, *De Wallen*. Satisfied, I showed him what I had written, "I think this is it."

He scratched his chin as he looked down at the paper and then at me. "De Wallen. The Dutch term for what foreigners call the Red Light District." Mark cleared his throat and continued, "Amsterdam is a beautiful old city and there are many diversions here for both its tourists and residents. De Wallen is perhaps the most famous.

"I would love to tell you more about my city and show you around. Are you busy tomorrow? I have the day off from work."

His warm dark brown eyes looked directly into mine. He smiled at me. I felt guilty having to say no to him.

"Thank y'all so much, but I already have plans. Someone else has offered to be my tour guide for the day."

"Oh, that man with the Rottweiler?"

"Yes."

"Paul Vermeer. Just be careful. American women are so innocent when it comes to dealing with European men."

"Spoken from experience, I hope a positive one."

He smiled broadly and said, "yes, a very positive experience or two."

"I am happy American women have made such a good impression on y'all. I'm from New York City. I doubt I'm as innocent as y'all think I am. Thank you for the information Mark."

"Anytime Deena anytime. But not originally from New York?"

"No, how'd y'all guess? From Baltimore, Maryland, born and bred."

"A southern girl. Known for your hospitality, aren't you? Just don't be too generous with that hospitality. So…..please take good care of yourself Deena. I look forward to seeing you again."

"Thank you for the advice. Y'all have been so kind. Bye for now."

I waved good-bye to Mark. As I got into the elevator, I

concentrated on translating what Paul had said in his phone conversation. "I am definitely not coming to De Wallen tonight." Not coming to De Wallen tonight? The man I was going to dinner with later this evening had previous plans to visit the Red Light District? For what purpose? To visit his club? No, it wasn't open yet.

There was only one plausible explanation. Paul had a date with a prostitute. And the prostitute was calling him? That probably meant he was a regular with the woman.

What! This is crazy! I thought as I got off the elevator and walked down the hallway. *Don't go out with that guy, he'll be nothing but trouble.*

By the time I entered my room, I had changed my mind. All I could think about was Paul, how sexy he looked and how hot he had made me feel when he kissed me. I was too excited to think clearly. Thoughts about his phone call and the Red Light District faded away.

Chapter 3
Ready for Him

It was time to shower, apply make-up, brush my hair, and decide what to wear. I chose a simple vee neck short sleeved dress in a pretty light green color that buttoned down the front. My mother had given me a gold chain and good luck pendant that was my grandmother's when she kissed me goodbye. Finding the family heirloom in my purse, I attached the chain with the pendant around my neck. The small egg shaped pearl encased in its delicate gold cage looked elegant with the dress, I decided.

I checked myself out in the full length mirror – the black wedge heeled sandals looked attractive with the dress, which was about five inches above my knee. Neck line, let's see – too much or too little showing? Much too much. Maybe the dress was too revealing. But I loved the color and the way it fit me, just a bit too snug.

Go with it. Why not please the man?

Damn it, Deena, I thought as I stared in the mirror, *look at this situation clearly. Paul Vermeer is a frequent customer of a prostitute. You are almost certain of it. Is he the type of man you want to get involved with? Oh, but he's really good looking. Sure, more good looking than any of your boyfriends back home ever were. And he treats you much better too. So comforting to me on the plane, when I was afraid of the turbulence. Really Deena, don't be such a big baby! Have a good time and see what happens.*

I looked at the clock radio. It was only half past eight but I was too nervous to wait in the room. I took the elevator down to the lobby. There were some lithographs on display and I began to examine them. I was happy to have something to do while waiting.

"I hope you are enjoying your stay here, miss," I heard a male voice say from behind me. I turned around to see who it was. "I'm Rolf de Jonge, the hotel manager."

"Hello, I'm Deena Green. This is a very nice hotel."

"Thank you. If there is anything I can do to make your stay here more enjoyable, just let me know, Ms. Green." Mr. de Jonge was tall, very thin with close cropped blonde hair, pale blue eyes and a narrow beak of a nose. He looked like a predatory bird.

"I saw you with Paul Vermeer earlier today in the hotel lobby," Mr. de Jonge continued. "I hope Mr. Vermeer treats you well. I would love to take you to dinner tomorrow evening. I know a cozy spot near……"

"Wait just a minute sir!" I raised my voice and interrupted him. "Let me be clear about one thing. I am in Amsterdam on a business project that is very important to me. I don't have time to juggle dates between competitive male peacocks. How rude of you!"

As I turned quickly away from him, Paul was there, blocking my path.

"Deena, what's the matter? De Jonge, how dare you upset this young woman! Let's get out of here," he said as he put his arm protectively around my shoulders.

My cheeks were flushed with anger. As we walked outside, Paul tried to calm me. "De Jonge is a trouble maker. I don't trust him. I have a lot of friends in this city, but also some enemies. Sorry I didn't arrive sooner."

"I'm all right. I can take care of myself. Y'all must think I'm just another dumb American. I'm not."

"I know that. You are both beautiful and intelligent. I want to hear more about your idea, your project, yes!"

I stopped for a moment and took some deep breaths. I couldn't stay angry at Paul. It wasn't his fault the hotel manager was rude. Paul wanted to help me.

"Let's go to the restaurant and have a drink. We can relax and talk there," he suggested.

"OK," I said, relenting.

"You are very lovely tonight. Too lovely!" He looked me over slowly, spending extra time on my low cut scenic view. "How will I keep my attention on food and drink when you are so enticing?" He moved his arm to my waist, and held me close to him as we walked to the restaurant.

"You'll find a way I'm sure," but I wasn't certain if I could concentrate on anything but him. He looked devastatingly handsome in a tight dark blue dress shirt and black slacks that fit snug and low on his hips. *Courage, Deena, courage,* I reminded myself as we strolled together, enjoying the warm Amsterdam night.

Chapter 4
Dinner Date

"I hope you will like the food. We have many Indonesian restaurants in Amsterdam because of the Dutch colonial history there. The restaurant we are going to, Tempo Doeloe, is the best in all of Amsterdam, yes!" Paul said, and smiled at me.

As we took in the sights along the Prinsengracht canal, he pointed out the architecture of his favorite private residences and shops along the way. Each building was different, although attached to the one next to it. Most were four stories high, some with simple roofs, others with more intricate details. Many of the wooden doors were elaborately carved. Some had such large windows I could see inside to the high ceilinged interiors.

Paul pulled me close to him, as hordes of bicycles appeared from seemingly nowhere.

"The bicyclists control the roads and the bike lanes too. Just be careful and stay near me," he warned and held me even closer.

"Can we stop here for a moment?" I asked, as we approached a small bridge spanning the canal. "The view is so perfect. The bridge frames the scene over the water. Don't you think so?"

"I think Deena you're what is so perfect tonight," he said and turned to face me. "You enjoy the view and so will I."

I tried to concentrate on the Amsterdam scenery, but I

couldn't, not with Paul near me.

"Mmmm I'm hungry aren't you?" I said.

"Yes, I'm very hungry," he said as he put both his arms around me and focused his attention on my mouth. He bent down and kissed me with his sensual lips. I was caught in the web of his kisses, and felt that I could never fly away. I wanted more of him, so much more. Too soon, we stopped kissing and continued walking to the restaurant.

"Ah we are here, I'll just ring the bell and someone will let us in," he explained as we arrived at the restaurant at Utrechtsestraat 75. The door opened and a middle aged Dutch man greeted us. "Good evening Paul. So nice to see you."

"Hello Franz! This is my lovely American friend Deena. Where is Suzette hiding?"

"Paaauuulll, helloooo," a female voice sung out. "Soooo happy to seeee you. I have missed you soooo much. How was your trip to New Yoork?" The Indonesian woman who owned the voice appeared in front of us, seemingly out of nowhere.

"I have missed you too, Suzette. New York was good, yes, very good. Even better though, I've met a beautiful woman. This is Deena."

Suzette's dark brown hair was chin length, framing her pleasingly plump face. She was round everywhere, from her café au lait cheeks to ample breasts to her full hips. She scrutinized me from head to toe, paying special attention to my cleavage. I straightened my back so as to give her a good look. *Might as well give her her money's worth*! I thought.

After what seemed like an eternity, Suzette started to laugh. She hugged me to her, then released me and said, "Finally, my plaayybooyy has found just the right woman for him! I can tell you two are simpatico, I have a sixth sense about these things. I reserved my favorite table upstairs just fooorrr youuuu. Except for the waiter bringing your food and drinks to you, you will have your privacy."

I smiled at Suzette. Then I surveyed the intimate restaurant. The walls were covered in a light bamboo wood. The many plants gave the place a jungle look. Indonesian bric-a-brac decorated the walls – colorful sconces of men and women embracing each other. Ceiling fans and dark wooden floors completed the East Asian décor.

All the tables were filled with people talking loudly, enjoying their food and drink. The very aroma of the place was enticing.

We followed Suzette through the restaurant and up a steep flight of stairs. The heel of one of my sandals caught on a step halfway up. I would have fallen but Paul grabbed my rear end with both of his strong hands and pushed me upright again.

"Thank you," I said gratefully.

"Thank you very much, yeesss." He laughed and squeezed my rear gently. "Only a few more steps Deena, do you need me to keep holding you?"

I glanced back at him over my left shoulder. Even in the dim light of the staircase I could see the intense glow of his eyes. Their warm royal blue had turned a deeper color, and they were hot with passion. His wide mouth formed a lopsided, devilish grin. I gripped the railing with my right hand and said, "I think I can manage by myself now," and negotiated the rest of the stairs.

What I could not manage to do was control the heat wave that had started at my lips, enveloped my breasts, my stomach, and quickly traveled to the place moistening between my legs.

Suzette showed us to our table, which was so intimate our knees touched as we sat down across from each other. "I'd love a glass of ice water please," I said to her.

"Of course," she said and went back down the stairs. I tried to concentrate on Paul's eyes, and forget if possible the way his intimate touch had made me feel. He was seemingly unaware of how good looking he was – his focus was outward, towards me, not inward.

I wanted to lean over the table and kiss him. Not on his mouth. No, I wanted to kiss his imperfect nose and the dark scar on his right cheek. I wanted to heal whatever had hurt him, to make it all go away. To make it better for him.

But hadn't I promised myself I'd be careful? I pushed aside my misgivings about his connection to the Red Light District. I could only focus on how much I was anticipating having Paul all to myself in this private place.

Suzette returned with a pitcher of water. As she filled two glasses for us, she explained sadly, "This weekend is the last one that this upstairs room will be ooopennnn to the publiccccc. They say the old staircase is not so safe. You will be one of the last to experience the intimacy here. I will bring you your usual dishes, yes Paaauuullll? And what wine would you enjooooyyy? Savignon blanc from Chili?"

"Too bad, Suzette, I love this room," Paul said, shaking his head. "Deena and I will give the room something to record in its history this evening, yes! We will have the Soto Ajam to start, that's spicy chicken soup, Gadon Dari Sapi, beef in a creamy coconut sauce, and white and yellow rice. How does that sound to you Deena?"

"It all sounds wonderfully erotic, I mean exotic!"

"Yes, and the white wine will be great too Suzette. Please tell the chef to add some extra spices. You know how much I enjoy the flavor of nutmeg."

"Of course, Paul. Nutmeg, nature's aphrodisiac!" she said in her musical sing song. I could hear Suzette laughing as she went down the stairs to place our dinner order.

"Is it true? Nutmeg is an aphrodisiac?" I asked.

"Yes. It was at one time a very valuable commodity. Grown originally in Indonesia. There are still nutmeg plantations on the Molucca Islands there. A beautiful place with beautiful people."

"The people. Y'all mean the women."

"Yes, the women. So naturelle, the beaches and the women."

Paul leaned towards me across the table, looking at me intently. "Deena, tell me about this special project that has brought you to Amsterdam."

"OK, but first I have to know how you feel about something."

"What something?" he asked as he reached for my hands with both of his.

"Well, I'm Jewish. I want to know if my being Jewish bothers you."

"Bothers me? In what way?"

"Well...in an anti-Semitic way." I waited for his reaction anxiously.

"Now it's my turn to be angry with you," he said as he held my hands tightly. "Your religion has no bearing on my feelings for you. So you are a beautiful Jewish woman. I had several Jewish girlfriends when I lived in Manhattan, yes. None as striking as you though. None."

"Several?"

"Quite a few." He grinned slyly at me. As he stroked my fingers, he noticed the ring on my right pinky. "Beautiful diamond.....from a boyfriend?"

"From my Uncle Alan. Although he's not really my uncle. Alan is my boss and a close family friend. He's the reason I'm here in Amsterdam."

I then told Paul all about Uncle Alan's idea. I explained his plan to establish a new diamond cutting and polishing business and have Jewish artisans relocate to Amsterdam from New York.

He listened carefully to what I had to say. "How many workers were you thinking of?"

"Alan has planned for twenty five or so initially, with the goal of expanding to approximately one hundred artisans, plus their families."

"It certainly would be a good way to enhance the Jewish

community here. My brother Rick and I have been looking into redesigning the interior of an old factory building on Nieuwe Uilenburgerstraat. The city of Amsterdam owns it and has been renting it to various manufacturers. The most recent tenant has just moved out. We are also renovating residential space in the Plantage, which at one time was a Jewish neighborhood. I think some of the Jewish artisans could make it their home. Now I can see a purpose to our work.

"You will need to obtain government work visas for the diamond artisans to emigrate to The Netherlands, as well as approvals for the new business venture. I have a meeting in The Hague on Tuesday with Chris Bucholtz, Deputy Minister of Trade. If you accompany me, perhaps you can convince him to consider your proposal. Chris has a particular weakness when it comes to attractive women."

"Thanks so much! That sounds like a wonderful idea."

"Rick and I usually have a late lunch together on Sunday afternoons. He has several friends in the jewelry industry. I know he would love to meet you and hear about your ideas."

As I told him about the project, he reached over to touch my left hand with his right. He pressed his fingers on mine, as if to reassure me that all would go well. I felt his touch deep inside me, and I thought everything was possible.

While we talked, first the wine and then our food was served. The Indonesian cuisine was delicious.

Paul kept my plate and glass full. "Try the Gadon Dari Sapi, Deena, it's unlike anything you've ever tasted!" he said as he took a spoon, filled it with the beef and coconut sauce and brought it to my lips. I bit into the sweet meat and tried to lap up some of the sauce with my tongue. The liquid ran down one side of my mouth. "Here, let me help you." He brushed away the liquid with his fingers, and then said, "good, yes?"

I couldn't help myself as I brought his fingers to my mouth, licking my tongue over them. "Yes, very good. Delicious." I stared at his mouth as he smiled at me. *Kiss me, Paul, kiss me now.*

And as if he could read my mind, he said, "soon Deena very soon."

We learned more about each other. He told me how much he loved New York. After studying architecture at Pratt Institute in Brooklyn, he had interned with a firm specializing in restoring landmark buildings. Paul had lived in New York for a total of ten years.

"A long time to be away from home," I said.

"Yes," he agreed. "Since I returned to Amsterdam I've been able to work on many renovation projects because of what I learned in America."

I told him about my family history. My German Jewish ancestors had emigrated to Baltimore in the 1840s from Wurzburg, Bavaria. They had followed Rabbi Price, a revered Orthodox Jewish leader, from Europe to America. Both Jewish and Christian German immigrants had found the bustling American city a good place to establish successful businesses. The Jewish community had started small but grew rapidly.

As we talked, I felt a sensual undercurrent pass between us. Was it jet lag, or the wine, or was there some other reason I felt like I was floating? The more I tried to fight it, the more I was caught up in his aura. The smell of his musky cologne and his natural salty scent were making me dizzy with desire. I was being pulled towards him by an unseen force. He reached for both of my hands with his left one and held them.

"Your hands are so small and delicate. Mine are clumsy Belgian farmer's hands. Who would believe these hands belong to a descendant of Johannes Vermeer?"

So, I thought, *it's true. He is from the famous artist's family.* "I believe it. You write in a beautiful old world script. I saved the paper you wrote your name and phone number on. That piece of paper reveals more than just letters and numbers. I mean to find out your secrets, Paul Vermeer."

"Do you? Well, I mean to find out some of your secrets too. I want to know how this makes you feel," he said, his voice low, as he took each of my fingers in his mouth.

"You are my dessert Deena, sweeter than the sweetest of fruits." I could feel myself being swept away by him, with nothing to hold onto to bring me back to reality. I didn't want to come back either.

He stood up and pulled me close to him. He held my chin gently and kissed me hard on my mouth with more wet heat than I had ever thought possible from one kiss. His full lips and thick tongue took over my life at that moment. Our kiss seemed never ending. My knees went weak, and a pulsating sensation in between my legs was gaining strength. I pushed him away for a moment so I could try to rein in my desire for him.

"Your kisses should be illegal," I whispered to him.

"Nothing is illegal here in Amsterdam, love. Nothing."

We explored each other with our lips and tongues. His taste was even more intoxicating than his scent. He was wine, nutmeg, mixed with searing sweet breath. Time stood still for us. The more we kissed, the more kisses I wanted from him. We were in a paradise of our own, there in the little Indonesian restaurant.

"Closing timmmme, lovers, it is midnight alreadddy! Our atelier room is going out in blaze of passionate lovvve! I can feeeel the firrrre !" Suzette sang out to us.

"Suzette, just a few more minutes, please!" Paul called to her, still holding me. We heard her footsteps retreating back downstairs. "Deena, are you alright? I can carry you down the stairs, yes? You look so beautiful, your hair is so fiery!"

He took a handful of my long hair and brought it to his lips. I saw it had changed color, more reds than yellows. Maybe it was the lighting, maybe it was the late hour. Or maybe it was something else entirely. He touched the soft flesh of my breasts before pulling his hands away reluctantly.

As we made our way down the stairs, I leaned on him for balance and sanity. Paul quickly paid the bill. "Bye Suzette," we both called to her. We left Tempo Doeloe and glided down the street holding onto each other, never wanting to let go.

Paul talked about our plans for tomorrow. First he wanted to show me the factory and the Plantage building he was renovating. He suggested we visit the Portuguese Synagogue. "I think you will love the beautiful old house of worship. It would be a good idea to wear a skirt since we will visit the synagogue on your Sabbath. We'll be traveling around the city on my motor bike, which has a nice comfortable seat."

I looked up at Paul, and said, "I can't wait! It all sounds so wonderful!"

With our arms held tightly around each other's waists, we walked the fifteen minutes it took to get back to the hotel. I didn't think about the fact that I only knew this man a very short while. I was with a man who had cast his spell on me. Of that I was certain.

When we arrived at the hotel, Paul insisted on escorting me up to my room. "I don't want you to run into de Jonge alone. I've got to protect you from him."

We didn't say anything to each other until we arrived at my hotel room door.

"Thank you Paul," I said, as I looked up into his blue eyes.

"I should do the thanking. Do you want me to stay with you tonight?" He was extremely convincing. I almost said yes, but I realized my energy was spent. I was too tired to be the way I wanted to be for him, very sexy in bed.

"Not tonight...."

"Tomorrow night, yes?"

"Maybe."

"You are so beautiful, Deena."

"Thank you!"

"Very very lovely. I like you a lot, yes."

"Mmmm, tell me more tomorrow," I said.

"Just one more kiss for tonight?"

"Yes one more."

He kissed me, first on my right cheek, and then twice more on my left and right cheek.

"That was a Dutch kiss. Three times on the cheek. Now you must kiss me back. Dutch treat, yes? When a man gives a woman something, a woman must give a man something in return."

I wasn't sure that was the definition of a Dutch treat, but I was under his spell once more. I kissed him three times on his cheeks, and then on his lips. He held me tightly in his arms, our bodies pressed together. It was a breathtaking kiss.

We couldn't get enough of each other's lips and tongues and tastes. With each button he opened on my dress, he unlocked more passion and desire hidden within me. He licked his fingers, reached down my dress, and then caressed my taut nipples. I kissed the scar on his cheek, trying to hide from him my short panting breaths.

"I have another scar. Would you like to kiss it, too?" he whispered.

"Where?" I asked.

"Here," and he pointed to his right side just below his waist.

"Not tonight," I whispered back. "Tomorrow night…"

I finally had the resolve to put the key card in the door. "Good night Paul. See you tomorrow morning at ten."

"Good night, my sweet. Until tomorrow."

I quickly undressed, telephoned the front desk for a wake up call for the next morning, and crawled under the covers, naked. I squeezed my breasts, licked my fingers and then rubbed my nipples. I wanted Paul doing that to me. Harder. More. Yes Paul. Oh yes. Here, between my legs…yes stroke me there there faster faster…..oh oh oh oh oh OH OH oooooo...

Chapter 5

Exploring New Territory

"You are beautiful Deena. But I can't stay, can't...." It was Paul's voice, but he wasn't with me. Where was he? Why wouldn't he stay with me?

Later that night, I woke up, got dressed, and took the elevator to the lobby. Paul was in the hotel bar, having a drink. Then he left, and I followed him. I kept a safe distance between us. I didn't know where I was. He walked swiftly with a sense of urgency. There were crowds in the streets, men and naked women.

He stopped at a narrow doorway and disappeared. Curiosity got the better of me. I tried to open the door. It was unlocked. I carefully entered. I saw him ascending a flight of stairs.

"Paul," I heard a woman say, "I can tell you have missed me!"

"How do you know that?" Paul said. "I haven't even gotten undressed yet."

"Oooo, there it is," the woman replied. "Ah yes, that big boy of yours has a mind of its own."

"Stop talking woman! Let's go inside. On your knees and get to work!"

The telephone rang and woke me. *Was it nine o'clock already? I must have been dreaming.* I would be seeing Paul in an hour. But I was still uncertain. *Had he gone to the Red Light District last night after our date?*

I quickly showered and then picked out some clothes. I chose a black knee length skirt, which was appropriate for synagogue, and comfortable black flat sandals. A light pink short sleeved blouse, a bit too tight, completed the tourist outfit. I added my mother's necklace and pendant. If the pearl egg was indeed a good luck charm, I decided it couldn't hurt to wear it while I was spending the day with the man that had awakened untapped feelings and desires in me.

It was early but I was too nervous to stay in the room. I went down to the hotel cafe to wait for Paul. He was already seated there, sipping coffee. I watched him undetected for a few minutes. Many of the waiters and waitresses came to his table to say hello. It seemed just about everyone knew him. I waited another minute or two and then could wait no longer.

"Good morning, Deena!" he said when he saw me. He stood up and gave me three kisses on my cheeks and one longer one on my mouth. "You must have slept well. You look wonderful today. Let's get you some coffee. How about a croissant?"

"Coffee is fine thank you Paul. Good morning to you too! I think I'll just have some fruit if you don't mind. My clothes are snug on me," I said as I adjusted my skirt and sat down.

He stole a glance at my tight blouse. "You look just ripe, I mean right, Deena! Perfect, yes. I can't wait to take you on my tour! Pretty pendant you have around your neck," he said as he pointed to the pearl egg. "But then anything would look lovely if you're wearing it."

Paul looked even more gorgeous than he did last night, if that was possible. He was wearing a pale blue short sleeved shirt, and grey slacks. The shirt was made of a very light material. His muscular arms looked so inviting. Soft strands of black hair showed from his unbuttoned neckline as well as coating his arms.

"Thank you. This is my mother's good luck charm she gave me just before I left. I can't wait to ride on your motor bike through your wonderful city!"

We finished breakfast and went out to his motor bike. It was black with chrome trim. Its highly polished surface glistened in the morning light.

"Where are the helmets?" I said.

"Helmets? Nederlanders, we don't use helmets. We like to feel the fresh air, yes!"

The seat was barely big enough for two people. He helped me get on and then straddled the seat in front of me. I noticed he was wearing his black boots. My pulse quickened. I held onto him tightly and felt his hard body through his shirt.

Paul was right, the breeze felt great blowing through my hair as he drove the motorbike at what seemed like breakneck speed along the narrow streets. The buildings, most not more than four or five stories high, were reflected in the canals. I could almost hear the history of the old city whooshing in my ears as we arrived at our first stop.

The factory on Nieuwe Uilenburgerstraat was down the street from the former Boas jewelry complex. Paul explained that before World War II, the Boas family had employed hundreds of Jewish diamond artisans. Now most of the space was a diamond showroom owned by the Glassman family, with only twenty polishers employed there.

The building that Paul had suggested as a workplace for our diamond artisans was taller than Glassman's. "It is hard to envision what it will look like when renovated to the specifications that you require," Paul explained. "But I have been inside several times, and I think the flooring will be able to support heavy machinery. And it is near the Plantage neighborhood, where we can provide housing for some of the workers."

We walked around to the back, so Paul could show me the depth of the property. I was very pleased that he thought it could be refitted for our needs. It was made of red brick, and looked like an impregnable fortress.

"Let's stop at the Dutch Resistance Museum," Paul suggested as we walked to the street and got back on the motorbike. "I'm very proud of my grandfather Henrik Vermeer. He arranged for hiding places for Jews throughout the war. Yes, so here we are already. I will let the exhibits speak for themselves." He put his arm around my waist as we walked to the museum.

The security guard tipped his hat to Paul. "Good morning Mr. Vermeer. How are you? Go right through the security checkpoint sir and your lovely lady friend as well."

"Good morning, Herman. Nice to see you again. I am fine, thank you, yes."

"Is Herman friend or foe?" I asked as we entered the first exhibit.

"Oh Herman is a friend for sure. By the way, my brother Rick is much more well known than I am in Amsterdam. He's involved in many charitable organizations. I'm just basking in his glory."

Paul proudly guided me through the museum. "My grandfather did so much to help the Jews of Amsterdam. He obtained forged documents, used his own money to bribe officials and arranged for safe places to hide for many Jewish people. He always wished that he could have done more........" His voice drifted off, and he seemed lost in thought.

We had completed our tour of the museum. "Next stop, the residential building that Rick and I are working on in this neighborhood. We can walk there."

The sun was stronger now than it had been earlier in the day. Paul took my hand in his. Having him so close to me made me feel protected.

The neighborhood was quiet. Soon we arrived at a residence which was at the end of a block. I liked it immediately. It was five stories high and had a view of the Artis Zoo across the street. It seemed to be wider than others nearby. I asked Paul about that.

"Yes it is wider and the windows are more generous than most in the Plantage. We can't go in, because there are supplies and equipment everywhere. We can walk around this way, though," he said as he led me around the back.

"It was built in the 1870s for a wealthy Jewish family. The original owner liked its proximity to the Botanical Gardens. Let's walk there, it's just a few blocks away."

We strolled along holding hands. He paid the admissions fee and we explored the indoor gardens. Plants and trees were everywhere, beautiful and fragrant. We stopped for sodas at a small café, surrounded by jungle-like foliage.

"So, Deena, what do you think, yes?" he said as we sat on chairs close to each other.

"I think the factory building is perfect for our project. I can envision the artisans working comfortably near the windows in the natural light. The neighborhood seems quiet and safe. And the Plantage residence will be convenient to travel to and from work for the artisans."

He hugged me. "Thank you," he whispered in my ear and then kissed my neck gently. "I somehow feel that by helping you, I am carrying on my grandfather's work." He then kissed me on my lips, gently at first and then more insistently. His lips would not relinquish mine. His tongue refused to leave my mouth. Finally, sadly, our mouths parted. "Deena you are more fragrant than all the flowers and trees in this garden! When I am with you I am in paradise!"

I felt the same way about being with him.

We lost track of time. We walked around the gardens enjoying the serenity there. He told me about his brother Rick, his beautiful wife Rachel and their only child, Vanessa, a lovely seventeen-year-old girl. Rick and Rachel were very concerned about their daughter. Lately she was sad and withdrawn. She stayed out late and didn't come home weekends. Paul thought she was still mourning her grandmother, Paul and Rick's mother Sonya, who had died suddenly two years ago. Vanessa and her grandmother were very close.

We left the Botanical Gardens and walked to the old Portuguese Synagogue. The courtyard entrance was protected by plate glass gates. Paul looked up at the security camera, and a moment later the gates opened for us.

"Thank you Avi," he said to the security guard. "This is my friend Deena from New York. How long can we visit here?"

"Mr. Vermeer, stay as long as you like. I am on duty all afternoon. Even the Rabbi has gone home for lunch so you have the whole place to yourselves."

"Great, thank you again Avi. Regards to your family."

"Same to yours sir."

I had given up asking Paul how virtually everyone in Amsterdam knew him. I would have to wait until he was ready to tell me why he and his family were so well known.

We stood before the main synagogue, which was constructed of old reddish brown bricks and adorned with graceful windows. As we walked into the main sanctuary, natural light from the windows lit up the whole room.

"Isn't this a fascinating place? There is no heat or electricity. Candles are lit in the evenings, just as in the 1600s," Paul explained.

It was very quiet inside the synagogue. The outer courtyard buildings protected the main building from any of the usual city sounds.

The architecture in the large imposing sanctuary was very graceful. I gazed at the beautifully sculpted wooden ark, which held the Torah scrolls, containing the Five Books of Moses.

After we had explored the large synagogue and some of the smaller courtyard rooms, I felt a strong connection to the Jews that had worshipped in the Portuguese Synagogue for centuries and still did. The history of the Jews in Amsterdam was now not just a story in a book. It was here before me in this sacred place.

Chapter 6
Lunch and Dessert

Paul looked at his watch. "No wonder I'm so hungry – it's past three o'clock! Can I interest you in a late lunch?"

"Sure." I still felt like I was time traveling back to the 1600s in the beautiful old synagogue.

"We'll pick up some sandwiches and beer, yes. I know a great place to cool off and picnic too. My favorite place in all of Amsterdam!"

"I would love to see your favorite place, Paul!" I was back in the twenty first century, and happy about it too. Happy to be with this attractive, attentive man.

We walked hand in hand to the Dutch Resistance Museum where we had parked the motorbike. Paul took off at a fast clip. *He must be hungry!* We stopped to buy lunch, got back on the motorbike, and finally arrived at a street right on a canal.

Paul parked in front of an attractive houseboat. It was painted pale yellow. Trees gracefully framed the entrance. The front door was made of old mahogany, trimmed in lacy iron scroll work. The entrance was decorated with an ivy covered trellis. Yellow rose bushes and red tulips flanked the front door.

"Welcome to my home!" Paul said proudly. "I've named it Spice Island."

"Why do you call it that?" I asked as I admired the surprisingly large houseboat.

"A distant relative of mine was a spice trader in Indonesia in the 1800s. I decided to name the houseboat Spice Island to honor him. His name was Daniel Vermeer. My full name is Jean-Paul Daniel Vermeer. From some old pictures my grandfather gave me, I can see a strong resemblance between Daniel and me.

"I'll give you a tour of the interior soon, but first let's relax on the deck and enjoy the cool breeze. I'll get some things for our picnic. We've had a busy day, yes?"

I nodded my head in agreement. I followed Paul to the deck which was around the back of the houseboat. I was grateful to be able to relax. I made myself comfortable on a chair and rested my feet on an ottoman while Paul went inside. There were many houseboats on that particular canal, but Paul's was definitely one of the larger ones. The deck ran the length of the boat and had plenty of room for a table and several chairs. I put my head back and looked up at the thickening clouds. Soon my eyes were closed.

I felt something wet on my cheek. Was Paul kissing me? I woke to find two big brown canine eyes staring at me. It was Pandora. She had given me a doggy lick.

I petted the friendly girl behind her ears. She seemed to love it, pushing her head against my hand for more when I stopped.

Paul appeared with a tray filled with our lunch. He had changed his clothes and looked rugged in a black tee shirt and tight jeans.

"I see that your competition is here too!" he said as he put the tray down on a nearby table. "Pandora is lovely, isn't she?" He sat close to me and the affectionate dog quickly moved in between us. He began rubbing her massive chest. "Yes girl yes. We know you were lonesome today."

I couldn't help but laugh at how this most masculine of men was putty in Pandora's paws.

"I'm funny?" he said, smiling.

"Oh yes very. Your puppy love for Pandora is charming."

We ate the sandwiches and started on our beers. Paul told me he found Pandora by contacting the German Rottweiler Club four years ago. Mr. Hans Schneider of Rheinberg, Germany was a regional breeding supervisor of Rottweilers and had invited Paul to his home to meet a litter of six week old puppies. Paul had picked out Pandora because she was the most affectionate of all the pups. Two weeks later he returned to Rheinberg to take Pandora home, and became fast friends with Hans and his wife Giselle.

"That reminds me, Hans and Giselle have invited Pandora and me to spend a few days at their home this coming week. I hope you will join us there. They live in a castle on the Rhine, and have a private lake as well. It's a great place to take a break from the heat wave I hear we're expecting……."

We were so involved in our conversation that we didn't realize it had started to rain. Almost immediately it came down heavily and we were drenched.

Paul took my hand and we ran to the front door and into the houseboat, Pandora right behind us.

We stood in the living room and laughed at each other. We were both soaking wet from head to toe. My blouse, bra and skirt were clinging to me. Paul stopped laughing as his gaze focused on my chest.

"I'll get some towels so we can dry off," he said after a moment. "Why don't you go into the bedroom and make yourself comfortable."

After he left, I quickly surveyed his living room. It was very modern with highly polished light wood floors, a navy rug and a matching navy sofa.

I found the bedroom at the rear of the houseboat. It was sparsely furnished with a blonde wood platform bed and two sleek night tables. The bed was covered in a furry brown blanket. There was a black and white zebra striped rug on the floor.

I looked at myself in the large full length mirror on the wall opposite the bed. Nervously, I tried to push my long hair into place but it was no use.

This is the moment you always dread, Deena, I thought as I stared at my reflection in the mirror. *Now you will either have to reveal your body to Paul, or run out the door into the rain, and away from the promise of passion he can give you.*

You're a coward! You should be proud of your body. Instead, you are ashamed of your imperfections. Pandora jumped up on the bed and stretched out on the blanket. There were no covers for me to hide under.

And you're afraid of what he'll think of you. He's used to the pleasures a prostitute can provide him. He won't find me sexy. He'll laugh at me, I know it.

Paul entered the bedroom, wearing only a towel thrown over his shoulder. "Take your clothes off and I'll dry you, yes!" he commanded playfully. His stance though was anything but playful. His hands were now on his well defined hips, which were thrust towards me as if to confront me, to challenge me to look at him there.

I was not prepared for what now had me mesmerized. Paul was naked, his raw sexual power displayed before me.

Should I run away from him, from his broad shoulders, the left one tattooed with a large arrow? Run away from his strong muscular chest? Run away from legs that were so powerful looking? Run away from the black Gothic heart tattoo on his right side below his waist, with another arrow pointing the way to his manhood? Was it possible, could he really be that large or were my eyes playing tricks on me?

He threw the towel on the bed and walked over to me within kissing distance. "Your clothes, Deena, give them to me," he demanded. I was spellbound by him. My fingers reached for his chest, touching the silky damp hair circling his nipples. Then I traced the tiger line from his chest to his navel. I continued towards his thick erect masculinity. Suddenly I realized where my fingers were headed. I withdrew them quickly as if I had touched something red hot.

"No I can't," I said.

"Why not? Don't you want me?"

"Yes I want you. Very much. But I'm not perfect the way you are. You are Adonis, sculpted like a Greek god." I looked up at his face, down to his chest, and then to his incredible sexual display, which was even larger now.

"I think that you are perfect baby!" he said.

"No I'm not. I'm not thin enough. I'm not tall enough. I have sex under the covers. My body. It's ugly." My eyes welled up with tears.

"Come here Deena, let me help you." He began unbuttoning my blouse. I felt desire for him mounting within me, along with fear that he would reject me.

"Look, look at me! Covered with spots. Don't you see?"

I stripped off my blouse and bra. I opened my arms wide and showed him the landscape of light freckles that coated me from my shoulders to my hips. I turned around to show him more of the same on my back.

"Is this what you think is ugly?" he said as he massaged my back and then reached in front of me to caress my breasts. "Deena, you are more beautiful and more wonderful than anyone I have ever known." He turned me around and looked at my face. He let out a sound which started with a rumble in his chest, and grew to a roar as it escaped his lips.

"You are my jungle cat!" He bent down and covered my breasts with passionate kisses. Then he stood up and stroked my hair. "I love this thick fiery mane of yours, your exotic green feline eyes, your beautiful silky skin, your soft lips, your sweet full breasts, your nipples.... Mmmmmmm. How much more convincing do you need? I am wild with desire for you and have been since the moment I met you!"

"But....."

"I am bewitched by you! Here... I will prove everything I say to you, yes..."

He quickly pulled off my skirt and panties. Gently cupping my breasts in his hands, he teased each of my nipples with his tongue, licking little circles around first one dark pink pleasure trove and then the other. He then slowly suckled them. I wanted more, so much more. My nipples responded to his lovemaking and became hard and erect. I put my head back and enjoyed the pleasure he gave my body. I forgot my ugliness. I had put on a cloak of beauty for him.

"But Paul..."

"Yes Deena?"

"Where is the scar I haven't kissed yet?"

He took my face in his hands and gently pushed me down below his waist so I could kiss his scar. I kissed it, and then I got down on my knees and stroked his overly generous erection.

It was thicker than any other I had experienced. Different! I realized why. Paul's cock was intact. The foreskin covered his penis to almost the very tip of it in glorious fleshy splendor.

My eyes widened with surprise. I stood up to face him. I continued stroking him and said, "I'm a virgin when it comes to an intact lover!"

He looked at me with amusement and said, "my innocent American angel, so you have never had this pleasure before, yes? Let me show you, let me teach you."

Transfixed by the desire in his eyes, I said, "Yes, show me, teach me."

"Obey me. Get down on the floor next to me. You are my tigress and I am your tiger." He was on his hands and knees, and I imitated his stance next to him, waiting for his next command.

He licked his lips and said, "Will you obey me?"

"Yes," I purred. I kissed his shoulder submissively.

"Now, approach me from behind until you find this new source of pleasure for you," he demanded.

I crawled to his rear, and began licking and biting his firm round ass. I didn't need any further instructions from him. My primeval instincts charted my course. His musky scent reached me, intoxicating me. I lowered my mouth and began licking and kissing the two round sources of musk over and over again.

Paul was panting and pawing the ground. I knew something else was waiting for me, and not patiently at all. I crawled in front to face him, and we kissed each other's lips.

"Now, my tigress, I will show you what to do. Now!"

He rolled onto his back. I moved quickly to his cock as he reached for it and held it for me. As he slowly pushed down the foreskin, I saw what was gift wrapped beneath it. The dark pink round head of his penis emerged from the foreskin swollen and ready for my waiting lips. "Here you are my little cat. Now suck me!"

I did as I was told and began licking and sucking the tip of his cock. My hand encircled his penis tightly as I played with his foreskin, rubbing it with my fingers, sliding it slowly up and down. I made little circling licks and love bites around the edge of it.

He pulled away from me. "Ooo Deena, you learn too quickly. I must pleasure you too."

He rolled me onto my back. He licked me between my legs gently at first and then more forcefully. My pussy was pulsating, aching. I couldn't wait much longer. He was driving me crazy.

He kissed me on my mouth and said, "I'll get a condom, my

pussy cat." He quickly retrieved one from his night table and returned to the floor next to me.

"I hope it's extra large. You're incredible in every way!" I said.

"Extra large is the only size sold in Amsterdam! I'm going to make this extra special for you, yeess!" he growled.

Before I could respond, he entered me. He was gentle no more, his manhood deep within me. "I'll put the condom on soon, but first I want you to feel what real pleasure is like."

He thrust his huge erection in my pussy over and over again. He made me feel like a sexual goddess. He came away from me for a moment to put on the condom.

"Give me now what I've been waiting for," I begged him.

"Yes yes yes I will," he said as he drove his cock into me. My pussy squeezed him, shuddered, squeezed, again and again. I shook with the force of my orgasm.

Chapter 7

More

Afterwards, we lay on the floor in each other's arms, laughing and kissing.

"Not enough kissing the first time," I offered.

"I agree, baby, yes. We were in a bit of a hurry. Let's slow it down next time. And I need more of those big beautiful breasts. Come on top of me and let's see if we can correct that."

"Not just yet. I want my first Dutch lesson. Teach me how to say - I want you! Now! More! I need you!" I needed to know his words.

"Greedy witch! You are teasing me! I'm lucky I can remember my own name! But OK..................."

Now I could tell him what I wanted from him in Dutch, just like all the other women in Amsterdam. I mounted him and pressed my nipples to his waiting mouth. "Repeat after me," he said. "*Ik willen jü!!! Nu!! Meer! Ik nodig heben jü!!!*" I repeated the Dutch words as best I could and then reverted to English. " I need you and want you now! More! Suck them hard. Don't stop!" I shouted.

He kissed and sucked my breasts, and bit them none too gently. Then he pulled me lower so we could delight in each other with our tongues.

I was hungrier for him with each kiss. Each time he pleasured me I felt I was losing control. I was all wet heat between my legs.

Our appetite for each other was insatiable. I reached for a condom, and put it on him hurriedly.

"Deena what are you doing to me? I can't keep up with my desire for you. You have enchanted me!

"Come with me baby. Come and never leave me," he moaned as I pulled his erection into me. I thrust my hips to his and I rode him in and out with increasing speed. I kept up with his need for me, my hips meeting his. My pussy was throbbing.

"Paul, Paul!" I said, as I climaxed and so did he.

We both tried to catch our breath. "Was that supposed to have been slow and leisurely?" I joked.

"We'll have to try until we get it right," he said, laughing.

Chapter 8
Guess He Likes Me

The second time was even more incredible than the first. I never thought I could satisfy a man so accomplished in bed. But I did!

"Pandora has been very patient with us, but she should have her dinner and a walk, no?" Paul said as he stroked my breasts. "Why don't I shower and dress and take her out. I'll get us something to eat too. Just feed her three cups of her food, love. It's in the kitchen."

He flashed a huge smile at me, all white teeth and loveable mouth, as he headed towards the bathroom. I went into the kitchen, found Pandora's food and dish, and fed the grateful dog.

While Paul and Pandora were out walking and shopping, I drew a warm bath and soaked leisurely. I couldn't stop thinking about the unbelievable love making we had experienced together. Maybe for him it was a normal occurrence, but for me it was unique.

I was beginning to think I was developing a sixth sensual sense. My body was stronger and more easily aroused than before. Something unusual was happening to me.

Paul returned with pizza and beer. He came into the bathroom to dry me off. We then spread our dinner out on the bed. He took his clothes off and we enjoyed the food. Our appetites were temporarily satiated.

"Are you up for some dessert?" he said.

"Yes…..what did you have in mind? Something sweet?" I teased him as I noticed his masculinity was erect.

I moved close to him so he could play with my breasts as I stroked him. "I think I'll just help myself," I said as I bent down to lick him. He tasted salty and musky and sexy.

He started to push me away saying "Let me do you…."

"No," I interrupted him, "let me make you come."

I sucked him. I couldn't get enough of that most intimate part of him. I had never been so turned on by oral sex before. I climaxed even before he did. It hurt so much to feel soooo good!

We were finally satisfied. We fell asleep in each other's arms.

I woke up early the next morning- the clock read 5:15. Daylight was inching its way into the bedroom.

I looked at Paul and decided…. he was perfect. His thick black hair was tousled, inviting me to run my fingers through it, which I did. Just doing that simple act aroused me. Even in his sleep he had the power to excite me.

His lips were full and beautifully shaped. I touched them gently with my fingers.

My gaze now concentrated on his body. Paul's skin was smooth and lightly tanned. The artistry of thick black hair on his perfectly sculpted chest was amazingly sensual. His arms were muscular and similarly adorned.

His stomach coating was thicker and curlier. His muscles there were well defined too. I gently pulled the blanket away from him.

There was the scar I had kissed our first time making love. Right next to the scar was a tattoo. It was black and in the shape of a heart, with daggers encircling it. It looked Gothic. I wondered about the scars and the tattoo, and under what circumstances Paul had gotten them.

Then to his crowning glory, male perfection. Almost too large, but evidently I was able to handle it throughout a night of lovemaking.

I wanted to touch him there, to arouse him as the sight of his naked body aroused me. What could I give to this perfect man he didn't already have? Could I keep him from the Red Light District, away from the professional pleasures of a prostitute? I was brought back to reality when I heard a friendly snort – it was Pandora, eyeing me from her vantage point next to the bed. The snort was followed by a whimpering sound. The big girl had to go out.

I grabbed a towel that had been discarded carelessly last night, and wrapped it around me. "Here Pandora," I called softly. I opened the door for her.

I heard Paul say in a husky voice, "So what were you doing while I was sleeping, baby? Taking advantage of me, no?"

"Pandora and I need a bathroom break. I'll be right back," I said as I waited for Pandora and then let her inside.

I went into the bathroom and looked at myself in the mirror. My lips were swollen from Paul's succulent kisses. On my neck and breasts were several red bite marks. Our lovemaking was not a dream. It was real, intense, unforgettable.

I returned to his bed. "Can I ask you a question, lover? Please be totally honest with me," I said as I snuggled next to him.

"I will always be honest with you, the Dutch are too honest, yes," Paul said as he caressed my breasts.

"OK then, what's a magnificent Greek god like you doing with a mere mortal woman like me? You are perfection itself and well, I'm just me, with all my faults. Cute, but nothing compared to you," I said.

Paul smiled at me and said, "Promise you'll listen to me without interrupting, yes?"

"I promise."

"Good," Paul said as he stroked my left arm. "Deena, I have had relationships with many women. Beautiful women, some my age, some older, some younger. So I know when I have found someone special. You, my lover, are incredible. The other night on the plane I was expecting to read and nap. Instead I landed on planet Venus and found you. You have the most incredible green cat's eyes, wonderful tasty lips and amazing skin. I could get lost in your long reddish blonde hair. Your body is so warm and sensual, from your full breasts and pink nipples to the moist delicious place between your legs and everywhere in between." He fondled my nipples as he spoke.

"And my Venus, you have a sexual appetite to match mine. I give you as much pleasure as you give me.

"I'm not perfect Deena. No. But you are. You're perfect for me, yes."

"But I'm not fashionably thin...not attractive..."

"Don't say that. Don't ever say that again. Maybe I should use a word you will understand. *Zaftig*. You're zaftig."

"How do you know Yiddish?" I said.

"Every man in Amsterdam knows what zaftig means. Full breasts...wide hips... sweet soft ass. Delicious," he said as he kissed my lips. "Sexy," he continued as he sucked my nipples. He was exciting me, and he knew it. "And juicy," he said, and laughed as he moved further down my aroused body. His fingers found the pleasure spot between my legs.

For once I was speechless. It started to sink in. I'm his goddess. He wants me! Maybe he has even forgotten about the Red Light District!

He interrupted my thoughts by saying, "all this talking makes me hungry for you baby."

"Hungry?"

"It seems I have an insatiable appetite for you. I want you now, yes. I want that delicious treat surrounded by that beautiful fiery hair. Sit on my mouth, Deena. Feed me," he commanded me. I did as he asked, moving to position my pussy on his mouth, my body facing his penis. He grabbed my breasts as I moved first slowly and then quickly up and down on his mouth as he licked me. The passion I came with hurt me. It felt so incredible. I reached for his hard erection, pushed his foreskin down, and began sucking him there. He yelled my name and other things I couldn't understand. But I understood he was satisfied when he came in me. Even that part of him tasted delicious.

"We should rest now, baby," he said. "We are going to meet my brother Rick for lunch later. And then I am moving you in here with me. No more hotel. You belong in my home."

Paul took me in his arms protectively and we fell asleep, lulled by the sound of Pandora's light snoring on the floor next to us.

Chapter 9
Lunch at the Hotel with Rick

When I woke up again, I looked at the clock on Paul's night table. It said 11:30. "Paul," I said softly, trying to wake the wonderful man still asleep next to me, "when is your brother expecting us for lunch?"

"Oh Deena, we had better get up! Rick will be meeting us at one o'clock, and he is always on time. Let's get ready and then walk to the hotel. We'll meet Rick for lunch in the hotel's restaurant. The food is good and there is a great view of the canal."

"I'll have to change my clothes in the hotel room when we get there. Meet you in the shower," I said as I walked quickly into the bathroom and turned on the faucet. Paul was there in a second, with washcloths and soap in hand. We washed each other. I couldn't believe my good fortune once again in having met him. I rubbed my wet breasts on his chest, and savored the wonderful sensation.

The shower was over all too quickly. What had he said about visiting his friends in Germany this week? There was a lake on their property, and I began daydreaming about swimming with him.

Paul dressed in jeans and a tee shirt. I put on my blouse and skirt that had dried from yesterday's downpour. He let Pandora out on the deck, and said she would be fine there for the few hours we were away.

We walked to the hotel under a beautiful blue sky, with a slight breeze coming off the canal.

"Deena, I hope that you'll come with me this week to Hans' castle in Rheinberg. On our way we can stop in The Hague. I will call Chris Buckholtz tomorrow, and mention that you will be joining our Tuesday meeting. You're going to love Hans and Giselle, yes. I have some work to check up in Dusseldorf, near Rheinberg. We can stay until Saturday morning, and then I have the club opening on Saturday night. Of course you'll join me, I can not wait to show you off to my friends!"

"Won't I be in the way?" I asked.

"On the contrary, you will be an asset to my business negotiations in The Hague. I'm applying for permission to restore a landmark building in Amsterdam. The Dutch bureaucrats love Americans, especially pretty ones like you. In Dusseldorf I have to check on how the renovations to a museum are progressing. I always take Pandora, so I will have my two girls with me!"

"I'm your girl, Paul?"

"I want you to be my woman, yes," he said in a low, serious voice. "Will you? I can't bear the thought of leaving Amsterdam without you, even for a few days."

It was what I wanted to hear from him, what I was hoping for from the moment I met him. "I want to be with you too Paul."

Suddenly I felt a flash of fear creep up my legs. I stopped walking and started to shiver.

"What is it Deena? Are you ill?" Paul was alarmed.

"No, love. I believe I'm afraid. Afraid to go to Germany. I've never been there before."

"It will be alright, my sweet. Nobody will hurt you there, I promise. I'll be with you and when you meet Hans and Giselle you'll feel very comfortable with them. You will love them. Rheinberg and Dusseldorf will enchant you with their old world charm, I am certain of it."

I felt better about going to Germany, as long as I was with Paul.

We arrived at the hotel. We agreed to meet at the restaurant in thirty minutes. "Will you be alright without me?" he said playfully. "I can help you undress, no?"

"I'm sure of that," I countered. "It will be good for you to miss me." I went up to my room to change my clothes.

Truthfully, I needed a little time to myself. Now that I was fully awake and thinking a little more clearly I realized what had happened last night. I had made love several times with a man I had just met. I did know a little bit about him but there was much more to his story that remained a mystery.

Besides being so sexy and handsome, Paul was very generous. When we made love, he wanted me to feel as much pleasure as he did. Our foreplay was so wonderful and would have gone on longer but I couldn't control myself. I had never had a man that came close to his incredible lovemaking.

My cell phone was chirping its text message song. It was Ali Ackerman, my best friend back in New York. Ali was like a big sister to me. When her marriage broke up several years ago, she came to Alan's shop, wanting to exchange the remnants of her marriage, her engagement and wedding rings, for a pair of diamond earrings. We became close friends.

Ali's professional name is Dr. Alexandra Ackerman. She is a psychologist, and has helped me to discover a new sense of confidence in myself. She encouraged me to accept Uncle Alan's offer to work on his project in Amsterdam. Ali had lived in Amsterdam several years ago, and knew I would be charmed by the city.

Text from Ali: Deena, how is Amsterdam? Isn't it amazing?

Text from me: Too amazing!

Text from Ali: Really???

Text from me: Met a man. Wonderful. Sexy. Late for a date. Later. xoxo

I realized it was almost time for our lunch. I quickly dressed in a pastel floral print sleeveless dress and high heeled sandals. I put on a touch of makeup, brushed the tangles from my hair and headed downstairs.

When I walked into the restaurant Paul spotted me immediately. He stood up and walked over to me.

"I hope I'm not late," I whispered to him.

"It's OK, you look beautiful! Rick can't wait to meet you!" Paul said as he took my arm in his and showed me to their table.

Getting up from his chair to greet me was a man who could have been Paul's twin. Their facial features were almost identical – the large royal blue eyes, square masculine chin, full lips on a generously wide mouth. Of course, Rick did not have the facial scar that Paul did. Rick's hair was black too, but graying at the temples. Paul was taller and thinner than Rick.

I walked up to Rick and kissed him three times on his cheeks. "I am so sorry I'm late. Please forgive me. I'm Deena. So wonderful to meet you Rick!" I said hurriedly. I admit I was caught off guard by his uncanny resemblance to Paul.

"So nice to meet you Deena, think nothing of it. You are certainly worth waiting for, is she not Paul?" Rick said.

"Yes she is!" We all sat down and Paul pulled his chair close to mine. "Deena is both beautiful and very intelligent as well," Paul continued to stroke my ego. I loved when he stroked me.

"My brother has told me about your reason for traveling to Amsterdam," Rick said. His manner of speaking English was excellent, but his accent was definitely more Dutch than Paul's. "I think your Uncle Alan's plan to revitalize the diamond cutting and polishing trade here in Amsterdam is a good one. So he wants to have many Jewish people employed in that trade?"

"Yes. It's Uncle Alan's mission to bring back both the people and the industry to Amsterdam that died during the war."

"I must tell you his idea sounds very important to me. I am not sure if you will be able to get the approvals, but I will do everything I can to assist you in this plan," Rick said. His eyes looked intently into mine. He was serious and sincere.

"I believe that you have struck a chord with my brother. Rick is very much the moral conscience of Amsterdam these days," Paul said.

"And Amsterdam needs some morality. My experience of being a father to our teenage daughter has taught me that. Our Vanessa is seventeen, and has been keeping company with a wild crowd from her high school for the past year or so. I am afraid her latest boyfriend is a very bad influence on her."

Rick looked directly at Paul as he continued. "Nessa came home at six this morning. She wouldn't speak to us at all. She went into her room, closed the door and locked it. We heard her crying a little while later. She won't take calls from anyone. A boy named David Coen keeps calling our house, wanting to know if Vanessa is all right. She won't speak to him. My apologies, Deena, but I must return home soon. My wife and I are frantic with worry."

While we were having coffee, fruit, cheese, and croissants, we made small talk. "How is my favorite dog Pandora?" Rick asked. "I would love to bring Vanessa over to see her, but she doesn't want to leave her room. You know Pandora always used to calm Nessa."

"It's that big heart of hers that always works, yes," Paul replied. "She has won Deena over."

"Pandora is a wonderful dog," I said.

"I will make some calls this evening," Rick said. "Hopefully I can arrange a meeting tomorrow with Solomon Grossman, who owns the largest jewelry exchange here in Amsterdam. He employs a few diamond cutters and polishers. I think he will like Alan's idea of expanding the trade in Amsterdam, and increasing the Jewish population in the city as well. I will call you later Paul. I apologize for leaving so soon, but Rachel and I must see what we can do for our daughter."

We all stood up and Rick gave me three quick kisses on my cheeks. Paul hugged his brother tightly to him, as if to give him the strength he needed to deal with his family's problems.

"I hope they can find a way to help Vanessa," I said to Paul as we watched Rick hurry out of the restaurant. "Teenagers can be so difficult."

"Nessa wasn't always this way," Paul answered. "When I first brought Pandora home she was so eager to help with all the demands of puppyhood. Sometimes Nessa would sleep on my couch for a night or two, with Pandora curled up in her arms. She accompanied Pandora and me to obedience classes given by a woman that trains large breed show dogs. I also had another trainer teach Pandora protection commands. She is very obedient despite her happy go lucky demeanor. Rottweilers are known for their devotion and loyalty to family members. And here in Europe, they have been bred for good temperament, not like many in America bred only for aggressiveness. I've seen her protectiveness only a few times. It's there, just beneath her thick coat of fur."

I took Paul at his word. Pandora didn't just walk down the street with us, she commandeered it like an army tank. I felt very safe with her.

I signed the bill, and then we headed to the front desk so I could check out of the hotel. Paul gave his credit card to the desk clerk.

"Paul," I protested, "what are you doing? I should pay the bill."

"I insist. Alan can repay me. He already has, by sending you to Amsterdam and into my life."

Chapter 10

First Sunday Evening

Paul came up to the room with me to help me pack my things. When I opened the door, he looked around and laughed.

"I'm funny?" I questioned him and then started laughing too. I realized how the room must look to the male eye. Clothes and shoes were scattered everywhere.

"You haven't given me much time to organize," I said in my defense.

"I will take all the blame for your lack of control over your wardrobe. Looks like you've planned to be in Amsterdam for a long time judging by the amount of …..of things here, no? Ah ha, so I've found your one flaw. Too much fashion. Can I help you? I think I may have to purchase another houseboat just to accommodate you."

"Believe it or not, I can pack all of this up in no time. Why don't you turn on the TV and relax," I suggested.

Paul sat on the bed with his long legs in front of him, his back propped up on the pillows. He clicked the TV remote and found the Amsterdam news channel.

I organized my clothes and put them neatly in suitcases. I went to the bathroom to gather up my beauty supplies. On impulse, I undressed and entered the bedroom in just my black lace bra and matching thong panties.

Paul was intently watching the TV with a frown on his face, not paying any attention to me. "Bad news, Paul?" I said.

He didn't answer me for a minute or two, and then turned off the TV. "Yes bad news, but it's just more of the same in Amsterdam. The Deputy Mayor has been making things difficult for Mayor Jacob Ruben. Jacob wants to get tough on crime. On the books, as you say in America, our laws have been revamped to allow for stricter sentencing of violent criminals. However, the law has not been followed to the letter in practice. Criminals involved in rape and other violent attacks have gotten off with very brief jail time. For some reason which Jacob and I have yet to figure out the Deputy Mayor likes things the way they are."

"Sounds like you are in the Mayor's corner."

"Yes I am. Jacob is a personal friend of mine. He needs more support in the City Council. Elections are next March and Jacob wants me to run for a seat on the council. If I am successful I can help him fight the criminal elements here."

"Then you are taking Jacob's request seriously." I was seeing a different side to Paul than he had revealed to me before.

"I am thinking about it. Rick and I have been discussing the possibility. I don't know if I'll be successful. The Deputy Mayor's law partner Niels Niemands will be running for the seat as well. He is older than me by five years and well connected.

"Deena, where are your clothes?" he said as he finally noticed what I was wearing, or actually, not wearing. "I thought we would leave here as soon as you were all packed up."

"I've been standing here like this for the last five minutes. Too warm to wear clothes!" I said as I bent down over his feet and started taking off his socks.

"Now what? Don't take my socks off. I hate when a woman surprises me."

"Relax, I'm just going to massage your feet before we leave.

You're so tense after watching the news."

I checked the expression on his face. He didn't seem to be suffering. His right eyebrow shot up as he glared at me.

"So you have a foot fetish, do you?" he said.

"Ah no, more of a full frontal phallic fetish," I replied.

"I see."

"It starts lower though," I said as I took his socks off and rubbed his feet, and then kissed his big toes. I massaged his calf muscles through his slacks, and then moved to his incredibly powerful thighs.

"Any objections so far, Paul?" I asked innocently. "Still hate what I'm doing to you?"

"I hate every second of it, yes," he groaned.

"Good," I laughed as I unzipped his slacks, and pulled them and his underwear off.

He was ready for me. His masculinity was extra large.

"That part of you seems to love it," I said and blew a kiss towards his erection.

"What a fool he is then, my sweet, a fool for you."

"Then stay out of it, this is between him and me," I giggled and kissed his testicles. I inhaled their strong musky aroma. His manhood quivered with each kiss.

I needed more of him…..I needed all of him. I unbuttoned his shirt and buried my nose under his right arm, and then his left. Soft thick black hair greeted me, sweaty, salty and delicious. I got my fill of him there, and travelled south to the fur surrounding his penis. A growl reminded me that his erection deserved and required my undivided attention.

I encircled his foreskin with my thumb and finger, and then slowly moved it up and down. I licked the tip of his penis with my tongue and then my mouth closed over it. My pussy was throbbing, aching, my panties wet from being so turned on by him. His manhood became liquid in me, sending me streams of him. He tasted so good to me.

After giving him what he needed, I wanted him even more.

"What have you done to me?" he said.

"Oh so now you like it?" I challenged him.

"Come here crazy woman," he demanded as he pulled me up to face him. "Don't do that again. Not unless you want me to kiss every part of you. Your mouth," he whispered as he kissed my lips. "Your breasts," he growled as he unfastened my bra and buried his face between my two soft mounds of flesh. "The sweetness between your legs," he groaned and he nuzzled his nose in my panties, inhaled their fragrance, and pulled them down. He kissed and licked all of my wild wet places. He knew where I needed him, and his lips and tongue found the secret spot that soon brought me to a pulsating climax.

As we showered together, Paul said, "Last night on my way to get the pizza, I stopped at my friend who is an apothecary. He gave me some birth control pills for you to take."

"Y'all just think of everything, now don't you honey," I drawled. "I'll take one as soon as we get back to your place."

After we got dressed, we finally organized my things. I pulled the lighter of the large suitcases, and Paul took charge of the heavier one with all the shoes and accessories. When we got to the lobby Paul stepped outside to arrange for a taxi.

While we waited, he chatted with the two hotel doormen. All three of them were joking and laughing together like old buddies. He waved at me and continued his conversation. I could see that Paul would be able to run a successful political campaign in Amsterdam. He knew everyone, everyone knew him and most people liked him very much. And he knew who his enemies were.

The taxi arrived in a few minutes and Paul and the doormen loaded all my things into the trunk. The taxi driver said, "Paul, your friend must be opening up a store with all the clothing she has here!"

"Alberto this is Deena my American girlfriend. Now take us to my houseboat, you know where it is." I couldn't help laughing at Alberto, as we got into the taxi.

When we arrived at Spice Island, Alberto parked and insisted on bringing my things inside. Pandora was waiting for us, and entertained Alberto by sitting and giving him her paw. "She is my friend for sure Paul," Alberto said. "Deena, enjoy Amsterdam. Going to have a heat wave this week I hear," the friendly man said.

"Bye Alberto! Give my love to your wife and children!" Paul said as he waved goodbye.

"Everyone is your friend," I said to Paul with admiration.

"And you my sweetheart, are more than just a friend I hope. We will have to get you a dresser or two for all those things. In the meanwhile, let's relax. For some reason, I am very tired. Not too much sleep last night!"

I agreed. As we took off our clothes and got under the covers, he said, "I promise to leave you alone for one hour. After that, I am not responsible for my actions!"

While we cuddled together, Paul's cell phone beeped. It was a text message from Rick. He had arranged for us to have an eleven o'clock appointment tomorrow with Mr. Grossman at his jewelry exchange. I was to meet Rick at ten at a cafe called De Beste Koffie in the Plantage neighborhood near the exchange.

I was happy I was making some progress with Uncle Alan's project, and happier still that I was in Paul's arms. I fell into a deep sleep.

The loud chirping of my cell phone woke me. Paul was no longer in bed with me, probably out walking Pandora. I looked at the clock - - six o'clock in the evening! I must have been catching up on my jet lag! When I answered the phone, I was pleased to hear Uncle Alan's voice.

"So, what trouble have you gotten into now, Deena? I see from my City Lights online statement that you have checked out of the hotel. And where may I ask are you? Or shall I say who are you with? My too friendly favorite young woman, what are you up to?" he said.

I was so delighted to hear his harsh but endearing Brooklyn accent I didn't even get angry at what he was implying. Of course Uncle Alan knew me too well.

"I have met a wonderful man named Paul Vermeer. He is a Dutch architect. His brother Rick has made arrangements for me to meet with the head of a large jewelry exchange here tomorrow. And Tuesday, Paul and I have an appointment with the Deputy Minister of Trade in The Hague. Yes my favorite Uncle, I love and miss you too!" I truly did. "When can you come to Amsterdam?"

"You know I'm too busy to travel, my sweet girl. I am proud of you. You have already made a few connections. One too many, maybe. Who is this Vermeer? The name sounds familiar."

"Paul is a descendant of the famous Dutch artist Johannes Vermeer. He is a very nice man, educated at Pratt Institute in New York. He and his brother work together in their architectural firm," I explained.

"And are you staying with him?" Uncle Alan asked.

"Yes I am. The hotel manager was coming on to me. Paul and I are dating. Well I guess it's gone a bit further than just dating. He is a very good friend of Jacob Ruben, the Mayor of Amsterdam. And his grandfather helped to save many Jews during the war. You'll like him Uncle Alan, I know you will!"

"I am not happy about you jumping into a relationship so soon. But at least this time you've chosen wisely. Prominent friends couldn't hurt our cause, my love."

"That is not what brought us together. We sat next to each other on the plane. After our meeting in The Hague, he is taking me to Dusseldorf. He has a wealthy German friend there. We're going to stay in his castle. I am nervous though Uncle, nervous about going to Germany."

Uncle Alan was quiet for a moment. Then he said, "Don't be anxious my love. I have met several German business people and they're very much like Americans, friendly and wanting to please."

"Thanks, I'll try. I'll call you Tuesday afternoon, this way I can tell you about both meetings. Love you and miss you Uncle Alan. Tell Mom and Dad I'll call them Tuesday as well."

"Love you too Deena. I am indebted to you, my love, for helping me get the project off the ground. Bye for now."

I will love Uncle Alan forever, I thought. I heard Paul open the houseboat door and come in with Pandora. Will I love Paul forever? I certainly did love him now, I decided, as he entered the bedroom. He walked over to me, took me by my hand and led me into the bathroom.

"Get ready, my lady, I've arranged with a friend to take us on a private boat ride through the canals this evening!"

I washed up and freshened my hair and makeup. I attacked the suitcases and found a pair of tight jeans, low cut pink tank top and black heels. Paul looked at me as I put on my clothes. "You will even stop the bicyclists in their tracks with that outfit, yes!" he said.

He was surely stopping me in my tracks. He was wearing a tight fitting tee shirt in royal blue, the same color as his eyes, and snug fitting jeans. I almost pulled him back into bed, but the thought of a romantic boat ride took precedent for the moment.

"We will take the scenic route to my friend's boat," Paul said. I smiled at him as we left the houseboat. Paul signaled to Pandora to wait for us inside by putting his hand up in front of him.

"I haven't seen a view in Amsterdam that isn't scenic," I replied, as we walked along the canal route.

"There are parts of Amsterdam that are not pretty at all, I am afraid. I fear my niece Vanessa has been hanging out with her boyfriend in some of those questionable places. Rick and I think her boyfriend is her loverboy."

"Loverboy? That doesn't sound so terrible to me."

"In Amsterdam, a loverboy acts as if he is in love with a vulnerable, lonely girl. He then gets her to make money for him by forcing her to be an underage prostitute. He becomes her pimp. Happens all too often here," Paul explained.

"Vanessa has been troubled ever since her grandmother died two years ago. My mother lived with Rick, Rachel and Vanessa. Nessa was especially close to her. They shopped, went to dinner together, attended concerts and theater all the time. When her grandmother died, Nessa lost her best friend.

"Right now Rick and Rachel are trying to keep a close watch on Nessa. Her school has been alerted. They are unfortunately familiar with this type of behavior from other students. The late nights are taking a toll on her parents. We are hoping she will break up with her boyfriend before it is too late."

We walked with our arms around each other's waists until we were at a canal with several boats lined up at the dock. A tall, dark haired man with a full beard waved to Paul from one of the smaller boats. "Hello, my friend!" he said. "You are late! Now that I see your beautiful companion, I don't have to ask why!"

"My friend, how are you? Deena, this is Jaap. He is an old sailing dog. I told him to clean up his act for you this evening," Paul retorted.

"Nice to meet you Deena," said Jaap with a big smile. He looked me over from stem to stern, and his smile grew bigger still. "You are every bit as pretty as Paul has said, and more so. You haven't done this woman justice. Allow me to make you comfortable." He held out his arm for me, and I took it. His dark brown eyes sparkled as he took me aboard his boat. There were comfortable chairs and a small outdoor sofa arranged around a table, where there was a bottle of wine and glasses waiting for us. Paul and I sat next to each other on the sofa, facing the stern of the boat. "It is going to be a lovely evening my friends," said Jaap as we cuddled up close to one another. "We will leave soon. Help yourselves to some wine. Paul, you know where I keep the food when you are hungry. Come forward and visit me in the bow when you two have had enough of one another. Guess I will be mighty lonely up here tonight!" Jaap said as he made his way to the controls.

Soon the boat was moving slowly but surely on the canal. The sun would be setting in about an hour. The fairy tale scenery of Amsterdam and the incredible man I was with made me feel like I was in a magical place.

The magic continued as we drank the wine and witnessed a glorious sunset of red hued colors. We kissed lightly and then passionately. Soon we were hungry and Paul went to find the sandwiches Jaap had prepared. He spent a few minutes with Jaap before returning to me. We ate leisurely, and then Paul wrapped me in his arms as we were lulled to sleep by the rhythm of the boat. I dreamt I was a sorceress. I had cast a spell upon my prince and he would be mine forever.

"Time to get up children!" It was Jaap, and he was gently patting my arm. We were both still sleepy, but said goodnight and thank yous to him.

As we walked back to Spice Island, I enjoyed the warmth of the Amsterdam night and the much warmer feeling of being near Paul. We were soon at the houseboat. Paul said, "we both have a busy day tomorrow. You are meeting Rick at ten o'clock and I have some work to catch up on in my office before our trip."

We let Pandora out for a while, and then undressed each other in bed and tried to go to sleep. But we started kissing. I greedily sucked on his bottom lip. I felt his masculinity ripen against my leg.

"Can't sleep," I whispered in his ear, licking it gently.

"Neither can I," he whispered back.

A loud canine groan could be heard from the rug. "Pandora has had enough of our lovemaking, I guess," I giggled.

"Have you?" he said.

"No not yet," I said. *Not ever.*

"Make believe we are still on Jaap's boat," he said. "It is night. We can see the stars. Give me a kiss for each of the stars you see, Deena. I love you. Kiss me now!"

"Just kisses my love?"

"Start with those. Who knows where the boat will take us?"

Kisses. On our lips. On our bodies. Show him how much you love him. He is telling you how much he loves you with every wet hot touch. Forget everything everyone. Only him. Open yourself. Wide. Hard. Strong. Harder, stronger, faster, deeper. Oh oh oh never ever was it like this. He is groaning, panting, coming. So am I. So am I.

Chapter 11

The Jewelry Exchange

In the early morning, in the time between sleep and wakefulness, I hugged Paul tightly. In his sleep he kissed my forehead. We belonged to each other. It felt so wonderfully right to be with him. My doubts about him and his involvement with a prostitute in the Red Light District had faded away.

Later on we woke up, and showered together. "Are you really here with me Deena, or is this a wonderful dream?"

"Yes, Paul, I am here with you."

"I will miss you today," he said as he kissed me goodbye. "Miss you very much. Say hi to Rick. Yes?"

"Yes," I said as I kissed him back. I didn't want our lips to part. But I let him go, knowing we would see each other at the end of the day.

I met Rick for breakfast at Best Koffie in the Plantage neighborhood, near the Grossman Jewelry Exchange. "Thank you for taking time out of your day to accompany me, Rick. I really appreciate it," I said, after we had been seated at a cozy table in the rear of the restaurant. It was not the same as having Paul with me, but their likeness to one another made me feel that, if Paul was not with me, he was nearby.

Rick had arranged a meeting for me with Mr. Solomon

Grossman, the owner of one of the largest jewelry exchanges in Amsterdam. He explained that Mr. Grossman was very influential in the diamond industry. He hoped he would be able to steer me in the right direction. Mr. Grossman did have a few skilled diamond cutters and polishers in his employ, but I thought Uncle Alan's proposal could enhance the industry in Amsterdam.

"Think nothing of it, Deena. I know Paul would love to be with you instead of me, but he had to prepare for his meeting at The Hague tomorrow. He can't wait to show you Rheinberg and Dusseldorf. Hans's castle and its lake and grounds make for a wonderfully romantic setting."

"Paul has told me about Hans and Giselle. I am looking forward to meeting them."

"You will see, the Dusseldorf area is lovely with all the old castles! You will like Hans and Giselle and their Rottweiler menagerie very much. Paul met Hans when he was searching for a Rottweiler pup for his thirtieth birthday present. That's how he found Pandora. Hans has a very good reputation as a breeder."

Rick continued on a more serious note. "Paul wants to be with you all the time, Deena. He is like a man possessed! I hope you have similar feelings towards him. He is my younger brother and I want only happiness for him. He hasn't been able to find it with any of the woman he has known."

"Ah yes, there seems to have been a lot of women in Paul's life," I said more to myself than to Rick.

"I won't deny that. Women find him very attractive. He doesn't trust the Dutch women though. He thinks all they are interested in is our family's money and notoriety."

"Notoriety?" This was the first time I had heard the word in connection with the Vermeer family.

"I will let Paul explain it to you himself." Rick looked at me with those big blue eyes of his, eerily like Paul's. "Deena, do you love my brother?"

"Yes Rick I do. We had an immediate connection to one another from the moment we met on the plane. He has been wonderful to me. I've only known him three days, and I already miss him when I'm not with him," I said honestly.

"I'm very happy to hear you say that. And now about our business meeting. I'm glad you will have an opportunity to meet Solomon Grossman. After the war, his family opened a jewelry exchange in the building where the Jewish diamond artisans used to work. Paul and I have helped Mr. Grossman obtain approvals for renovations of his building."

Rick and I walked to the Grossman Jewelry Exchange. Since we were a few minutes early for our appointment we had time to browse around the showroom. It was very elegant, with display after display of beautifully set diamond earrings, bracelets, pendants and rings.

"Do you mind if I look at a few of the rings?" I asked Rick. "I want to get an idea of the quality of the diamonds."

"Of course. We have some time," he said.

"Good morning," I said to one of the sales people. "How are you? I would like to see that piece," I said as I pointed to a large emerald cut diamond ring.

"But of course miss. For a special occasion?" The salesman asked.

"Just planning for the future," I said and laughed. Rick smiled at me.

"What do you think Rick?" I tried the ring on my left ring finger. The diamond appeared to be approximately three carats.

"Lovely... anything would look lovely on you!" Rick said.

"Thank you!" As I spoke, I took a jeweler's loupe out of my purse. "Let's see what we really have here." I put the loupe up to my right eye, and bent down to examine the ring on my finger.

The salesman started to protest, but then thought better of it.

I put the jeweler's loupe away, and said to both Rick and the salesman, "the quality of the diamond is excellent! I cannot wait to meet Mr. Grossman and tell him myself!"

Rick led me to Mr. Grossman's office. He was waiting for us. "Hello Solomon. How have you been? I'd like you to meet Deena Green, my brother's girlfriend. Ms. Green and her employer Alan Rosen of New York have an interesting proposal. I'll let Ms. Green explain it to you herself."

"So nice to meet you, Mr. Grossman. Please call me Deena," I said. "I've examined one of your diamonds this morning. It is quite beautiful, and of an excellent quality too!"

"Nice meeting you Ms. Green. I hope your family is well, Rick," Mr. Grossman said formally. "Please have a seat." Mr. Grossman pointed to two chairs facing his desk. Rick and I made ourselves comfortable.

"Well," I said, "My employer Alan Rosen's family members were Jewish diamond cutters and polishers here in Amsterdam prior to the Second World War. A few of those artisans survived the war and settled in New York. Alan's goal is to have a group of Jewish diamond artisans re-establish the industry here in Amsterdam. I am assisting Alan in that endeavor."

Just then Rick's cell phone rang and he excused himself. "Sorry Solomon, Deena, I need to take this call. I'll be back in a few minutes."

"Well, Mr. Grossman, what do you think of our idea?" I said as Rick left the office. I decided we might as well get down to business.

"I am not in favor of your idea, Ms. Green, if that is what you call it. We already have all the diamond artisans we need here in Amsterdam. Most of the diamond work is now done in Antwerp."

"We are aware of where diamonds are now being finished, Mr. Grossman. We believe that by bringing Jewish diamond artisans back to this city, we will add a new dimension to the community here. Aren't you the least bit interested in welcoming more Jewish families? We also think the economy of Amsterdam will benefit from the growth in the diamond industry," I said, a little louder than I had planned to.

Mr. Grossman was ready for me. He said, "Ms. Green, I don't agree with you in the least. We have enough people here already working in the diamond industry. You will be hard pressed to get the necessary red tape cleared with the bureaucrats in The Hague. And your association with Paul Vermeer is going to work against you. He is the bad boy of Amsterdam society. And his family's reputation……"

"But," I interrupted him, "Paul and Rick's grandfather was a respected member of the Dutch Resistance Movement."

"And their father, Ms. Green, don't you know about him?" Mr. Grossman said with a sneer.

"That's quite enough Solomon. What's gotten into you? Paul and I have helped you recently, and this is the thanks we receive in return?" Rick said loudly to Mr. Grossman. He had entered the office without Mr. Grossman or me realizing it.

"Let's go Deena," Rick said. "And Solomon, you had better think of a way to apologize to Ms. Green, a guest in our city. And to my family as well. Good day!"

When we were outside the exchange building, I breathed a sigh of relief. I was very upset by Mr. Grossman's words, and surprised at the mention of the Vermeer "family reputation".

"What was that all about?" I asked Rick.

"Paul is going to have to explain our family's history to you. I am so sorry Deena. I thought Solomon would be in your corner. I completely misjudged him."

I had a feeling Mr. Grossman was worried about the competition that another diamond business would bring. I was very upset about the things he said concerning Paul and his father.

"Rick, I feel in my heart and soul that Uncle Alan's project will succeed. Can we walk to the old Portuguese Synagogue, please? It's not far from here, is it? Paul and I visited there the other day, but I need to go back now."

As soon as Rick and I entered the courtyard of the synagogue, built in the 1600s, I knew I had to continue with my purpose in coming to Amsterdam. The synagogue was a symbol of the history of the Jewish community here, a community that deserved to be revitalized and renewed.

Chapter 12
Confession

Rick and I said our goodbyes. It was cloudy and dreary as I walked back to the houseboat. Although he tried to reassure me our meeting at The Hague with Chris Bucholtz would go much better than the meeting with Mr. Grossman, it was hard for me to be optimistic. But I promised myself once and for all I wouldn't let anything stand in the way of Uncle Alan's project.

Grossman's comments hinted at something dark and dangerous about Paul. It didn't make any sense though from what I knew about him, and how I felt about him. The mysterious scars did trouble me, as well as the phone call about the Red Light District. I was drawn to Paul, heart and soul. I couldn't get away from him. Some unknown force was pulling me under, not letting me surface, keeping me close to him.

But there was something very disturbing in Paul's family history, something he as yet did not feel comfortable sharing with me. I had a feeling I wouldn't have to wait long to find out the truth.

When I arrived at Spice Island, Paul was not at home yet, probably still working at his office. Pandora greeted me with her tail wagging. I could tell she considered me part of her family already. She waited patiently for her food. After she finished eating, I attached her leash to her collar, and we went out together.

Wherever we walked we encountered beautiful canals, which

were accented at every cross street with small bridges spanning them. Private yachts, larger tourist boats and of course houseboats filled the waterways. I realized I loved his city almost as much as I loved Paul. I felt very much at home in Amsterdam.

I stopped at a store to buy some fish for dinner, leaving Pandora to guard the entrance. Next door I bought two bottles of Riesling, collected the big friendly girl and headed back home.

When Pandora and I got in, I changed into something comfortable, a short pink sundress and pink thong panties to match. I started to prepare a salad for dinner, and bent down to get some vegetables from the refrigerator.

"I like the view, yes," a deep, familiar masculine voice behind me said. I started to stand up so I could kiss Paul hello. Instead he reached for my panties and pulled them off. "Now bend down again. Don't deny me that incredible view!" he demanded.

"But we have so much to talk about Paul. I have so many questions…"

"Not now. Later, I promise," he said.

I couldn't say no to him. That voice, the heat in that voice could melt the snow caps off the Rockies in February.

I did as he told me. I felt his tongue licking my pussy from behind me, as he held my rear tightly in his strong hands.

"Slow down, cowboy," I warned him. "This filly gonna be out of the corral before you can even saddle 'er."

"So you did miss me? How much baby? As much as I missed you, yes?" he said.

"So much, too much. What am I to do with you?" I responded.

"Prove it. Prove how much you missed me."

"Git outta my way then. I'm after you now!"

I turned around and pulled his slacks and underwear off. I got down on my knees and started licking his beautiful round testicles. They tasted like nutmeg spice.

"Easy baby easy," he warned me.

"You started this and I'm going to finish it. I just can't get enough of you, sugar, why do ya always taste so damn good?"

Paul responded by picking me up and carrying me into the bedroom.

" Woman, you make me crazy!" He sat down at the edge of the bed. He held me tightly as I straddled him. I pulled off my sundress and thrust my nipples in his mouth. He was making me crazy too. Knowing there was something notorious about him made me want him even more. If he was a bad boy, I was for sure going to be his bad girl.

I was amazed at how I wanted and needed him. He thrust himself in me as he lifted me up and down. My body shook with each wave of desire until we both climaxed. Every one of my sexual fantasies was coming true with Paul.

After we had both satisfied each other, he said "I need a warm bath. Want to join me? We'll relax. And then I'll tell you everything."

"Yes," I said. "Yes."

Paul prepared the bath. When it was ready we settled in facing each other.

"Deena, my love," he said as he washed my body all over with a soapy cloth, "I don't understand something. How could the guys in the States let you out of their sight? Any day now I expect some American boyfriend of yours to appear in Amsterdam and take you away from me back to New York."

After a few moments, I answered him. "There is no American boyfriend, Paul. Maybe it's my fault. But it seems most American guys I've met are interested in a woman for a short while, and then can't wait to get back to their male friends for what I call male bonding. In the U. S. many men go from one event with their guy friends to another. It doesn't seem to really matter what it is –

endless sporting events, poker nights, golf outings."

I dunked myself under water for a moment, resurfaced and then continued, "The women are supposed to be 'independent' and develop their own interests. That's not how I was brought up. I'm an only child, and my Mom, Dad and I went everywhere together on the weekends. My parents had many friends that were like family to me. I'm not used to this 'American independence'. I need more from a relationship than a date night once or twice a week."

Paul frowned, and closed his eyes for a moment. He looked troubled. Maybe I had said too much. I've scared him away, I thought. I'm so foolish, with my non-stop talking.

"Deena," he said, interrupting my thoughts, "your childhood with your devoted parents sounds wonderful. You were truly loved by them and the members of your extended family. I envy you, yes."

"You do?" I responded happily. I was so glad he understood what a treasure my parents were and are.

"Yes I do. I'm going to be honest with you and get my family secrets out in the open. I hope you'll still love me and trust me after I tell you about myself."

I reassured him by holding his hands in mine as he spoke.

"My mother was from Brussels, as I've told you. She was a beautiful woman, devoted to her family and her Catholic faith. My father, unlike his father, was an unscrupulous businessman. He amassed quite an empire in Amsterdam of real estate holdings, especially in De Wallen. My brother and I knew he was the owner of several brothels. Without going into too much detail, let's just say my father was a very frequent patron of those brothels.

"My mother tried to influence my father to lead a moral life. All of her attempts failed. A power struggle between my parents developed for control over their sons. My mother was forced to strike a bargain with my father. She took Rick under her wing, and my father took control over me. If she had fought him on it, my mother would have lost both Rick and me to his power. Rick grew up to be a devout Catholic, with a social conscience which he has to this day.

"My father never let a day go by without reminding me what a worthless boy I was because I didn't have a different prostitute every night. I had to invent an alternate life for myself, a secret life, something to escape to, to believe in.

"On my way home from high school, I would pass the shop of a gypsy fortune teller. One day, when I was sixteen, I stopped to look in the window of the shop. I was fascinated by the crystal balls, tarot cards and Ouija boards displayed there. The fortune teller saw me staring and motioned to me to come inside. Her name was Electra. She was in her sixties, with unlined olive skin, beautiful black eyes and long black hair.

"Electra told me she could see I was unhappy. 'Tell me your troubles, Jean-Paul. Maybe I can help you,' she said. I described to her how my father treated me. After I told her my story, she held my hands in hers and closed her eyes. I closed mine too. There was a searing hot charge that passed between us.

"Electra said she had seen into my past as well as my future. She believed I had lived before in another era, and I had had a wonderfully rich life then, filled with love. My future would at first be very difficult, but then would be filled with love as well. My astrology sign is Sagittarius, the archer, and she encouraged me to have an arrow tattooed on my arm, which I did. She said it would give me strength, and would eventually lead me to my soul mate, an Aquarian."

"Paul, that's my astrology sign! I'm an Aquarian!" I said.

"Electra was right then! And she was also right about how difficult things would get for me. My sixteenth birthday present from my father was a night with a prostitute. By the time I was seventeen, I was addicted to sex and drugs. I dropped out of high school. I had fallen in love with one of the beautiful young prostitutes, and she was in love with me. Her name was Tatiana. We were tattooed with identical heart tattoos as a testament of our love for each other.

"But her pimp found us in bed together one night. He came at me with his switchblade, and cut my face. He wanted to destroy our love tattoos, so he attacked me at my waist too. Tatiana was able to hide from him somewhere in Amsterdam. After a day or two she visited me in the hospital where I was being treated for the wounds, one of which was serious. Tatiana demanded I escape with her to Romania, her homeland. My mother had already made arrangements for me to leave Amsterdam for New York to stay with her friends when I was well enough. When I refused Tatiana's request, she became enraged. She then told me she was a sorceress. My prostitute was a witch as well, lucky, no? In her anger, she cast a spell on me."

"What kind of spell?" I asked.

"Her spell, her curse on me was that I could only fall in love with a prostitute. I should have known Tatiana would eventually be my undoing. The fortune teller's predictions of a good life filled with love seemed impossible, but I held onto her words like a lifeline."

"Have you fallen in love with another prostitute since then, Paul? Tell me the truth," I pleaded with him. I was afraid to hear his answer. I steadied myself for a confession about the woman in the Red Light District.

"No Deena, I have been in love with a few women, yes, but not a prostitute," he reassured me.

"Then maybe her spell has been broken," I said hopefully.

"Well, yes, maybe it has, if it ever existed in the first place. My Uncle Frederick, my father's brother, prevailed on my father to allow my mother to send me to her good friends in New York, two sisters named Pamela and Denise Sulzberg. They took me into their home in Manhattan and sent me to a private high school. They brought me to a psychiatrist who helped me with my drug addiction and emotional problems. They saved my life!

"Pamela and Denise are architects. I guess you could say they were my role models. I went to Pratt Institute to study architecture because of their example. I usually confer with them on special projects like the Plantage building. We had a meeting the week before you and I met.

"Turns out that I am a pretty talented architect. Also turns out I still have a very strong need for sex, yes."

"But you can control yourself, Paul, can't you?" I already knew all about that strong need, and realized I wanted him all the more because of it.

"Control myself?" he said and laughed. "Not around you I can't, no. And I don't want to control myself when I'm with you. From the moment I saw you on our flight, I knew you were the woman I wanted. I love your feistiness, your sexy beauty. I never know if Dutch women want me for my family money or my bad boy reputation."

For once I was speechless. I moved closer still to Paul and looked at his big blue eyes that were on the verge of tears. "I hope you can still love me and be with me Deena, still respect me. My reputation as a playboy in Amsterdam goes back to those days in De Wallen. Hard to live down, I guess."

"I love you Paul," I said simply. "I love the courage and strength you found to overcome your wounds and be healed. You had help, it's true, but you accepted that help."

"I'm not lonely anymore," he said to me. "Not since you've moved into my home and my life."

"How can a man as attractive as you be lonely?"

"Sex is easy to have, yes. But love, when someone loves who you are, and you love who they are, that's difficult to find. But I can stop looking now. Because I've found you. You are smart, caring, loving, sexy, giving. Why should I look anywhere else?" He kissed me gently.

We were quiet for some time.

"My father died ten years ago," he said after a while. "Probably from too much drugs and alcohol. I never made peace with him. Soon after he died Rick sold off all the properties my father owned in De Wallen."

"And your mother?" I asked.

"She passed away two years ago. She lived to see me move back to Amsterdam, lead a normal life and start working with Rick in his architectural firm. My niece Vanessa was devastated by her grandmother's death. They were devoted to each other. She has been withdrawn and secretive ever since. Rachel and Rick are very worried about Vanessa and her boyfriend. They fear the worst will happen to her."

His story was heartbreaking. I realized I loved him even more for trusting me to believe in him.

Paul climbed out of the bath tub, and then helped me. We dried each other and dressed in shorts and tee shirts. Paul prepared dinner while I opened a bottle of wine and poured us each a glass. By the time he had finished cooking, we needed a refill on the Riesling. We took the food and wine out on the deck. While we ate we looked at the beautiful night sky – the moon and stars reflecting their lights onto all of Amsterdam.

"Come here and hold me and kiss me," I said seductively after we had finished dinner. "I want to show you how much I love you."

Paul stood up quickly, and kissed me hard on my mouth. He held my left hand tightly as we quickly walked to the front of houseboat. The next thing I knew he was sitting on the bed and I was standing next to him. As I stood there stroking his hair, he stripped off my clothes and in a minute I was naked before him. He was on fire. He suckled my nipples hungrily and then got on his knees and licked me between my legs greedily as if it was our first time together.

His wild fire spread to me. I got down on the floor next to him and pulled his jeans and underwear off. I wanted his cock in my mouth. I couldn't stop pleasuring him. He lost himself in physical arousal. I stopped for a moment, he growled at me, and I continued pleasuring him until he came in me.

"Woman," he said when we both caught our breath, "we have to pack for our trip to The Hague and Dusseldorf. It will be hot this week, so bring a bikini, shorts and those sexy tank tops, yes! Also plan to wear a business dress for our meeting with Chris Bucholtz. I spoke to him today. He is of course looking forward to meeting you. I do not trust that guy, no. But he is the point person in the government for the approvals we both require."

We busied ourselves with packing. Paul went to Rick's home to pick up a car, and parked it in front of the houseboat. It was an understated BMW sedan, roomy enough for Pandora to be comfortable in the backseat.

Chapter 13

At The Hague

At eight o'clock the next morning, we packed up the car with a suitcase for each of us, Pandora's food, bottles of water and Pandora. Paul drove to The Hague in about an hour. At Paul's suggestion, I wore a simple black sleeveless dress, a white suit jacket with a black and white scarf to cover the low neckline of the dress. Our appointment with Mr. Bucholtz was for ten, so we had time to have a quick breakfast at an outdoor café overlooking a canal. Pandora curled up next to us as we ate and enjoyed the early morning bustle of The Hague, the capital city of The Netherlands.

We finished breakfast and walked to the office of the Minister of Trade. The security guard at the building greeted Paul with the usual friendly small talk and petted Pandora. Then we walked up the steps to the second floor.

A tall handsome man was there to greet us as we arrived at the top of the stairs. *I could get used to living in The Netherlands*, I thought. *The whole country is just chocked full of great looking guys!*

"Hello Vermeer," the man said with reserve. "So you are here once again. And you must be Deena Green. I'm Chris Bucholtz, Deputy Minister of Trade." He first shook Paul's hand and then took mine in his. He bent over very gentlemanly and gave my hand a quick kiss. "Welcome to The Netherlands. I trust Vermeer you are treating your American guest well. If not, Ms. Green, I am ready to take over as your host at a moment's notice." Chris had light blue eyes that looked closely at mine as he spoke.

Paul frowned as he watched Chris stare at me. I cleared my throat and said, "Hi Chris, so nice meeting you. Please call me Deena. I would love to see your office. The architecture in this building is charming. We have nothing like this in the States. And you, kind sir, are charming as well!" I put my arm in Chris's as he walked me down the hall to his spacious office. Paul reluctantly followed us with Pandora.

As we were comfortably seated, Chris said, "Lovely dog you have. From Rheinberg, yes? I am familiar with the breeders there. All of fine reputation." Chris's English was excellent, although he spoke with a noticeable Germanic accent.

"So," he continued, "I know what brings you here Vermeer. I still am working on your latest landmark building renovation request. Deena, tell me what I can do for you?" he asked with a smile.

His smile grew wider as I took off my scarf and jacket to reveal my décolletage. I dove right in and said, "Warm in here isn't it? Quite a heat wave y'all are expecting I hear. Chris, I'm so glad you are interested in what has brought me to your wonderful country. My employer Alan Rosen of New York and I want to bring the diamond cutting and polishing trade back to Amsterdam. We have Jewish artisans in New York ready to emigrate to The Netherlands with their families and their expertise."

Chris thought for a few moments as he turned from me and looked out his window. When he turned back to face me he said, "Very unusual idea, Deena. But a good one. I can imagine The Netherlands being famous once again for diamonds, not just tulips. Several steps must be taken. Visas for the workers and their families, approvals for the new business. I am going to give your proposal serious thought. I assume you have something in writing for me to look over."

"Yes I do. My email address and cell phone number are on the first page," I explained as I handed Chris a detailed outline of the proposal Uncle Alan and I had prepared in New York.

"Wonderful. I hope you will be patient. Government approvals do take time, as your friend here knows all too well," Chris said as he looked with disdain at Paul. "I will give your proposal the highest priority Deena. You will hear from me within the next month." Chris stood up and Paul and I did as well. We walked to the door with Pandora in tow, and Chris reluctantly shook Paul's hand. Chris then kissed me three times on my cheeks. "Deena, please call me if you need anything. Here is my card. I spend many evenings in Amsterdam and would love to take you to dinner if I may."

"Sounds great Chris. It has been a privilege meeting you. I look forward to seeing you soon, and hearing how the approvals are moving along. Bye," I said and waved to Chris as we walked to the stairs.

When we exited the building, Paul said to me angrily, "Did you have to show off your breasts to him? What were you thinking Deena?"

"I was thinking, Paul, the only way to get my proposal to be even considered by this very important man was to appeal to his baser instincts. I was just paving the way for both your project and mine. I'm not going to bed with him. I have all I can handle in that department already," I said sweetly as I kissed him on his lips.

His anger subsided a bit as he returned my kiss with a long seductive one.

"Let's get back to the car and head out to Rheinberg," he said. "I need some fresh air to clear my head."

Chapter 14

Arrival at the Castle

Paul couldn't wait to get in the car and be on our way. He was soon driving on the highway between Amsterdam and Rheinberg at a very fast clip. Everyone seemed to be speeding along as well, so I relaxed and reviewed our brief but important meeting with Chris Bucholtz.

Perhaps I could have handled it differently. Chris and Paul seemed to have some personal agenda between them. My "getting comfortable" by displaying myself may not have been politically correct, but I thought Chris would be more likely to at least give my proposal some consideration. I had a feeling he was somehow some way going to help me.

Other than Mr. de Jonge, the manager of the hotel, Paul seemed to get along with everyone until we met with Chris. I was curious.

"Paul, tell me sweetheart, what is the problem between you and Chris Bucholtz? I am guessing at some point you were both interested in the same woman," I said.

"You are correct, my little witch. About a year ago, he had a girlfriend in Amsterdam. She and I were having an affair at the same time. I didn't know Chris and Catrien were so serious, almost ready to become engaged. She finally confessed to him about us. They broke off their relationship, and Chris has blamed me for it. Difficult dealing with him on a professional level as you can imagine. Maybe he thinks he can take you away from me. I hope he is wrong," Paul said.

"He is wrong so wrong!" I sang the words to him. "Chris is nice looking I'll admit, but you are my man."

With that Paul increased his speed. "Does everything you say and do have to be so suggestive, woman? We'll be in Rheinberg in about one hour. Enjoy the scenery."

The landscape began to change. Rich forested areas flanked the highway on either side. Large lakes could be seen in the distance. As we drew closer to Rheinberg, I was getting more excited and nervous as well.

Paul said to me, "Look to your left. That's Hans's lake. Isn't it beautiful?"

We drove past the lake and soon made a left turn into a driveway. Paul got out of the car and walked over to a gate. There was an intercom system there. Paul pressed the button, and the gate opened for us. We drove up to the castle. It was painted pale yellow, with large windows covering the façade. There were turrets at the rooftop of the immense structure. I stared at each detail, taking it all in. I felt like I had entered a fairy tale land, with my prince, Paul, right beside me.

A stocky grey haired man came out to greet the three of us. He was followed by a large female Rottweiler that looked like an older version of Pandora.

"Welcome, welcome to our home. Come in come in, Deena! I'm Herr Schneider, but you must call me Hans. Deena is more beautiful than you described Paul. Why have you hidden this exquisite woman in that damp swamp of a city? She belongs here in our castle, among royalty! May I introduce Princess Juliana, royal mother of Pandora. Princess Juliana, meet Lady Deena," Hans said in a very formal way.

I bowed and extended my hand which Hans took and kissed three times. "It's a pleasure meeting you Hans," I said. Then I bent down and petted Juliana on her neck. She seemed to like me and moved closer, wagging her tail.

Hans responded with, "the pleasure is all mine." His light blue eyes twinkled. "Come in come in, you must see Juliana's latest litter of eight puppies. They grow bigger before my eyes."

Paul and Hans hugged each other like father and son. In the meanwhile Pandora was running circles around Juliana. She was so happy to see her mother, but would soon realize she would have to share her with the new puppies.

"Come right in, Lady Deena. Welcome to my humble home. Please stand under the chandelier so I can get a better look at you. Paul, fix us some drinks, please, my friend." Paul went into the very large adjoining room which featured an old wooden bar.

"So now fraulein, let us see what we have here!" Hans said as he tilted my chin up towards his face. "Light green eyes, yes, wonderful color just as Paul told me. Perfect full lips, and a magnificent figure as well. Very thick long red hair. Yes, the Slavic grace note is on your face that plays like a Chopin prelude to me. Your family is both Slavic and Polish, yes?" Hans asked.

"No, we are originally from Wurzberg, Bavaria," I said.

"Ah then yes a German princess! You are indeed a beauty. Paul discussed your attributes with me at great length. We are very close you know. He is like a son to me. So you will make lots of babies, you and Paul, you look very ripe for the task," he said.

"You must excuse my husband's forwardness," a female voice interrupted Hans. "He gets carried away sometimes. Hello, I am Giselle, and you must be Deena."

Paul walked quickly to Giselle and gave her three kisses on her cheeks.

"Giselle, Hans almost always gets carried away. This time though I don't blame him. Isn't Deena lovely?" Paul said.

I was getting a bit uncomfortable being on display. I took a second look at Giselle. I couldn't believe my eyes! She looked very much like me! I kept staring at her and then stuttered, "but you, Giselle, we….don't you think……think we resemble each other?"

"Yes Deena we do, now that you mention it. Is your family German?" Giselle responded.

"Yes, German Jews originally from Wurzberg. My family emigrated to Baltimore, Maryland in the late 1840s," I said.

"Well," said Hans, "Jews have lived in Germany since the 1300s. You may be descended from the same royal family that Giselle is. I knew it. You belong in this castle, Lady Deena. Let us move to the bar and drink to rediscovering your royalty!"

Hans took my arm and Paul took Giselle's as we walked to the bar. We all drank a delicious fruity liqueur. "Please Paul more schnapps!" commanded Hans. "Very good," he declared. "And now our two beauties will bring Juliana and Pandora to the kennel to visit the puppies. The men in the meanwhile will have a business chat."

I followed Giselle to one of the many rooms on the first floor of the castle. Three large dog kennels, all lined with thick bedding and blankets, were in the room. The eight puppies were fast asleep in one of the kennels, curled up against, and in some cases on top of, each other. They were so adorable, all black balls of fur with traces of the distinctive red brown Rottweiler markings. "Good girl," Giselle said gently to the new mother as Juliana settled herself in with the puppies. They crowded around her and began nursing.

Pandora made herself comfortable in one of the kennels as if it were her own. "She feels right at home here, and so does Paul. Ever since we met him four years ago when he was searching for a puppy, we have felt like he was part of our family. As you probably know, his parents are both deceased. We have one daughter, Ada, who is at university in Heidelberg. Hans and I are very fond of Paul," Giselle said as she looked at me affectionately.

"I am very fond of him too," I admitted.

"Paul tells us he loves you, Deena. And of course Hans is already planning the wedding here at our home," Giselle said with a smile.

"How very sweet of both of you. We only know each other a few days. And I am Jewish. I don't know how his brother Rick would feel about Paul marrying outside of the Christian faith. We haven't discussed it at all," I said, a bit overwhelmed.

"Unfortunately Paul's father made sure that he grew up without religion. Mr. Vermeer worshipped money and sex. There was no love in that man. We would be delighted, and so would Rick I am sure, if you brought the Jewish religion into Paul's life," Giselle said as she looked into my eyes closely.

"You and Hans are so special. I am overcome by your kindness!" I said.

"Think nothing of it. I will show you to your room where you can freshen up for dinner. Our housekeeper has brought your luggage upstairs. Let's leave our canine brood and follow me."

We walked to a large graceful staircase and up the stairs to the bedroom wing. Giselle led the way to a beautiful guest room decorated in pale blues and yellows. There was a large four poster bed with several decorative pillows, a soft blue blanket and a thick rug in the same colors covering the old wood floors.

"Make yourself at home, Deena. I know you have had a busy day. We will have a late dinner at eight o'clock, but before that I will have some fruit and teas sent up here for you and Paul. Rest well."

I was so taken with Giselle's kindness that I didn't know quite what to say. "Thank you!" was all I could manage as Giselle left and softly closed the door behind her. I lay down on the bed.

She was right, it was a busy day, and a nap was in order. There was a knock on the door, and the housekeeper came in with a tray of goodies. "I am Berta," she said. "If you need anything, please let me know. I hope you like what I have prepared for you and Paul."

Fruits, pastries, coffee, tea and juice generously filled the tray. "Enjoy, fraulein," Berta said as she left, too quickly for me to thank her.

The pastries smelled delicious. I couldn't resist them. I got off the bed and sat in a chair next to the table laden with food. I picked one that looked like cheese and cherry and took a bite. *Heavenly*, I thought, and was so absorbed in the taste I didn't notice Paul had entered the room. He was behind me and whispered in my ear, "Give me a bite of something delicious, baby."

I turned around and laughed as I put the sweet confection in his mouth. He chewed it hungrily and then sat on the floor at my feet and began eating the fruit, pausing to share some with me.

"And now to the real afternoon treat, my love. You grow more beautiful every time I am away from you. In the past two hours, your beauty has taken on mythic proportions," Paul said as he stroked my thighs, and then moved his hand higher.

"Whatever are you talking about Paul?" I asked innocently.

"Do not play with me Deena. You are an angel and you are also a calculating courtesan. No other woman has held me in their power the way you do. You fulfill my every dream, waking and sleeping. You are my prostitute, my companion, my whore, my lover," he said.

"Just the way Tatiana's spell said it would be for you. To love only a prostitute," I said, more to myself than to him. I didn't know if he was acting the part to seduce me or if he really believed what he was saying.

"Many famous beauties in history were courtesans," he said. "You know how to excite me so much I cannot even describe the pleasure you give me. Each time I am with you, I feel like it is our first time, yes! I love you Deena, and the many ways you are my woman."

He caressed me more insistently between my legs. He knew how to please me too, more than any other man I knew or dreamed of. But would he always be mine? Was I a match for his sexual needs?

"Mmm, you bring out the whore in me," I said to him. I moved to sit next to him on the thick rug.

As if he read my mind, he said, "I have no doubt you will please me forever and ever, yes." He smiled his slightly crooked, devilish grin.

"Dutch men like to be top dog. But Belgian men, we want our women in control, yes? I'm your bitch now, baby," he said.

His words aroused something hidden inside of me. Only my needs, my wants this time. I quickly took off my dress, my panties and my bra. I rubbed my breasts on his nose, and then moved them down to his mouth.

"Suck my nipples," I said as I pushed both of them to his waiting lips. He suckled them gently at first, and then harder, squeezing my breasts so he could more easily pleasure each dark pink treat. My pussy was wet, so wet. "Finger me. Lick me. Make me come, bitch," I commanded him. He knew what I wanted. Only my pleasure. And he gave me what I needed then. For the moment I was satisfied. But I knew I would want him again very soon, and so did he.

Chapter 15

Dinner at the Castle

We lost track of time after making love, falling asleep in each other's arms. There was a knock at the door, and Giselle's voice cooed "dinner in one hour love birds."

Paul said, "thank you Giselle we will be ready shortly."

We kissed our way through our shower together in the sumptuous bathroom and dried each other with the thick towels. We dressed comfortably in jeans and shirts. Paul's shirt was light blue and mine was pale yellow. We each left several buttons open. We were both looking forward to making love again after dinner.

Paul led the way to the magnificent first floor dining room. Hans and Giselle were waiting for us. They both greeted us with kisses on our cheeks. "We trust you rested well. You both are glowing," Giselle said proudly. "The dogs have been fed and had some time outdoors."

"Please sit next to me, Lady Deena," Hans said from the head of the table. Paul sat across from me and next to Giselle.

When we were comfortably seated, Berta served the first course, soup and dumplings. Hans tasted his, and said "scrumptious, just scrumptious. Please everyone, begin. I will pour the wine, a Riesling from our vineyard."

As we ate our soup and dumplings and sipped the excellent

wine, Hans said, "so Deena, Paul has told me about your special mission to Amsterdam. I would like to help you in any way that I can."

"Thank you Hans, that is so thoughtful of you. We have presented the proposal to Chris Bucholtz, the Deputy Minister of Trade. It is his decision now."

"Yes, Paul told me that you have charmed Mr. Bucholtz. And I am also charmed by you and inspired by your idea. So much so I am going to contribute a large sum of money to help the artisans once they arrive in Amsterdam. I will also help fund the renovations to the building in the Plantage."

"Oh, Hans that is so generous of you!" I said. I couldn't believe what I was hearing! I jumped out of my chair and rushed over to Hans and gave him a big hug and a kiss on his cheek. I did the same to Giselle, and then kissed Paul on his lips, perhaps a little too seductively for the dining room. Hans and Giselle were enjoying the show however and smiled huge smiles.

"We are just happy to help your cause Deena. We are thanking you for giving us the opportunity to help the Jewish community of Amsterdam," Hans said respectfully.

I don't remember too much of the dinner after that. The food and wine were delicious. I couldn't wait to get back to the bedroom and celebrate with Paul.

We collected Pandora, and then went up the huge staircase to the bedroom. Paul carried me over the threshold and gently placed me on the four poster bed. Pandora found a soft doggie blanket on the floor to curl up on. He slowly took off his clothes for me, first his shirt revealing his muscular chest. Then he took off his slacks and his underwear, displaying his manhood in all its magnificence. I thought his body, his virility, must be the most splendid the old castle had ever seen.

He gently unbuttoned my blouse, kissing my exposed rounded

flesh as he did so. He unfastened my bra and suckled my nipples. They were instantly erect. He unzipped my jeans and as he pulled them down over my hips, he kissed and licked my stomach. He quickly finished with my jeans and panties and found what he was searching for, the spot between my legs, the spot that moistened at the very thought of him. Now I had the sight and smell and taste of him too. He was first gentle, but then grew more forceful as he entered me. "Love me. Love me like I love you, yeesss," he commanded me. And as my hips rose to meet his again and again and again, I did.

Chapter 16
Call from Uncle Alan

Paul kissed me goodbye early the next morning. "Go back to sleep my love, I am going into town to check on a museum project. When I return, we will go to the lake together."

I snuggled next to Pandora who had joined me in bed. Giselle must have fed her and let her out because she seemed satisfied to rest with me.

I thought of what Paul said last night. I was hoping to be Paul's girlfriend, his partner. Now he wanted me to be his courtesan, his prostitute.

I knew from the beginning that Paul's need for sex was very strong. Could I satisfy his sexual appetite the way prostitutes had in the past? Would I be able to be everything he wanted me to be?

Perhaps Tatiana's spell was a reality after all. Maybe Paul could only truly love a prostitute.

Pandora's soft snoring lulled me back to sleep. I would need to be well rested for our afternoon swim and more at the lake.

The ringing of my cell phone startled me at ten o'clock. It was Uncle Alan. *Oh no! I had forgotten to call him after our meeting at The Hague yesterday.*

"So sleepyhead, wake up! I want to hear all about the meetings at the jewelry exchange and The Hague," he practically shouted.

"Love you too Uncle," I said, still groggy with sleep. "You're up early!"

"Early – I never went to sleep last night. What on earth have you been doing?" he demanded.

"Calm down Uncle. Paul and I arrived at his friend Hans' home in Rheinberg yesterday afternoon. Hans and his wife Giselle have been wining and dining us since then. Sorry I didn't call you. The meeting at The Hague went very well. Mr. Bucholtz seemed very interested in our idea. I left the written proposal with him for his review. I think I established a good rapport with him," I explained.

"Rapport? You mean, dearest one, you charmed the pants off of him," Uncle Alan laughed.

"Something like that. Paul was jealous," I laughed too.

"Good! And Grossman the jeweler?" Uncle Alan said.

"The meeting with Grossman didn't go well at all. I think he's afraid we will somehow become his competition. And he doesn't have very nice things to say about Paul. But Hans has pledged a large sum of money to help us financially. He and Giselle are very generous people."

"Ah yes, the good Germans. We'll need all the assistance we can get. By the way, how is your friend Paul?" he asked.

"He is out this morning checking on some projects in town. The weather here is hot, we'll go for a swim in Hans' private lake this afternoon."

"I guess it's too late for me to say this, Deena, but don't get in over your head with this man," he warned me.

"You are right, Uncle, it's too late for that. Paul and I are very close."

"I don't want you to get hurt, my sweetheart. I am very concerned about you."

"I know, Uncle, I know. How is Scott doing, by the way? I hope I was able to give him enough to go on to get started with sales.

He's very smart so I'm sure he'll do well."

"Scott is doing fine, Deena. He has already brought in another account."

"That's great Uncle Alan. Well, bye for now, I hope to have good news in a few weeks. In the meanwhile, Paul is designing workspace in an old factory building for us."

"OK, love, take good care of yourself."

"Love you, Uncle."

Chapter 17

First Day at The Lake

After my conversation with Uncle Alan, my cell phone rang again. It was Ali. I had been so busy I had neglected to call or text her.

"Ali, hi, so sorry I haven't called you," I said.

"Well, Deena, tell me everything! I want to know all about this new man of yours. Is he Dutch? The Dutch guys are so sexy," she said.

"Well, Paul is part Dutch, part Belgian and very sexy. I feel like I'm living a dream, Ali, a dream I never had the courage to envision before. He is wonderful, and has been introducing me to people I hope will help Uncle Alan's project become a reality. How are you, sweetie?"

"I'm fine. I broke up with Jeffrey last week. Thank goodness it's finally over. The relationship went on about a year too long. Anyway, I'll be coming to Amsterdam in another few months. The contract with the Dutch government to start a counselor training program to help troubled teenager girls is all set. So what's Paul really like?"

"Ali, he's just incredible. Tall, and very good looking. Since we've met he hasn't paid any attention to all the women that flirt with him. Not like Steve, my last boyfriend. Remember, he was always flirting, using that oh so tan, handsome face and sweet little smile to get attention?"

"That's because Steve felt inadequate," Ali said.

"Well Paul is just the opposite. He is very confident of himself, in and out of bed. He doesn't look at any other women, but could have anyone he wanted, I'm sure. But..." I said.

"But what, Deena?" Ali said.

"He's superstitious. He believes when he was a teenager, his girlfriend, who was a prostitute, was also a sorceress and placed a curse on him. Plus, I overheard a telephone conversation in Dutch which he didn't realize I understood. I think he was breaking a date with a prostitute."

"Look Deena, it sounds like Paul is in love with you. Why wouldn't he love you? You're cute, down to earth, sincere, loving, and sexy! Don't worry so much about a prostitute. It's only for sex, that's how it is in Amsterdam. He's with you now, isn't he?"

"Maybe you're right Ali. You always make me feel better about things. Well I'm going back to sleep. Got to get my rest before Paul comes back. I want to have lots of energy for that man!"

"OK love, just enjoy yourself when you're with him. Love you!"

"Love you too!"

I fell back into a deep sleep. I was awakened with dreamy kisses from Paul.

"Wake up, sweet Lady Deena! Your royal servant is here with a sexy European bikini for you to wear today," Paul whispered in my ear, and then licked it. He pulled the blankets from me, and tossed over a tiny sky blue two piece suit. "Put this on please, my love!"

I was barely awake, but complied with his request. He was so happy anticipating how I would look in the bikini. As I tried the suit on, I realized the top barely covered my breasts, and the bottom was just a hint of fabric around my front and rear. "Perfect!" said Paul.

"What about you?" I countered. He took a dark blue men's

bathing suit from the shopping bag that was little more than a thong.

"Voila!" he said proudly, and quickly took his clothes off and donned the mini suit. It showed his tight lower abdomen muscles off to best advantage.

I was grateful I would have him all to myself at the lake. "Absolutely breathtaking! Men actually wear those suits in public?"

"Of course, baby, after all this is Europe, not America, no? Let's get the picnic lunch that Berta has prepared for us and walk to the lake."

We put tee shirts and shorts over our suits, and slipped into sneakers. In the kitchen, Paul made sure there was wine for us and water for Pandora in the picnic basket. We thanked Berta for preparing our lunch, and set out for the lake.

We followed a well worn path through a wooded area, which led to an open meadow covered in wildflowers. While we walked Paul filled me in on his morning meeting at the Goethe museum that was undergoing renovations. He was pleased with the progress. Hans and Giselle had gone out to do some shopping. I told him about my conversation with Uncle Alan, leaving out the comments about Chris Bucholtz.

Soon we were at the lake. Paul picked out a grove of trees near the shore and spread out the blanket underneath them. He put out a bowl of water for Pandora, told her to "stay" and left her to guard the picnic basket. We took off our shirts and shorts and plunged into the water, which was refreshingly cool.

We swam towards a miniature island in the middle of the lake. Paul was a strong swimmer, but I was surprised that I was able to keep up with him. When we got to the island, we stretched out on the grass and sunned ourselves. Paul fell asleep and I was left to observe him secretly once again. His wet manhood was barely hidden from sight by the suit. I couldn't get enough of it and of him.

He woke up and caught me staring at him. He took off his suit and said "There, now you can get the full view, yes?"

He pulled at the strap of the bikini top which barely covered me. He cupped his hands, scooped up some lake water and gently wet my breasts. "Now you are the goddess of the lake. Your hair is so untamed, you are wild. Show me all of you, my goddess, yes!"

I took off the top and bottom of the suit. I dipped underwater in the lake for a moment or two. I came out and lay my wet body on top of his. We stayed still for a while, feeling each other, breathing in the lake scents and our own. Paul smelled like pine trees, and felt like fire beneath me.

Soon our french kissing began. Tongue kisses led to nipples being licked and suckled. Our mouths found the wet hot places between our legs. Arousal overcame reason – we were lost in each other. Our lovemaking went on and on, deeper than the lake, hotter than the sun.

When we were temporarily satisfied, we put our suits back on and swam to shore. We were hungry and gratefully devoured the sandwiches and drank the wine. We shared our food with Pandora and gave her more water.

After lunch we swam leisurely near the shore of the lake. Pandora joined us in the water and proved to be an amazingly agile swimmer. She loved swimming next to Paul, nudging him with her snout from time to time affectionately.

We swam to the shore of the lake and dried off in the warm sun. Paul mentioned that Hans and Giselle wanted to take us into town for dinner. We packed up our things, got dressed and walked through the meadows and woods with Pandora at our side.

Chapter 18
Evening in Rheinberg

We arrived at the castle. Hans met us at the door and said, "we hope you would like to have dinner with us. There is a special restaurant our friends own in town."

"We would like nothing better Hans," said Paul. "We will shower and dress and then we are all yours for the evening. Is one hour good?"

"But of course, my friend. Take your time. I hope you enjoyed yourselves at the lake today," Hans said.

"It was lovely, Hans," I replied. "Like paradise."

"I believe you two create your own paradise. See you in one hour. I will tell Giselle," he said.

We brought Pandora into the kitchen to be fed by Berta, and then we went upstairs to wash up and get dressed. "Do we have time for a bath, baby? I would love to relax with you," Paul said.

"Of course, love. Anything you say," I said. And that was the truth. I was under his spell, his power.

I drew warm water for the bath, and we got into the enormous tub together. We washed each others' hair, scrubbed each others' bodies. I massaged Paul's back. He purred with satisfaction.

"Seems a shame to wash away the lake water from our bodies," I said. "It was a wonderful day."

"Tomorrow we'll explore Dusseldorf with Hans and Giselle, and on Friday I had planned a day for just the two of us at the lake. Before we have to return to Amsterdam, yes," Paul explained. "How does that sound to you?"

"It sounds amazing, just like you," I said as I kissed him before I got out of the bath.

We watched each other reluctantly get dressed. Paul wore black slacks and a black dress shirt. I put on my light green dress, too short too tight but just right for him.

"Here is the young couple!" said Giselle as we descended the stairs. "They look so much in love, don't they Hans?"

"Yes my precious one, they do indeed," agreed Hans. "I hope you two are hungry, Gertrud and Laurenzo have prepared a feast for us!"

Hans held the back door of his Mercedes sedan open for Giselle and me. Paul sat in the front passenger seat and Hans drove us to Rheinberg. "Tomorrow we will show you the old castle ruins in Dusseldorf. Ah here we are already at the restaurant."

We parked in front of an inn that looked like a small Tudor home, and walked through a doorway that Paul had to duck under to enter the restaurant. Once inside, it was as if we were in a cottage straight out of a fairy tale. Old wood beams graced the ceiling, the walls were of stucco and the floor was made of stone.

An older couple came to greet us with hugs and kisses. The man was tall with white hair and dark eyes. The woman had dark grey hair, blue eyes and was short and pleasingly plump. "You must be Deena, Paul's new love. You are quite beautiful," said the man. "I am Laurenzo, and this is my wife, Gertrud. We hope you are hungry and thirsty. Welcome to our restaurant, The Cottage."

Laurenzo and Gertrud seated us at a cozy round table. They brought us beer, red and white wine, and a huge basket of bread with butter and cheeses. We helped ourselves.

GOING DUTCH

Laurenzo and Gertrud served us heaping platefuls of German delicacies – savory bread soup, followed by schnitzel, potatoes, noodle dishes and vegetables.

They were assisted by a waitress with long blonde tresses. She hurried to our table with a full tray of steaming German sausages, which she placed in front of Paul.

"Hello, it is you, you finally came back to see me!" she said as she adjusted her low cut peasant blouse, the better to show off her plump breasts. "What are you doing after dinner?"

"We're going back to the castle, Hans, Giselle, and my new girlfriend, Deena. We are very serious with each other. Deena, this is Zelda. Zelda, meet Deena."

"Oh, too bad, Paul. I was going to give you a repeat performance. Remember last time we were together? How can you forget, you were so…..…

"Zelda, enough already!" Gertrud said. "Our friends are here to relax and have a nice dinner. Go back to the kitchen."

Paul looked at me, his eyes pleading for forgiveness. "Another notch on you belt, lover?" I whispered.

"I guess so."

"You are forgiven. So we are serious, are we?"

"Very serious, my love," he said as he kissed my lips.

When the cheesecake and fruit were served, I said, "Oh my favorite, but where am I going to put it?"

Paul took a forkful of cheesecake and fed it to me. "There my sweetheart, a bite for now. We will take the rest home for later, yes?" he said.

Laurenzo and Gertrud packed up the desserts and with hugs and kisses sent us on our way.

"Let's take Pandora and Juliana out for a walk. I need to work off some of that incredible dinner," I said when we arrived at the castle. "Hans, Giselle, thank you so much for a wonderful evening."

We found mother and daughter dogs. We put on their collars and leashes and took them outdoors. The evening was beautiful, the stars lit up the sky. The country air was perfumed with the scent of flowers. I held Pandora's leash and Paul held Juliana's. We walked with our arms around each other. Soon we stopped to admire the sky and the stars and he turned towards me and kissed me. "Deena do you have any idea how much you mean to me? I can't believe I have fallen so deeply in love with you," he said.

"I love you too, Paul. So very much," I replied as I kissed him back.

"One kiss for you for each of the stars in the sky," he said and kissed me again and again. His tongue found mine. We forgot about everything but pleasuring each other with our tongues and lips. Only the ageless stars knew our secret - our love was timeless, without beginning or end.

Pandora's whimper brought us back to the present. We walked the dogs for a while longer and then headed to the castle. Pandora wanted to stay with Juliana, so Paul told Berta to take both mother and daughter dogs to the puppies.

In the bedroom, the cheesecake and fruit were arranged on a table, with plates, knives and forks, a teapot and cups.

"Bring that cake to me, please, and leave your clothes on the floor!" I purred at Paul as I took off my clothes and got into bed. "I think I can handle both you and the cake."

Paul did as he was told. He brought the cake and a fork into bed as I had requested. He slowly fed me the rich creamy confection. Soon it was my turn to give him something he hungered for. I spread some of the cake on my breasts. He licked it off and suckled my nipples. Then he moved lower and pleasured me in between my legs. He didn't need any further direction from me. He knew what I wanted and needed from him all night.

Chapter 19
Dusseldorf

We slept in each others' arms all night. It wasn't until 10:00 o'clock the next morning that we looked at the time. Paul said sleepily, "Let's get up, my sweet. I know that Hans and Giselle are anxious to show you the sights, yes."

"Oooo, OK…..how about a good morning kiss?"

One of Paul's kisses was never enough for me. He gave me several long lingering ones. Reluctantly we made our way to the bathroom. We washed each other in the shower, and then dried off with the luxurious towels. I chose a tank top and a short skirt with a sweater in case it was cool in the museum. Paul dressed in lightweight tan slacks and white short sleeved shirt.

Coffee, rolls and cheeses were waiting for us in the dining room along with Hans and Giselle. "Food again!" Paul said. "I think we could manage it, it looks so wonderful. You two are really spoiling us, yes!"

"And we are loving every minute of it," I added.

We ate breakfast and then met Hans and Giselle in the library, where they were having coffee. "We will explore the ancient ruins of Barbarossa in Kaiserwerth first and then spend the rest of the day at the museum," explained Hans.

"And we have four tickets to the Dusseldorf Symphony

Orchestra for tonight," added Giselle. "It is the world premiere of a new work entitled 'Roma Fantasia'. We were lucky to obtain the tickets through our subscription to the symphony. There will be a wonderful guest violinist. Would you two like to join us?" Giselle asked.

Paul and I were looking forward to spending a romantic evening just the two of us after sightseeing all day with Giselle and Hans. But we just couldn't say no to them. They had been so kind to us.

"But of course," Paul replied as he saw me nod my head yes to him. "Deena and I would love to accompany you. Dinner will be my treat at your favorite Indian restaurant near the Tonhalle, Hans."

We were soon at the ruins of the Barbarossa Castle which overlooked the Rhine. Many of the original red brick walls were still standing, having survived for hundreds and hundreds of years. It looked like mythic giants had inhabited it. After a couple of hours of exploring the ruins and an old churchyard nearby, we got back in the car and headed to the Goethe Museum in Dusseldorf.

The museum was a graceful contrast to the Barbarossa ruins. Rows of trees on either side of a long driveway led to the elegant eighteenth century former hunting palace. It was situated on a park like meadow.

We were grateful for the cool temperature inside the museum, and the beers that quenched our thirst in the café. Accompanied by some chips, that was all we needed to get us through the day.

Paul gave us a tour of the new wing of the museum he had helped to design. Even though it was not quite completed yet, it was beautiful, more modern than the rest of the museum, but still on a grand scale. I was so proud of him for being involved in such an important project. Goethe's newly discovered poems and letters would be housed there.

After spending two pleasant hours in the museum, we all decided we were hungry. We drove to the Indian restaurant, Spices.

Beautiful exotic looking Indian waitresses, dressed in tight fitting, revealing saris, were very attentive to us throughout the dinner. The waitresses flirted with Paul of course. But he sat very close to me, making certain that I was delighted with the food and drink and him. And I was.

After dinner we walked the few blocks to the Tonhalle. Hans held my arm in his and gave me a brief history of the unusual building.

"Tonhalle was built in 1926 as one of the first planetariums in the world," he explained. "After the war, it became a concert hall, and now it is a place of beauty for both the eyes and ears," he said proudly.

Hans showed us to our third row center seats. I sat between Giselle and Paul. Giselle leaned close to me and whispered. "It seems the Romanian guest violinist and the composer are very close. It is rumored that they are having a secret affair."

The orchestra took their places and so did the conductor. The attendees in the sold out concert hall rose to their feet in applause, and stayed that way to greet the solo violinist.

She was tall and lovely, with long dark hair and pale skin. As we sat down again, I noticed that Paul was staring at her. He seemed spellbound all through the captivating music. I enjoyed the performance, but I was worried about Paul. He was in a trancelike state.

During the intermission, Paul ran out of the nearest exit without a word to any of us.

"What is the matter with Paul?" Giselle asked me in a concerned voice.

"I'm not sure," I replied. "The violinist seems to have hypnotized him...."

Paul did not return to his seat after intermission. I concentrated on the Chopin etudes. They offered beauty and peace and I tried to grasp at that.

He was waiting for us when we left the concert hall. "I apologize," he said. "Not feeling all that well. Perhaps it was the Indian food, no?"

"You'll rest up at the castle," I said. I knew Paul's absence had nothing to do with the food, and everything to do with the violinist.

Hans and Giselle made small talk on our drive home. Paul and I were unusually quiet.

When we arrived, Pandora followed us to our bedroom. Paul perked up a bit as Pandora snuggled next to him on the bed.

As we undressed, I challenged him. "Did the violinist look like her?"

"Like who?" he said, feigning innocence.

"Like your Tatiana from Romania," I countered.

"You know me too much. Too well. I don't know what to say," he said.

"Just tell me. Tell me about Tatiana. Start at the very beginning," I suggested, as we lay down on the bed and held each other.

"Maybe it is best that you know everything, yes. So…my father left me in the care of one of the madams of a brothel in De Wallen. I was just seventeen. She turned me over to the younger prostitutes. One day while trying to wake up from my stupor sipping coffee in a cafe, I met Tatiana. She was twenty, several years older than I was and already an experienced prostitute. She sent money home to her family, who lived in poverty in Bucharest. I fell in love with her beauty, her long black hair, dark eyes, her tall enticing body, full breasts. She loved me too, I believe. I dropped out of high school, and Tatiana instructed me in lovemaking several times a day. She soon neglected her clients in favor of me. Her pimp became enraged with both of us because of all the time she was spending with me. And so he attacked me, and tried to attack Tatiana."

He continued, "Yes, the violinist looked just like her, she could have been her twin. But not related."

"You asked the violinist?" I said.

"Yes," he admitted.

"Are you still looking for Tatiana? If so, I'll get out of your way," I said as I searched his eyes for an answer.

"No, Deena, no, I love you. You must have had a first love, yes? What would you do if you thought you saw him somewhere?" he questioned me.

I thought for a moment. "If I saw someone that looked like John, I probably would have done the same as you did," I admitted.

"What was he like?" Paul asked.

"We were high school sweethearts. He was a football player, tall like you are, husky, handsome, brown hair, dark eyes. Very smart. John went to an expensive private college in New England, and I attended NYU on scholarship. He met a girl from a prominent Boston family and married her soon after graduation. I sometimes read about him on the internet. But he doesn't want to see me, not even for a quick drink."

"He broke your heart, yes?" Paul sympathized with me.

"Yes he did, he really did," I said sadly.

"I won't baby. I couldn't. I love only you, my temptress." He stroked my hair as he spoke. "So, this John, was he a good lover? Not as good as me, no?"

"We were just kids. He was not as experienced as you are. Given time, he would have been almost up to your standards," I teased him.

"Never!" Paul said emphatically.

"Well, he was almost as large as you are," I said playfully, as I started to caress his erection. "Almost...."

"No, not an American! Didn't you say American men have sports on their minds, not lovemaking?" he said and then caressed my breasts and kissed me long and lusciously on my lips.

"True," I laughed. "Now, my big handsome lover, no more talking. Kiss me some more, more, more…"

I was lost once again as he kissed me and massaged my ass, gently at first, and then not gently. I forgot about Tatiana and John, and reason. I could feel only my want and need for him.

And then he entered me, holding my ass tightly and making love to me. His lovemaking made me throb, hurt, ache between my legs. Sweet release when I came to him, so sweet.

Pandora was asleep next to our bed. I heard her gentle snoring as Paul said, "I want the next twenty four hours to last forever, my lover. When we go back to Amsterdam, our lives will be busy once again. I've already received too many texts and emails. Let's get up early and spend the whole day at the lake."

"I agree, Paul. Let's make this time last forever."

"Pandora will be with Juliana and the puppies tomorrow. It may be too hot for her at the lake," he said as he bent down to pet the big girl. "She will forgive us for leaving her behind."

"Forgiveness comes easy to the women who love you. But I won't forgive you if you don't make love to me again!" I hissed at him.

"Making love to you comes easy to me, yes." He began kissing me all over, from my head to my feet, and everywhere I wanted and needed him to in between.

Chapter 20

The Last Day at the Lake

Paul woke me early on Friday, with delicious kisses on my lips. We got ready to go to the lake, and asked Berta to pack up some food and drinks for us. She fed Pandora and brought her to Juliana and the puppies. Soon we were on our way to the lake once more.

Arriving at our usual spot, we decided to spend the day in the nude. We stripped off our clothes and took a swim before breakfast. We then spread out the blanket and ate under the shade of the trees.

"Deena," Paul said as he stared at my breasts. "I have a big problem with you."

"Really, why haven't you told me before?" I asked.

"I just realized it, yes. I am equally obsessed with your lips, your breasts and your pussy. I want to kiss them all now. I want to kiss every part of your smooth creamy skin. I can't get enough of you," he said.

"And I can't stop looking at you, handsome man. You've got a great tan from being in the sun the other day. I like your darker, exotic look."

"I like the difference between us, the lovely milky white you and the darker me." He pressed his body on top of mine.

The day turned into one wonderfully long lovemaking session. We kissed every moment we were on land, and while we swam as well. We made love on the island.

As we swam back to the shoreline of the lake, Paul grabbed me by the waist. "I have been waiting for this opportunity. You are my bitch now. My mermaid bitch." He pushed me gently onto the ground, with my upper body on land and my lower body in the lake. He was ready for me. Ready to have all the pleasure. He rubbed his hard manhood on my ass, and in between my plump cheeks.

"So sweet, so sexy, bitch. Open wider for me. Now," he commanded me as he entered my pussy from behind. I raised my ass up to allow him to come in me. Wave after wave of him crashed into me. I yearned for each new stroke beating in me. I felt him finally lose control, and reach orgasm. And then my throbbing aching pussy climaxed too.

We ate lunch, drank wine, swam, and made love once again. We lost track of time.

> I composed a poem to Paul. I entitled it "Dreaming"-
>> I dream about you every night
>> When I first saw you
>> I looked into your eyes
>> And caught a glimpse of your soul
>> Your body is there before me
>> Sweet and giving
>> I surrender to you
>> I trust you
>> You protect me
>> I love every look
>> Every touch
>> Every kiss
>> Every touch
>> Every kiss

GOING DUTCH

We watched the sun set over the lake, a glorious fireball of brightness. Then a crowd of stars looked down on us as we headed back to the castle.

Paul knew the way in the darkness – I held on to his hand tightly. Too soon we reached the castle. We were still holding hands. We knew this day was special. We would remember its perfection no matter what the future held for us.

"So you two had a wonderful day, yes?" Hans said as he greeted us both with hugs and kisses. "We missed you terribly."

Hans and Giselle had waited for us to have dinner. We quickly went upstairs to put on dry clothes and then joined them in the dining room. The cook had gone all out to make a wonderful feast for us.

We dined on German delicacies - beef, spaetzle, potatoes - and apple strudel for dessert. We were planning to leave the castle early in the morning. I was ready to go back to Amsterdam, the city I had fallen in love with. The sound of Paul's cell phone ringing woke me from my reverie.

"I have to take this call. Excuse me for a few minutes," Paul said. He seemed very upset. I wondered who it was.

Hans, Giselle and I made small talk but we were all curious to know who Paul had rushed out of the room to talk to.

After a few minutes that seemed like an hour, Paul came back into the dining room. "That was a friend of mine. Deena, we must leave right after dinner. I need to speak to her in person." He composed himself and then after a minute continued. "This friend of mine, Lorraine, is a prostitute in De Wallen. She says she has information about Vanessa and her boyfriend. I have to go to De Wallen to question her."

"Paul, take me with you. We can drive right there from Rheinberg," I suggested. I didn't trust Paul alone with her. I didn't trust any of it. I wanted to make sure the only reason he would see

Lorraine would be to get information from her about Vanessa.

"It can be a very dangerous place, De Wallen, yes," he said. "You'll wait for me at the houseboat."

"I'm coming with you. I want to help you and your family. I'm with you wherever and whenever you need me."

"We'll see. Let me think about it."

"No, I insist!"

"OK we'll take Pandora with us. She'll protect you."

"Deena," said Giselle, "let's go up to my room for a few minutes, while the men finish their coffee. I have some clothes of mine to give you. They will look very pretty on you."

We stopped by the kennel and each picked a puppy to take upstairs with us. Giselle and Hans' bedroom was enchanting. It featured a huge four poster bed draped in a white canopy, richly appointed rugs in blues and yellows, an antique dresser, night tables and an armoire. The puppies, Teddy and Selena, fell asleep on a blanket on the floor.

"Deena, let me explain to you something about Paul. He has friends everywhere in The Netherlands and Germany. There has been talk of him entering the political arena in Amsterdam, or even the European Union," said Giselle. She went into her huge walk in closet for a moment, and brought out some pretty white eyelet blouses, and several skirts in black and navy blue. "I think these will fit you. You can wear them to synagogue, the skirts are of a modest length."

"Thank you, Giselle." I took the clothes from her and spread them out on her bed. "So Paul has friends in government, and in the Red Light District, too."

"It seems many men in Amsterdam have ties to De Wallen. He is yours now though, Deena, I can tell," Giselle said soothingly. "I hope you have enjoyed your stay here. I will miss you."

"I love being here in your home. Thank you for your hospitality.

You and Hans are wonderful, as are Princess Juliana and her puppies." I sat down on the floor and put Teddy in my lap. "It must be fun to watch the puppies grow right before your eyes."

"It is. And it has been wonderful to see your relationship with Paul grow deeper every day!" Giselle said.

"I do love being with Paul, and I think he enjoys being with me too. We can't seem to get enough of one another," I said as I thought for a moment or two. More hesitantly, I continued, "may I tell you something in confidence?"

"But of course, liebkind. It will be between the two of us."

"That's good," I said as I petted little Teddy. "I don't know quite how to describe it. But something unusual has been happening to me. I feel my body has somehow been changing since I arrived in Amsterdam."

"In what way are these changes occurring darlink?" said Giselle, very concerned, as she sat next to me on the rug.

"I feel stronger than I have ever felt before. It started my first day in Amsterdam. I jogged for an hour without tiring at all. I'm not a natural athlete, so I usually feel winded after jogging for so long. Wednesday, Paul and I swam for hours in the lake. I would usually not be able to swim anywhere near that amount without tiring."

"Perhaps it is the European air. So good for one's breathing!" Giselle suggested.

"Well, there's more…"

"What else? Tell me, don't be afraid."

"Well….my sexual appetite has increased," I said. "At first I thought it was because of Paul, who has aroused me more than I could ever imagine. I think part of the change is within me. I can satisfy him in ways I never thought I could satisfy a man. Especially given his, mmmm, physical attributes, his extra…large…"

"Yes," Giselle helped me, "Dutch men are quite well endowed."

"Well that's it, I guess. Maybe it's all in my imagination."

"I don't think you are imagining any of this. Has Paul mentioned anything to you about his days in De Wallen when he was a teenager? You have seen his scar and his tattoo?" she asked.

I nodded my head yes. Giselle continued, "Then you know about the spell, the curse, that Tatiana in her anger cast upon Paul. Here in Europe we still believe in the power of witches and sorceresses. But……"

"But what? I have very strong feelings for Paul. I have been thinking of the stories my mother has told me about a great great great grandmother of mine named Delilah. She had many men in her life, and seemed to have supernatural abilities with respect to predicting the future. She emigrated from Wurzberg, Bavaria to Baltimore in the 1840's with her parents and brother," I explained.

"Hans and I believe the spell has affected Paul's ability to truly fall in love with a woman. Paul goes from one relationship to another. Some last longer than others…….." Giselle's voice drifted off to a whisper. She seemed lost in thought.

"Deena," Giselle said after a few moments, as she took both of my hands in hers, "you are not imagining the changes that are happening to you. Sometimes magical powers come to the fore in a certain place, a certain time. I believe in your case you have discovered your family's ancient sorcery gifts here in Europe. Your passionate love for each other has triggered those forces within you. Magic is brewing, I can feel it when I am near you and Paul. Even the egg shaped pearl pendant you wear around your neck is magical, an old European amulet that stimulates fertility."

"So this family heirloom really is a good luck charm in more than one way. Do you think my hidden powers of witchcraft are doing battle with Tatiana's spell?"

"I think so. I do. Just be patient. Don't let him leave you. Magic is a gift. Discover the power that I believe is within you."

I hugged Giselle by way of thanking her. I felt better and more secure about my relationship with Paul. After Giselle had reassured me she had a special feeling about us, I felt a strong bond with her despite the fact that I knew her only a short while. We exchanged phone numbers. I promised to call her in a few days.

"And now go back to your man. Use your powers. Love him, Deena, love him," she said.

Chapter 21

Goodbyes

I went to the guest room to organize my things, carrying the clothes Giselle had given me. Paul was already busy packing. Pandora was fast asleep in the dog bed, snoring softly.

"Deena, please do not think it was my idea for this meeting with Lorraine. I am desperate to help my brother and his family and others like them. People are tired of how the sex trade has affected teenage girls. I just spoke to Rick. Nessa came home this morning at 4:00 AM. Rick picked her up from school early so as to keep a close watch on her today. They are thinking of hiring a private detective to find out what she is up to. They fear her boyfriend has been using her as a prostitute. Other people have similar problems with their teenagers. So it is very important I find out what I can about Vanessa tonight from Lorraine.

"Rick wants to have coffee with me tomorrow morning, so we can discuss what I have learned tonight."

"Of course. I'll help you pack," I offered.

We organized our things and Hans came up to help us bring everything to the car. Giselle, Princess Juliana and a wagon full of puppies were at the front entrance waiting to see us off.

We hugged Hans and Giselle. I kissed Princess Juliana and each of her little pups. Berta gave us a basket of food for our breakfast the next day. Pandora licked each puppy and saved her most affectionate kiss for Juliana.

Soon we were on our way to the city I loved, with the man I adored, on a mission whose outcome I could only guess at.

.

Chapter 22
Questions

On the drive back to Amsterdam, I tried to fall asleep for a little while but I couldn't. I had a lot on my mind.

I thought about my conversation with Giselle concerning witchcraft. Perhaps I was a witch, perhaps I had supernatural powers I could use to make Paul mine, and break the spell that Tatiana had cast on him.

But if I did have magic at my fingertips, did I want to use it? I believed in the power of love, the power of religion. Witchcraft and magic and spells were new concepts to me.

Still, I didn't want to lose Paul to Tatiana's curse, or something or someone else that would come between us.

Was I willing to experiment with sorcery? Could I be sure those gifts, if I even possessed them, wouldn't backfire?

And what about the prostitute that Paul was going to De Wallen to talk to? When he saw her, would she entice him to come back to her? I decided I would stand my ground, and accompany him.

I had no easy answers to the questions that troubled me.

.

Chapter 23
In De Wallen

Paul interrupted my thoughts as we were driving back to Amsterdam. "Let me explain some things to you, my love. About witchcraft, about prostitutes, about me, yes. Please listen and be patient with me. We have another hour or so before we reach Amsterdam. I hope in that time you will come to understand me.

"Every time I am with you, making love to you, declaring my love for you, I have to fight off the witch's spell Tatiana cursed me with. That is why every time we have sex, it is as if we are on fire. It is my way of trying to fight the power she still has over me. Fire against fire, sorcery fighting sorcery. It is a duel between Tatiana and me as to whose power is the strongest, who will win in the end."

He took a few deep breaths and continued, "Please forgive me for what I tell you now. When I am not involved with a girlfriend, I admit I do go to Lorraine in De Wallen. It is just for sex."

Well there it was. He finally admitted his involvement with a prostitute. I loved Paul, but I despised the idea of him going to De Wallen, even for one night, even though it was before he met me. I turned my face away from him.

"You're angry with me, aren't you?" he asked. "What are you thinking about? Tell me Deena, please, tell me."

"Right now I hate you, Paul," I said. "What do you mean, just sex? How could you have sex with someone you don't love? To me there is no sex without love, and no intimate love without sex."

"Maybe men are different than women," he said. "I can have sex with someone and not love them, and forget about them the minute my physical needs are met. But lovemaking is different. It's sex and love and intimacy. Like what we have together. But tell me, you have never had sex with someone you didn't love? Think about it. Maybe you have."

Why did Paul always have to be right about everything? He was correct in this case. I did have one or two relationships that were purely sexual in nature. It freed me from having to worry about whether the whole thing would work out. It was, as Paul said, just sex.

"OK, I hate to admit it, but you're right. I am not going to leave you because of your past. When you are with me, you are with me only. No other girlfriends, no prostitutes. I will be everything for you. I will love you even more," I said.

I vowed to myself I would use my love and desire for him and the power of witchcraft within me to help me fight Tatiana's spell.

Paul reached for my left hand, and gently kissed each of my fingers, just as he had on our first night together in Tempo Doeloe. And just as on that first night, I was his.

When we arrived at the houseboat, Paul brought in our luggage.

"I've got to go now, Deena."

"Not without me you're not." I wanted to see who this prostitute was. I knew after I met her I would be angry, and jealous too, but I was willing to take the risk.

"You are stubborn, you know that Deena. OK, let's go, but keep close to Pandora and me. You'll see I'm right about De Wallen."

We began a fast paced walk down the Prinsengracht. Paul was anxious to find out exactly what was happening to Vanessa. I could

GOING DUTCH

barely keep up with him. His strides were effortless and determined. He knew the way to De Wallen very well.

For me the streets and their surroundings at night were different than anything I had ever experienced. The closer we got to the Red Light District, the narrower the streets were. Crowds, mostly men, spilled out onto the sidewalks from the many bars and shops selling marijuana. It seemed everyone was either drunk or high. People were laughing, talking loudly.

I knew we were in the District when I began to see women on the sidewalks and streets dressed in very skimpy outfits that revealed their bodies shamelessly. Wherever Paul walked, at least two prostitutes followed him, trying to entice him with their barely covered breasts.

There were prostitutes standing in the first floor storefront windows, displaying themselves to the men shopping for who would be their sex partner for the short time they would be allotted. The women were mostly young, of different races, sizes and shapes. They had in common the prominence of their breasts, the perfection of their bodies and the hard look in their eyes. Everything and everyone was for sale.

With Paul leading the way, holding me with one hand and Pandora's leash with the other, we negotiated the alleyways. The crowds were so dense at one point I became separated from Paul and Pandora. I panicked when I realized I had lost them. I froze. Men were pushing me, touching my hair. One man yelled, "Hey, Red, how much do you charge?" I felt nauseous, dizzy. A tall slim man appeared, Rottweiler in tow. It was Paul. Relief, I was safe again! I reached up and hugged him tightly around his neck.

Finally we stopped at a doorway and Paul rang the bell. Someone buzzed us in. We went up a long narrow flight of stairs. Evidently Lorraine did not find it necessary to be on display in the windows.

A tall, slim brunette with large breasts barely held in check by her skimpy black bra greeted us on the first floor landing. She wore black thong panties that left little to the imagination, black lace stockings and mid thigh height black boots. Paul didn't seem to notice her body. He stared straight into her large dark brown eyes and said, "I hope you have some information for me. I don't want to be here in De Wallen for no reason Lorraine. This is my girlfriend Deena from New York."

"So Paul…you have left me for this short chubby woman?" Lorraine said, pointing a long red nail accusingly at me. "You will come to your senses soon, and be back in De Wallen with me. I will reserve a special three hour session for….."

"Stop dreaming," Paul shouted, "and start telling me what you know."

"OK OK don't shout at me. After all the pleasure I have given you, please treat me with a little respect! I saw Vanessa on the street around the corner here last night, with a boy about her age. The boy was pushing her into a doorway, saying something like, 'now Vanessa, get to work….I need the money and you promised me…' yes, something like that."

"What street? What address? What did the boy look like?" Paul demanded.

"I don't recall. Give me a kiss, maybe I can remember." Lorraine held Paul at the back of his neck, pulled him down to her, kissing him hard on his lips. With her other hand, she squeezed his crotch. "That's better," she said. "Yes, I saw them on the Trompettersteeg. I noticed them because the boy called out 'Vanessa' and I knew it was your niece's name. I didn't get a good look at him but I knew she was related to you. Tall thin girl, long straight black hair, eyes as pretty as yours."

"That's it?" Paul demanded.

"That's it lover," Lorraine said, puckering her lips seductively at him.

"Okay Lorraine. We will be going now. Here is something to thank you for the information on Vanessa." He reached into his pocket and pulled out a one hundred euro note. "Please let me know if you find out anything else."

"Oh, I will let you know Paul. Come see me again, very soon," she crooned to him, as she licked two of her fingers, pulled out one of her breasts from her bra and traced a circle around her nipple. "Very very soon."

I gripped the railing of the staircase as I followed Paul and Pandora to the street. I had to take a few deep breaths of air when we got outside. "Quite an actress, your friend Lorraine," I said. "She definitely would be cast in the role of a prostitute in a Hollywood movie."

"I couldn't agree more. She was being very dramatic for your benefit. Just ignore her," Paul said. "So just as we thought. If Lorraine is to be believed, Vanessa's loverboy is forcing her to act as a prostitute. Not good news to give Rick tomorrow morning."

We walked back to the houseboat, through the noise, the crowds, the prostitutes. It all felt so foreign to me, as if I had entered another world.

I was relieved when we arrived safely at the houseboat. Paul went into the bathroom to take a shower.

There was only one way I could keep him from returning to De Wallen. I would be even more attentive to his every sexual need. I took off my clothes, and put on tiny red bikini panties. I took two red ribbons from my suitcase and tied one around each of my breasts tightly with a knot. Many Jewish women believed that red ribbons brought good luck to those who wore them.

When Paul came into the bedroom, naked and glistening with dampness from his shower, I was waiting for him, lying on the bed. He said, "Well, lady dressed in red, what did you do, gift wrap yourself for me?"

"Yes, open your presents when you are ready, lover."

I saw the now familiar dark look in his blue eyes. "I'm ready now." And from the size of his erection, I could tell he was. He lay down next to me, and taking one red ribbon in each of his hands, pulled my breasts to his waiting lips.

"I love my presents, anything else for me?" he said after he had suckled both of my nipples together in his mouth.

"Don't forget the red panties, they are gift wrapping something else you may want," I said.

He moved lower, his mouth near my panties as he took them off. "You smell so sweet, lover," he said.

No more words were spoken between us that night. Our mouths and tongues were too busy to speak. We made love all night long.

Chapter 24

Prayers

The next morning, when Paul and Pandora returned from their walk, he took off his running clothes and changed into a white dress shirt and navy slacks. He as always looked very handsome. Rick arrived about nine o'clock and we took our coffees and croissants out on the deck.

"I wanted to talk with you both this morning," said Rick. "Deena, I apologize for involving you in our problems with Vanessa. Paul thought you should be included. Perhaps you have some ideas?"

"Have you asked her about her boyfriend? Do you know who he is, Rick?" I asked.

"We have questioned her many times. All she does is run into her bedroom, lock the door and doesn't stop crying," he answered, very upset.

"We've even questioned this boy David Coen, who keeps calling and asking for Vanessa. But he won't give us any information either."

"Ordinarily I would think this is just normal teenage behavior. But Paul has told me about the loverboy situation," I said.

"Rick, things are serious," Paul said. "A prostitute in De Wallen last night told us she has seen Vanessa recently in the district with a boy. He was shouting at her and seemed to be forcing her to act as a prostitute."

"Oh Paul, this is horrible, more horrible than I even could imagine," Rick said. "I will tell Rachel. We will arrange for a private investigator. Now I must leave you and go back home to my family. Paul, we will talk more on Monday."

"Yes, give my love to Rachel and Nessa," Paul said as he hugged his brother and kissed him on his cheeks.

After Rick left we cleaned up the breakfast things. Paul said, "Get dressed my love. We are going to the old synagogue for services. I know Giselle gave you some clothes that would be appropriate. I think we could use some prayer in our lives right now. Pray for Vanessa, yes?

"Avi the security guard is a friend of mine. I will call him and tell him we will be there. He has always wanted Pandora to help him with security. Now is a good day to give it a try, yes."

I quickly got dressed in the clothes that Giselle had given me, a simple long sleeved white eyelet blouse and navy skirt that fell just below my knees. It was a beautiful clear morning. The thirty minute walk to the Plantage neighborhood took us along the canals which glistened in the sunlight.

Soon we reached the synagogue and stopped at the gate. Avi let us in and was so pleased to see Pandora. "You know Paul, I would feel safer if Pandora was here whenever there are services," Avi said. "The Rabbi and congregants would feel safer too."

Paul explained to Avi how to instruct Pandora if there was ever a potential threat to the synagogue and its congregants. The instructions and commands were in Dutch, so I could not understand them. Avi looked very confident with Pandora by his side.

Paul and I entered the synagogue courtyard which was filled with people greeting one another. The men and women were a diverse group. Many wore modern clothes and several of the men were dressed in the black suits and black hats worn by Orthodox Jewish men throughout the world. As we walked further along towards the main building, the group of people parted and made a narrow path for us to walk through. Paul was greeted by many as we passed by. He stopped several times to say hello and shake hands with the men. The Rabbi was waiting for us at the entrance to the synagogue.

"Shabbat shalom Paul. I am glad that you and your friend will be joining us for services this morning," the Rabbi said as he shook Paul's hand.

"Good morning to you Rabbi. May I introduce to you Deena Green from New York. Deena, this is the famous Rabbi Hidalgo."

"Pleased to meet you Deena. Shabbat Shalom. I hope you enjoy our services. Do you read Hebrew?" the Rabbi said.

"I am honored to meet you Rabbi. Yes I read Hebrew and know the prayers." I remembered everything I was taught in religious school at our synagogue in Baltimore.

"Paul, please find a seat in the front row of pews. You and Deena will have to part from one another until after the services. This is my daughter Rebecca. She will accompany Deena to the women's section of the sanctuary," the Rabbi said kindly. "As you know, in an Orthodox synagogue, the men sit separately from the women."

Before Paul left me he squeezed my hand, donned a head covering and then walked towards the front of the sanctuary with the Rabbi.

Rebecca was very friendly, smiling at me as she took my hand and led me upstairs to the women's section. We sat down next to each other. Rebecca whispered to me, "You and Paul Vermeer make a handsome couple. Even though Paul is not Jewish, he is always welcome here to pray with our congregation. I think he had even learned some Hebrew when he lived in New York. A most interesting man, wouldn't you say?"

Yes, I thought, *Paul Vermeer is a most interesting man. He is extremely handsome and unbelievably sexy, loving and talented. A prostitute in the Red Light District would do anything to have Paul return to her as a favored customer. Also, he may still be under the spell of a prostitute/sorceress that he had an affair with when he was a teenager.*

I decided I'd best pray fervently these next few hours. I opened the prayer book and couldn't wait to hear the Hebrew melodies sung by the Cantor who had just ascended the altar.

I was not disappointed – the Cantor chanted the liturgy and the congregants prayed with him. Some of the melodies were familiar and some were new to me. I was so enthralled with the service the time went by too quickly.

After the final prayers, Rebecca led me downstairs and out of the synagogue. In a room in one of the courtyard buildings, the congregants were gathering, waiting for the Rabbi to arrive and bless the wine and challah bread. Paul was having a heated conversation with several of the men. They listened intently to what Paul had to say. No doubt they too were interested in the safety of the citizens of Amsterdam.

As the Rabbi said the blessings over the wine and challah, Paul appeared at my side. "I hope you enjoyed the service, yes?" he asked.

"I did, I really did. I'd like to attend services here often. Ah here comes Rebecca." She gave us each a cup of wine and a piece of bread. We enjoyed the sweetness of both.

We said our goodbyes to the Rabbi, Rebecca, and several of the congregants and left to retrieve Pandora. Avi was rewarding her with some homemade dog biscuits his wife had baked. He said she was calm but alert throughout the time she was with him. "I think I will take Pandora with us to the club opening tonight," Paul said. "She will be an asset to the security team we've hired. Avi, I am sure we will be here for services often. Deena has been inspired this morning in the synagogue, yes?"

"Yes, I would like to pray here often, my love."

As we walked back to the houseboat, I said, "Now I am ready to rest this afternoon so I can dance with you all night at your club opening!"

Chapter 25
From *The Amersterdam Post*

Shocking news - Paul Vermeer seems to be faithful to one woman and one woman only these days. And who is this person that has stolen The Netherlands sexiest man from us? Does New Yorker Deena Green think that she can keep Paul from the boudoirs and bordellos of Amsterdam for very long?

We doubt it. In the meanwhile our city's night life is boring without you Paul! Come back!

Chapter 26
Telephone Call from Chris

As we got closer to Spice Island, Paul put his arm around my waist and pulled me close to him. "My Jewish friends tell me it is a good deed if you have sex with your lover on the Sabbath, yes? So, are you ready to be a good Jewish woman for your man all afternoon?" he said.

"Have I ever said no to you? Of course, love, I can't wait to get you home," I said. I reached up and put my hands around his neck, pulling him close to me. I kissed him quickly on his lips, and then slipped my tongue into his mouth.

"Let's go! You're walking too slow!" I laughed.

As Paul opened the door to the houseboat, I heard my cell phone ring. I had left it on the table in the kitchen. I answered it saying, "good afternoon, Deena here," as Paul gestured for me to follow him into the bedroom.

"Good afternoon to you Deena," said a man with the unmistakable accent of Chris Bucholtz. "Chris here. I have been trying to reach you all morning. I hope I am not disturbing you."

"Not at all Chris. We just arrived home. Nice to hear from you. How can I help you?" I was trying to figure out why Chris was calling. It had been less than a week since our meeting in The Hague. I hadn't expected to hear from him so soon.

"It is I that can help you," he said. "We have made a lot of progress with your trade and immigration applications. I am planning to be in Amsterdam this evening. Can we talk about all of this over dinner later?"

Chris's voice was as smooth as silk. I knew I had to keep the man happy. He was the key to the successful start-up of our diamond artisans project.

"Dinner would be lovely Chris. Where and when?" I said softly. Paul would not be pleased with this.

"Deena, I can barely hear you. How about nine o'clock at Le Pecheur? I have some paperwork for you to look over. Of course, it will be just the two of us," Chris said insistently.

"Wonderful Chris, sounds great. See you at nine o'clock tonight. Le Pecheur, mmmm, can't wait!"

"Deena, I very much look forward to tonight," he said rather formally. "Good-bye for now."

Paul had come back into the kitchen and said, "who was that?" He practically roared at me. Pandora echoed Paul's unhappiness by growling at me as well. He had evidently overheard part of my conversation.

"Take it easy, love. That was Chris Bucholtz. I can't quite believe it, but he says he has made progress with my applications and has some paperwork for me to look over. I am meeting him at Le Pecheur at nine tonight. Then I'll see you at the club at eleven," I said.

"So now he is taking you to dinner? At Le Pecheur, no less, very expensive. Maybe he will ask you to pay your share, no? Chris is rather stingy." Paul was clearly annoyed.

"Do you mean Chris and I will have a Dutch treat?" I asked innocently.

"Dutch treat? What are you talking about?" Paul growled again, Pandora in true Rottweiler fashion echoed his mood.

"It's when you share the expenses," I explained. Then I started to laugh. He was so funny when he was jealous.

"Oh right. Look, baby, this is not funny. Chris will get you drunk and then try and get you in bed with him, no. I am worried."

"Please Paul you have nothing to worry about. I'll only have one glass of wine. I promise. Why don't you stop by the restaurant about eleven?"

"I will be there then if not before. Just be careful around him. Then we will go to the club." Paul was more relaxed. Pandora went back to her favorite activity, snoring.

"Wonderful! I'll wear my new black dress and boots that you bought me in Dusseldorf!"

"You are going to have to put something over that dress, it's too revealing for dinner with Bucholtz, no?" he said, the anger returning.

"OK, lover!" I knew just how to calm him down. "We have all afternoon together," I said suggestively as I took his hand and led him to the bedroom. I pushed him onto the bed and lay down on top of him. "Do you know what I want to do, my Dutch treat? I want to show you what I like most about going Dutch. It is your Dutch lips?" I said as I planted urgent kisses on his mouth and then explored further with my tongue.

"Or maybe it's your Dutch chest?" I whispered as I unbuttoned his shirt and moved lower, burying my nose in the thick hair on his chest, and then licking his nipples.

"Your tight Dutch abs perhaps," I continued, kissing him lower still. I unzipped his slacks and pulled them and his underwear off.

"I've found it, the best one of all," I said, "my very large, very erect Dutch treat. The sweetest I've ever tasted!"

He stroked my hair, groaned and said, "you *are* a witch. I am under your spell, yes!"

Chapter 27
Getting Ready for a Busy Night

We stayed in bed the rest of the afternoon, making love like it was our first time together. Paul needed constant reassurance I was not going to have more than just dinner with Chris. At five o'clock Paul and Pandora left to go to the club to check on last minute details and to help organize things for the opening.

I decided to use the time I had to myself to telephone my mother and get to the bottom of the witchcraft question. I called her number using the international codes and she answered on the first ring.

"Deena, my precious child. How are y'all? You must be so busy….how is that handsome boyfriend of yours?" Of course Momma was more interested in my love life than the status of the business project.

"I'm fine, Momma, and so is Paul. We just came back from spending a few days at his friends' castle in Germany. Lots of romantic hours by the lake, if you must know the truth," I confided in her.

"Sounds wonderful, just wonderful!" she responded in her charmingly enthusiastic way.

"It truly was, Momma. I have to ask you some questions. I have noticed some changes in me since I arrived in Amsterdam. I seem to be stronger physically. I feel something powerful is happening within me, in romantic ways as well, if you know what I mean, Momma," I said. I didn't like to talk about sex with my mother but in this instance I had no choice.

"Oh, you mean sex, my love. Y'all are having lots of great sex? Wonderful!" she replied.

"Yes it is very wonderful. Our German hostess Giselle thought perhaps there is a history of witchcraft in our family. That might explain why I am experiencing things differently." I couldn't wait to hear her response.

"Well, yes, ma precious one yes," Momma said. All of a sudden my talkative mother was choosing her words carefully.

"Yes? Please explain this all to me," I said. I was getting very frustrated.

"In America, witchcraft is not understood. It could be very dangerous to be discovered as a sorceress in America. I am sorry but I had to hide my ancestry from you," my mother said. "I did tell you about Delilah, and her ability to predict the future."

She was silent for a moment or two. Then she said slowly, "I also felt I didn't want you to rely on magic or sorcery. I wanted you to develop your intelligence and your skills without the help of witchcraft. I had a feeling you would discover your powers on your own, after being in Europe for a while. You did not have to wait so long.

"I can feel what you are feeling Deena. A witch who was Paul's lover has cast a spell on him. You want to use your powers to break the spell. Is that it?"

"How do you know all that Momma? I love him very much, and want to know that he will be mine always. Should I use witchcraft to counteract the spell?"

"That's your decision, my precious daughter. Discover what your strengths are. Use your powers to show your man just how much you really love him. Gotta go, my love. Good bye for now," she said and my mother hung up.

I was amazed at how much she knew about Paul. Discover my powers. Good advice, but I didn't know the first thing about it.

Instead, I sent an email to a lawyer that Rick had recommended, Henry Burken. I outlined the details of the project to Mr. Burken and advised him I was having a dinner meeting with Chris Bucholtz. I told him I hoped to have something concrete to report to him after the meeting.

Nerves got the better of me. I was anxious about how I would be able to keep my dinner with Chris on friendly terms, without giving him the wrong idea. I hoped I could walk that fine line.

I decided to take a ride on Paul's bicycle to distract me. As I rode through the streets of Amsterdam, I thought about how I should dress for the evening. Should I show off or cover up? Maybe a pretty scarf over the revealing neckline of the dress would do. I stopped on a street crowded with beautiful boutiques. I wandered from one shop to the next. I noticed a small store with the name "She's the One" over the doorway.

Something caught my eye in the store window, but it wasn't the clothing on display. A very attractive man with dark hair and big brown eyes was rearranging some of the dresses in the window. He saw me staring at him, smiled at me, and waved. I walked into the store.

"Hello, miss. Lovely day isn't it? Welcome to our shop," he said in a friendly way.

Yes! I thought, *you are very handsome, with your perfect dark brown eyes, smooth dark skin and friendly smile.* He was a bit shorter than Paul, and broader too.

"I'm Diego. Can I help you with anything?" he asked. "Perhaps my girlfriend Karime can assist you?"

"Ven aqui corazon, sweetheart!" he called out.

A female voice responded in Spanish, "Un momento mi amor!"

A young woman with long black hair fashioned in a braid that was swept over her left shoulder approached me. Her black eyes danced with happiness as they fixed their gaze on Diego.

"Si Diego," Karime said and smiled a tantalizing smile at him, with lips painted a beautiful dark red. "Ah yes miss, how may we help you today?"

"I'm not creative when it comes to fashion," I confessed to the friendly young woman, "and I have to make a good impression this evening. I have a business dinner with a gentleman at nine, and then I'm meeting my boyfriend at his new club later on in De Wallen. All of Paul's friends will be there, his ex girlfriends, everyone he knows. I'm so nervous, really I am!"

"Don't worry, don't worry. I'm sure we can find the perfect little dress for you. My name is Karime."

"Hi, I'm Deena. I was going to look for a pretty scarf to go with my black dress," I explained to her.

"No, no, black is not a good color for your creamy skin. You need red for this special evening, and I have just the dress for you, in your size too!" she said, assessing my figure as we walked together to the back of the shop.

"Here!" She stopped and picked out a short red dress. "Try this on, you will love it!"

I followed her to the dressing room. As I tried on the dress, I thought, *do I have the courage to wear this?* The neckline was plunging, the hemline was mid thigh, the back was low cut. It had long sleeves.

Karime came in and looked at me admiringly. "Perfecto, Deena!" she said. "Si, red is magnifico on you! With your beautiful hair color, wonderful! And your figure looks stunning, just stunning!"

"Not much left to the imagination, Karime! Dare I?" I asked her nervously.

"Yes you must, and here, some black heels to show off your pretty legs just right!" she said.

She convinced me. I thought Paul would love showing me off to his friends at the club in this revealing, sexy dress. I changed quickly and hurried to the front of the store to pay for my things. I was excited about getting ready for the evening! I thanked Karime, exchanged phone numbers with her, and said goodbye to Diego.

As I biked back to the houseboat, I thought about all the things I loved in Amsterdam, the museums, the parks, the architecture, and of course the old Portuguese Synagogue. I was enthralled with the canals encircling almost every street. I stopped for a moment and gazed at the city reflected in its waterways. I wanted to have a future in this city, a future with Paul.

Finally I was back at Spice Island. As I got dressed, I thought about how concerned Paul was with my having dinner with Chris. I had to admit I liked that he was jealous. I didn't think he was used to the role of being the envious one in a relationship.

I carefully took inventory of my clothes, hair and makeup. I was pleased with the way the red dress and black shoes looked on me as I gazed in the full length mirror in the bedroom. Karime was right, the dress highlighted the best parts of my figure, my breasts and my rear. I made sure I had just the right amount of color on my eyelids, a little blush on my cheeks and a soft red lipstick on my lips.

All in all, I thought I looked pretty. Paul was right – Chris would be attracted to me, no doubt about it.

I grabbed my purse and walked to the restaurant.

Chapter 28

Dinner with Chris

It was Saturday evening, and the city's residents and tourists alike were filling the outdoor cafes, anticipating a night of reveling in what only Amsterdam could offer.

I arrived at the restaurant on time. The host greeted me. "Good evening, welcome to Le Pecheur. Are you Deena Green?"

"Yes I am. Is there a problem? I am meeting Mr. Chris Bucholtz here at nine o'clock," I replied.

"But of course Ms. Green. Mr. Bucholtz phoned and said he will be a few minutes late. He tried to reach you on your cell phone, but you did not answer. Would you be more comfortable waiting at the bar or at your table?"

"I think I'll wait at the bar. Thank you." The people seated there looked interesting, dressed in casual but fashionable clothes.

I made myself comfortable on a bar stool. On my left was a young man holding hands with a pretty woman, and on my right a middle aged man. He looked me over from head to toe. His gaze was intense. The bartender was about to take my drink order when the man said, "Can I buy you a drink, miss?" He stared at my chest.

"No thank you," I said emphatically. "I'm waiting for a friend."

"A friend? Very nice for an American woman to have a friend in Amsterdam."

"I will have a glass of Riesling, sir," I said loudly to the bartender, trying to ignore the man.

"Please, miss, I mean no harm," he pleaded with me. "My name is Lotewik." The bartender said something in Dutch to the man, ending with Chris Bucholtz's name.

"Ach, so you have very prominent friends in The Netherlands! I am impressed," Lotewik said as he touched my upper arm none too gently.

He looked like everyone's bear of an uncle, round faced, chubby, light grey hair cut in a closely cropped crew cut, bright almond shaped blue eyes. He appeared to be in his late 60s.

"Yes, well, I know everyone in politics in The Netherlands. I'm a retired scientist. I worked for your C.I.A. for five years in both Eastern and Western Europe. You will like the food here. There are some other nice restaurants in Amsterdam that you should try. The Oysterbar, for instance, has wonderful clams. La Oliva is great for Spanish tapas. De Kas has the freshest vegetables in the city. And Beddington's is my favorite, I know the owner Jean personally."

Lotewik touched my arm a second time to get my attention. The bartender served me a glass of wine. I drank some. He began his monologue again, as he rested his hand on my lower arm. "Now, miss, you know you must savor the wine. Let it breathe first, before you sip it. Here, let me show you the proper way," and he took my glass and began sniffing the wine's bouquet.

Chris came in at the just the right time – I was getting a bit bored with Lotewik. Chris rushed over to the bar and said "Deena, so sorry that I am late. Are you alright? Ah, Lotewik, how are you? Keeping my friend entertained, no doubt." He put his arm gently around my waist and helped me off the bar stool. "Henry, please show us to our table," Chris said to the host.

As we followed Henry to the back of the restaurant, Chris said, "Lotewik is harmless. Did he convince you he was once a C.I.A. operative? He is a very good talker."

"Yes he is," I said. "New York bars are filled with characters like him, I'm used to his type."

Chris stopped me before we sat down at the table. "Deena, you look beautiful. What a lovely dress. Sorry....I haven't greeted you properly." Chris leaned towards me and kissed me once on each cheek, and then gently on my lips.

"I can not help myself when I am with you. Your mouth begs me to kiss you!" he said. Chris and I both laughed as we sat across from each other. He exuded confidence in himself. The restaurant was elegant, with fine linens, silver, china and glasses arranged beautifully on each table.

"Henry," Chris said to the host when he came to our table, "please bring us your best bottle of Chardonnay. We have a lot to celebrate."

Chris proceeded to tell me about what he had accomplished in the past week for the diamond artisan relocation project. All the approvals were completed for the Plantage building renovations. The old factory building could now be used for the diamond industry. The commercial section had approved the establishment of Uncle Alan's diamond cutting and polishing business, and work visas would be issued for anyone connected to the project, including me.

"All that in such a short time? Paul thought it would take months to clear everything with your government," I said.

"Deena, I must be honest with you. Your project has become something of a personal mission for me. I feel the Dutch have not done enough to compensate the Jewish people for the extreme hardships they endured during the Second World War. I have spoken with Jacob Ruben, the mayor of Amsterdam. He has become an enthusiastic supporter of your plan to bring Jewish diamond artisans back to Amsterdam.

"Both Mayor Ruben and I have brought our influence to bear on the necessary government agencies. I will admit we have had an extraordinary amount of success in such a short time," Chris explained.

Henry served us the Chardonnay, which was wonderful. "Henry, my friend and I are famished! Please order some of your delicious seafood bouillabaisse for us!" Chris was very happy, and so was I.

"Let me toast you, Chris," I said as I raised my glass of wine. "To you, my friend, thank you for working miracles for us!" We clinked our wine glasses together, and looked into each other's eyes. His gaze was intensely personal, very inviting. I quickly looked away.

As our food was being prepared, Chris and I drank the wine and ate hors d'oeuvres. I had ample opportunity to observe him. He was a classically handsome Northern European man – very tall, thin, with light blonde hair and pale blue eyes. I thought intermingled with his Dutch ancestry was something else.

"Chris, I'm curious about your family's history. Are you originally from The Netherlands? Or perhaps another country?" I asked.

"Hmmm, you are both beautiful and smart too," he replied. "My father is Dutch and my mother is German, from Berlin. They met in college in Heidelberg. He is an engineer, and started his own firm in Amsterdam when he graduated.

"Mother's family hid Jewish people during the war. Many escaped unharmed as a result of their efforts. After I met you last week, I called my parents and told them about you and the diamond artisans project. My mother urged me to help you in any way I could. I hope I have done that Deena. I hope I have made you happy! I would do anything for you!" he said, emotionally. I was surprised, because up until now I had thought Chris a cool, level headed man.

"Chris, I am very happy. I am eternally grateful for all you have done. When my Uncle Alan first told me of his idea, I thought it was just a pipedream. You have made it a reality. You are my hero.

How can I repay you for all this?"

Chris took my small hands in his large ones.

"I know that you and I are friends Deena. But I want more from our relationship. I want you to be my lover. I can give you all that Paul Vermeer gives you and so much more," he said, begging me with his handsome blue eyes.

"Oh, Chris, one man at a time is all I can handle right now! I must be honest with you. I love Paul, and he says he loves me.

"I value my friendship with you," I continued. "You've gone above and beyond for me. Lovers come and go, but friendships last a lifetime."

"I know, Deena, I know. I guess that I will have to settle for that for now. But I will never give up trying to make you mine. Never."

The waiter hovered near us, ready to serve us our dinner. Chris reluctantly released my hands from his.

The food was delicious and so was the conversation with Chris. He was well-read, and loved the theater and music. We had a lot of interests in common.

Chris excused himself for a few minutes as an important call had come through on his cell phone. I took the opportunity to send a short email to Uncle Alan. I wrote: "Uncle Alan, I just found out we have the approvals. Great news! I will call you tomorrow." He responded simply: "Thanks for the miracle, Deena. Love you and so proud of you, Uncle Alan."

Chris soon returned and apologized for the interruption. Over our after dinner coffee, Chris brought up Paul once again. He started questioning me. I tried to stop him, feeling that Paul was close at hand, my sixth sense alerting me.

"What do you see in him?" Chris asked. "Is it the physical attraction? Does he have some strange hold over you? He is too young for you. I am just right for you, mature and knowledgeable.

Give me a chance to show you how truly happy I can make you......"

Paul had come into the restaurant and was at our table, just as I knew he would be. He had evidently overheard the conversation. Paul's face was bright red with anger. He said to Chris, "I have no hold over Deena. She has me under her spell. We are lovers. Forever. Do you understand me?"

Chris stood and said, "Forgive me for my rudeness Deena. I meant no harm." He glared at Paul. "Please explain to him all the approvals are in place thanks to Mayor Ruben and me. I will send the paperwork to your attorney on Monday morning. I am leaving now."

I stood up and took Chris's hand. "Thank you for everything, Chris, for all the work you've put into the project for us. Dinner was lovely. I will call you on Monday." I wanted him to know how much I appreciated his help.

"Yes, Deena, yes," Chris said as he bent down to give me a Dutch kiss and then moved closer still and kissed me on my lips.

"Vermeer, I hope you realize Deena is a diamond, a gem. You are a very lucky man," he said and left quickly.

Paul and I sat back down at the table. He lowered his voice, but his face was still red with anger. "What was that all about? I am very possessive where you are concerned. I knew Chris would try something to steal you away from me, no? He was looking for an opportunity to drive a wedge between us. Well, he did not succeed," he said as his blue eyes lit up with his need for me.

"Listen to me, love," I said. "Chris and I are just friends as far as I am concerned. I made that very clear to him earlier in the evening. He has gone out of his way to cut through all the bureaucratic red tape for the project. I am so thankful for all he has done for me. But I belong to you Paul, you alone. As you said, forever. Do you mean that?"

"Yes, baby, yes. I love you and only you." As his anger subsided, he noticed what I was wearing. "Where did you get that dress? What happened to covering your beautiful breasts with a scarf? Woman, that red dress is way too sexy for public viewing, except in the windows of De Wallen. I want to take you home and make love to you! Sleep with me, now, lover," he demanded, as he put his arms around my neck and pulled me close to him.

"I'm not tired Paul," I said sweetly.

"You know exactly what I mean," he said. "You are exciting me too much. Let's go home right now."

"What about the club opening?" I asked.

"They won't miss us for an hour. I can't concentrate on anything but you!" he insisted.

"OK, if you want me that much…."

"Yes, I do!"

I knew it was not just about my sexy red dress. Paul was claiming his territory, making sure I wouldn't think of Chris, but only of him.

We quickly left Le Pecheur. The speedy motor bike brought us home to Spice Island.

As soon as we entered the houseboat, Paul grabbed the hem of the red dress, pulled it over my head and threw it on the floor. "The only red I want to see is your full lips, and your hot nipples. Give them to me, only to me," he said, as he pulled off my panties and threw them on top of the discarded dress.

He wanted to possess me, all of me. No sweet kisses tonight, only lust filled bites on my lips and my breasts. Passionate suckling of my nipples. Strong squeezes on my ass. He wanted to claim me as his own.

Paul stripped naked and proudly displayed his manhood. "You want me and only me, yes?" he said.

"Yes." What else could I say? I was spellbound by his large

glistening erection. Aroused beyond conscious thought, I said, "Take me Paul, I'm yours and yours alone."

He laid me down on the living room rug. He entered me, one lust filled thrust after another after another. We climaxed together, my pussy squeezing his cock as his stream of hot wetness filled me. He had marked his territory, claiming me as his bitch. We tried to catch our breath, the steam and sweat rising from our bodies and filling the room.

"Let's shower, my love. Then we'll go to the club. Pandora will be wondering where we are," he said. He was back to the calm, self-possessed man that I knew. After we showered, I was surprised when he insisted I wear the red dress. "I want everyone to see my beautiful, sexy woman, yes!"

As Paul unlocked his motorbike and lifted me up on the back seat he said, "Pandora is with the security guards at the club. She is enjoying her job there very much. She is acting like she owns the place!"

We both laughed, it was just like Pandora to take charge. I held on to Paul as he sped off towards the club. I was in ecstasy! Paul wanted me even more now. Jealousy is sometimes a good thing, I thought. I was also grateful Chris had come through with what we needed for the diamond artisans project to get off the ground. Very, very grateful.

Chapter 29
At the Club

We arrived at the club and Paul parked his motorbike. We hurried to the entrance. Paul was greeted by Pandora and her wagging tail, and two very capable looking security guards. The younger of the two men, who looked like a bodybuilder, said "Your Pandora is definitely a very helpful assistant tonight. She has already growled at a group of noisy college students, and scared them off. Good work, girl," he said as he patted her large head.

"I didn't doubt her for one minute, Geoff," Paul said. "I will leave you in Pandora's care then, gentlemen. It sounds like the party has started without us, no?"

The older man, Maarten, said, "yes, a lot of people have arrived already. I predict this evening will be a great success for your club, Paul."

Maarten was right. We walked down a steep flight of stairs and were greeted by loud music. People were dancing, drinking, smoking weed, laughing, embracing and shouting at one another so as to be heard above the latest music. The room was large, with tables and chairs around the edge of the dance floor. The lighting fixtures in the low ceiling were made of illuminated slats with sayings in Dutch that changed every minute. Paul said, "Do you like those light sculptures, sweetheart? I designed them."

"I love them, and I love to dance!" I said.

"What's your pleasure then, woman?" Paul said in my ear, and then looked at me playfully with a devilish grin on his just-been-through-some-hot- lovemaking lips.

"Dancing with you, but of course, silly man!" I mimicked his expression and grabbed his hands. "Follow me!" I shouted.

We started rocking to the music of Cold Play the DJ was spinning. Dancing with Paul made me higher than any drug or drink. We couldn't escape the potent aroma of Netherlands marijuana, however, and we were soon enveloped by it.

I was near him, always near him. I held Paul around his neck as he seemed to lift me up as we danced. Soon I realized I was floating above the dance floor on my own. Paul looked at me with amazement, and I was surprised too. Magic!

Everyone cleared the dance floor and watched as Paul and I danced together. We were center stage, the main attraction.

Someone handed Paul a microphone and the music's volume was lowered. "Thank you for coming to opening night at The Flying Fox!" Paul said into the microphone. "Everyone, meet my one and only girlfriend Deena! I enjoyed designing this club, so now please, everyone enjoy yourselves, yes!"

The music was loud once again. Everyone crowded back on the dance floor. Paul held my hips and started dancing in a very suggestive way, swaying his hips from side to side, moving closer and closer to me. My dance movements matched his. He was a good dancer – he then pulled me really really close all in time to the music.

His arms kept me near him, and I couldn't get out of his grasp. But why would I want to?

It seemed everyone at the club wanted to talk to Paul, have a drink with him, smoke with him, dance with him. I relinquished him to his friends. I was happy to rest, sip some wine, and watch him mingle with the crowd. He was the most sought after person in the room.

A good looking man with brown hair and brown eyes, probably in his mid forties, walked over to where I was standing, a drink in hand.

"Hi, I'm Paul's girlfriend Deena Green," I said.

"Hello," he said in return. "I'm Luke Janssen. Taking a break from the dance floor?"

"Yes, I wanted to give Paul a chance to be with his friends."

"He does have many friends. Some of us think Paul has a future in politics in The Netherlands. Has he mentioned his political aspirations to you?" Luke asked.

"We haven't really discussed politics," I replied, stretching the truth a bit.

"No doubt you two have been busy with other things," Luke said with a smile. "Well, if Paul is interested in a public career, as some think he is, there are many in Amsterdam who would be willing to support him. Having a Jewish girlfriend could be an asset for him in some circles here, and a detriment in others."

"I'm a bit surprised Luke. I wouldn't have expected there to be anti-Semitism in Amsterdam," I replied.

"Amsterdam is a surprising city. Don't let it disturb you. Nothing that can not be overcome, should Paul choose the political route. Here he is now."

Paul walked quickly to me and put his arm around my waist. He kissed me on my lips. "Deena, has Luke been flirting with you? Or giving you his usual pep talk about how he would help with my political career, yes?" Paul said, and laughed at Luke.

"Luke is one of our city's alderman. I'm sure he also mentioned your being Jewish might or might not be an asset to me. May I remind you Luke, my friend, of my family's long standing commitment to the Jews of Amsterdam that my brother Rick and I have continued, yes? Luke, listen to me. I may be a bit high, but I am down to earth on this – Deena is the most important person in my life. She is beautiful, a talented business woman, and Jewish. If you have a problem with that, I have nothing further to say to you."

"Paul, calm down, calm down. You know I don't have any problems with your private life. But others in Amsterdam might."

"Then they will have to solve those problems quickly, yes. Deena, let's say our goodbyes. Good night, Luke. My lovely lady and I need some private time together." Paul was relaxed as we walked around the club for another half hour, saying goodbye to everyone. The party atmosphere in the club was still at full tilt.

A strikingly beautiful woman approached Paul and gave him a hug and then three long kisses on his cheeks. She was an inch or two taller than me, with light brown hair cut chin length. Her large light brown eyes scanned the room, Paul, and then checked me out from head to toe. Her round face, with prominent cheekbones, held a smile for Paul from ear to ear. She was very pregnant. Was she an old flame of his?

"Claudia, what a wonderful surprise!" Paul shouted at her, so he could be heard above the music. "I thought you weren't coming here tonight. Did the little girl keep you awake? And where is Bjorn?" Paul tapped her protruding pregnant belly lightly.

"You are right," Claudia laughed. "The baby wanted to go clubbing, even though her mother would rather sleep. Bjorn could not wait to see this place. I have to admit, it is fantastic!"

A very tall, handsome man with black hair and a full beard walked quickly to Claudia and kissed her on her lips. "Just had to dance one dance, honey. Paul, great energy here tonight. Congratulations! And who is this lovely lady?" Bjorn asked, inclining his head towards me, looking me over with playful dark eyes.

"Claudia and Bjorn, meet Deena Green, my girlfriend. She is from New York," Paul said as he drew me to him possessively with his strong arm around my waist. "She is beautiful and smart like you are, Claudia. Claudia is my unofficial political advisor."

"Ah yes, my friend, and when are you going to make it official?" Claudia asked.

"Claudia, please be patient with me," Paul said.

"Listen to me, I am due to have this baby in less than two months. Your would be opponents have already declared their intentions. By the way, where were you all last week? You didn't return my phone calls or emails."

"Deena and I were visiting with Hans and Giselle," Paul said.

"We had a wonderful time," I added.

Claudia's eyes narrowed as she looked at me. "Knowing Paul, all too wonderful I am sure."

"I have been trying to make a decision about running for City Council. Rick, as you know, is preoccupied with his problems with Vanessa. So he won't be able to help me with the campaign," Paul said in a troubled voice.

"Paul, I promise you I will run your campaign, through pregnancy and motherhood. Having advised Luke successfully in his last run, I know the ropes. Just make your decision very soon."

"OK, Claudia, OK. I will call you on Monday, yes."

"Make it Monday morning. I have an important meeting in Utrecht Monday afternoon." Claudia and Bjorn said goodbye and left quickly.

"My friend Claudia is tough, yes? We have known each other since childhood, and her older brother and Rick are best friends," Paul smiled as he waved goodbye.

"Are you leaning towards running for City Council?" I asked.

"Yes I am, but let's go home now. I'll think about my decision all night long, as we make love."

"I'm hoping to take your mind off of everything but us."

"Then I will think about politics in the morning," Paul said as he kissed me on my mouth. His kisses always felt as exciting as the very first one we shared, and this one was no different.

As we were finishing our goodbyes and getting ready to leave the club, I was overcome by the feeling our attention was needed elsewhere. I excused myself for a moment to check on Pandora. I went outside and asked Geoff and Maarten how everything was going, and how Pandora was holding up. Geoff said that for the last few minutes Pandora had been whining. He thought the loud music was bothering her.

I went inside the club and found Paul. His eyes lit up when he saw me. He came over to me and hugged me tightly. We heard the DJ's latest choice, the song "Black Magic Woman", which I loved.

"Let's have a last dance, my magic woman, yes!" Paul said. As usual, I couldn't say no to him, especially when he held me around my waist and pulled me very close to him. I was lost in his arms, in his rhythmic swaying to the music. I followed the movement of his hips, his legs, and we danced as if we were one.

He sang along to the music and then held my waist as he reached forward to kiss me. My back curved and I dropped my head in a backward arch, and kicked one of my legs up in the air. He kissed my shoulders, my neck and then worked his way up to my lips. The song was over and we continued kissing, our bodies entwined in a heated embrace.

Paul whispered in my ear something I couldn't hear enough of from him, "I want you woman, I want you now. Let's leave, yes!"

All eyes had been on us as we danced sensually. We waved to everyone, as Paul shouted, "have a great night and a great morning everyone! Come again soon!"

I needed him as much as he needed me. But I sensed someone else needed both of us, someone needed our help.

Chapter 30
Vanessa

On our way out of the club, we kissed passionately. "Let's go home, Deena, I need you so much tonight, yes," Paul said.

We heard Pandora's insistent whine, which brought our kissing to a stop. "What is it Pandora?" Paul asked the big girl. "Are you jealous of my attention to Deena? I love you too," he said as he reached down to hug her around her neck.

Geoff said Pandora had not been her confident self for the last half hour. He thought Pandora sensed some trouble, but both he and Maarten had taken a walk nearby to investigate and had not seen or heard anything unusual.

I pointed out to Paul the fur on Pandora's back, from her neck to her tail, was standing up, a sure sign she thought there was something or someone to be afraid of. Paul asked Geoff to take the motorbike home for him, and gave him the keys. We started walking towards the houseboat. Something caught Paul's eye across the narrow street. He waited a moment or two and looked more closely.

"It's my niece Vanessa," he whispered to me. "Look, just over there. The tall thin girl with black hair, leaning on that boy. Pandora, stil zijn, be still."

There was no doubt the beautiful teenage girl was related to Paul. Vanessa had the same thick black hair, large eyes and square chin as Paul did. She was painfully thin.

"Oh no! Nessa looks terrible. Let's go behind this doorway, I don't want her to recognize Pandora or me. Not that she could in the condition she is in. She looks drugged out of her mind," Paul said sadly.

Paul was right. The girl couldn't even stand up straight on her own. The boy she was with was walking her down the street. They were nearing an all night café.

We couldn't hear what he was saying at first, but then he shouted, "Vanessa, Vanessa, come on, snap out of it. You need to stay awake. I am going to get some coffee into you." He opened the door to the café.

Paul decided we should follow them, at a safe distance, to see if we could find out anything further.

First Vanessa and the boy entered the café, and sat down near the front windows. Then Paul and I went in, leaving Pandora to stand guard next door. We sat a few tables behind them. The café was dimly lit, so it afforded us an element of secrecy.

The boy was trying to keep Vanessa awake. "Hey Vanessa, wake up, you whore," he shouted at her. "You are no good to me asleep. We must have you practice your English, for the American and British customers. You've still got to turn a few more tricks before I let you go home."

I had to hold Paul by both arms to keep him from getting up and strangling the boy. "Paul, listen to me," I reasoned with him in a whisper. "Let's follow them after they've had their coffee. Maybe we can find out more about where she has been."

We ordered coffee as well. We needed to shadow Vanessa, if it took all night, to make sure we knew what was happening to her.

Soon, with some coffee in her, Vanessa seemed to be more coherent. "Finn, I have been with four men. Isn't that enough for you?" she wailed plaintively.

"No Vanessa, your quota is six for tonight. You need to do two more men for me. You are such a good prostitute. Pretty, but wasted. The men won't care, they all love young girls like you. Finish that coffee and let's get going. I don't have all night," he answered her in a threatening tone.

"Finn, I love you so much. Why are you forcing me to do these things? First you promised me I had to do it only once or twice. Now it is every night, more and more each night. I want you to love me too!"

"I told you I love you Vanessa. But I need the money. Now be a good little whore and listen to me. Admit it, you like doing this," Finn taunted her.

"No, I don't like this at all. I want to stop it now. Tonight. I have had enough. Please, Finn, please I can't do this anymore," Vanessa pleaded with him.

"Oh yes you can, just a few more men tonight," Finn shouted at her and pulled her up off the chair and out the door.

We left the café. Paul told Pandora to follow right behind us and be silent as he picked up her leash. We were about twenty yards behind Vanessa and Finn. She was crying. We heard her saying over and over again, "no more Finn no more."

We walked in silence, and Paul stopped to gather his thoughts. "Now they are turning towards the Grand Canal," he said. Paul hissed at Pandora, and pulled her close to him. I sensed something was going to happen very soon, and Pandora sensed it as well. Paul took off Pandora's leash, and whispered in her ear in Dutch. "I told her to be ready to protect Vanessa."

Vanessa ran to the bridge that spanned the canal. She screamed, "no Finn no I can't do it anymore! I won't!" She leaned over the bridge, which was waist high, and started to climb onto the railing. "Finn, I love you!"

Pandora was a streak of blackness as she ran towards Vanessa. She reached Vanessa just as she was about to leap off the bridge into the murky canal water. Pandora jumped up, caught and pulled Vanessa's shirt with her mouth, and then laid down on the pavement on her back, so that Vanessa landed on Pandora's ample belly.

Paul and I dashed to the bridge. Paul gently picked up Vanessa and held her in his arms. Finn had run away when he saw Pandora.

"Nessa, Nessa, my love, it's Uncle Jean-Paul. I am here. I am here for you. Pandora saved you my sweetheart she wouldn't let anything happen to you," he crooned to the frightened girl as he rocked her in his arms. "Deena, here is my cell phone, dial 112, the emergency number. When the operator is speaking to you hold the phone near me and I will instruct them."

I got the operator on the phone, and held it for Paul. He said, "Emergency on the Grand Canal bridge in De Wallen. Send the police and sex crime investigators as soon as possible. A child has been raped."

"Uncle Jean-Paul, what are you doing here?" Vanessa said. She looked into Paul's eyes and then quickly looked away.

"Nessa, you almost jumped into the canal. Pandora saved you. I saw you when I left my new club tonight in De Wallen. I have been following you and that scum Finn."

"Finn, where is he? Uncle Jean-Paul, I love him so much!" Nessa cried to him.

"Nessa, Finn is no good for you," Paul said softly as he held her.

"I know, Uncle, I know," she said. "He made me be his prostitute. He was my pimp. I love him. Why, why did he make me do those things? Why did I let him?" Vanessa's words tore at my heart.

"You needed love, Nessa. We all do. Now here are the police. Let's all go to my home. This is my friend Deena from America. She will help you too," Paul reassured her.

Two uniformed police officers stopped their car and met us on the bridge. "Hello, I'm Paul Vermeer," Paul said. "This is my niece,

Vanessa Vermeer. She has been raped and forced to have sex with men by her loverboy. The boy ran away when he saw us.

"How soon can you get someone to my home from the sex crimes unit to interview and examine my niece? She has marks on her face and arms and probably elsewhere which indicates she has been beaten. Also she should be examined for bodily fluids," Paul said.

"We will contact that unit now. In the meantime, please come into our car, and let us take you and your niece home. And your friend, and of course your dog," the officer said as he smiled sadly at me.

"She is a brave girl, my Pandora, yes," Paul replied. "That scum could have pulled a knife on her. My fearless dog. She saved Vanessa from jumping into the canal. Deena, help me support her."

We each held Vanessa under her arms. She was as light as a feather, even though she was much taller than me. We walked her slowly to the police car. She was sobbing and holding onto Paul's neck as if her life depended on it. And perhaps it did.

Chapter 31

Investigation

Paul and I settled into the back seat of the police vehicle, Vanessa between us.

Pandora was able to squeeze into the rear of the small SUV when the officer opened the back door. The brave dog gently nuzzled Vanessa's neck, and the frightened girl seemed to calm down. "Pandora, Pandora," she murmured as she leaned on Paul.

While Paul gave directions to the officer, I tried to hold Vanessa's hand. She pulled away from me and moved even closer to Paul.

We soon arrived at the houseboat. Paul, Vanessa, Pandora and I got out of the car, and Paul brought Vanessa into his bedroom and made her comfortable on his bed. "Deena," he said, "please stay with Nessa for a few minutes while I talk to the police officers."

Pandora jumped up on the bed close to Vanessa before I had a chance to sit down next to her. Vanessa turned towards the loving dog, and hugged her furry neck. "Why Pandora, why doesn't Finn love me?" Nessa cried. Pandora licked Vanessa gently on her cheek. Vanessa stopped crying. Soon both dog and teenager were fast asleep, Pandora's huge head next to Vanessa's thin face on the pillow.

Paul came back into the room. He was very angry. "I called Rick and Rachel and they are on their way. Damn it, the police just told me the sex crimes investigation unit may not be here until mid day. Then it will be too late to collect evidence. They said it is has been a busy night."

"At least Vanessa is resting with Pandora," I whispered to him, taking him to the side. "Paul, I have an idea. I am going to call Chris Bucholtz, and see if he can get someone here sooner."

Paul hesitated for a moment. He didn't like Chris, but he also knew we needed his help now. "I could call my friend Luke," Paul suggested, but he realized Chris had more clout than Luke did. Paul said, "OK Deena, call Chris. Thank him for me."

I found my cell phone and called Chris's number. It took a moment or two before he answered. "Deena," he said, "Are you alright? It is three o'clock in the morning. Where are you? I can be in Amsterdam in forty five minutes. What's wrong?"

"Chris, so sorry to trouble you at this hour. Paul's niece Vanessa Vermeer has been involved with a loverboy. We are pretty sure he is a Dutch teenager. We found her in De Wallen earlier this morning, raped and beaten. We believe he forced Vanessa to act as a prostitute and have sex with many clients. The police tell us they can not get a sex crimes unit here until the afternoon. We are at Paul's houseboat now on the Prinsengracht. Don't you think we should have some investigative police officers here sooner?"

"Deena say no more. I am going to make a phone call or two. I will get back to you very soon."

"What did Chris say? Rick and Rachel will be here in a few minutes. Dr. Halperin, our family physician, is on his way as well," Paul said.

I put my arm around Paul and said, "Chris is making a few calls right now. I know you are so worried about Vanessa, but she is resting with Pandora. I'll cover her with another blanket."

Chris called back and told me a sex crimes unit would be on its way to the houseboat in about a half hour. Even though it was a very busy night in De Wallen, Chris was able to pull some strings.

Rick and Rachel rushed inside the houseboat as we waited for the police officers. "Sshhhh, she is safe now, she is sleeping with Pandora," Paul soothed them as they held onto to him with whatever strength they had left.

"Yes," I said "she is calm now, she has Pandora by her side."

Paul got some glasses and whisky out of the cupboard, and poured shots for Rick and Rachel. "Here, drink this," Paul said soothingly. "I have been assured the special sex crimes police unit will be here soon to begin the investigation."

There was a knock on the door and Paul opened it. Two plainclothes officers, a man and a woman, entered. Pandora let out a gentle "woof" so as not to wake Vanessa.

The woman said, "Please sit down. We know that you have been through a lot tonight. I am Erika van Pelt from the sex crimes unit and this is my partner Henry Hoff." Rick and Rachel sat at the kitchen table, and so did Erika.

She was a tall thin blonde woman in her early forties, and Henry was shorter, with balding light hair and a husky build, also in his forties. "We know this is a very difficult time for you. Please bear with us as we ask you some questions. We will have to question your daughter as well and examine her," Erika said.

"Vanessa is asleep now with my dog Pandora, who saved her from jumping off the canal bridge," Paul explained to Erika.

"Thank you, sir, and you are, oh yes, Paul Vermeer. The girl's uncle," Erika said.

We heard Vanessa saying to Pandora, "Dora, Dora what have I done? I thought Finn loved me. I need his love."

Rick and Rachel ran into the bedroom. Paul and I stayed in the hallway, but we heard Vanessa say, "Mama, Papa, I am so sorry."

"We don't understand, Nessa," Rick said, as he sat down on the bed next to her and took her hand in his. "What happened? Why did you have that horrible boy in your life?"

"Papa, you know I was lonely after Grandmother died. Nobody was with me. I needed love, hugs, kisses. Finn loved me. I needed to love him so much," she said.

"You should have come to us if you were in trouble," Rachel said, bending down over Vanessa.

"You are both so busy," replied Vanessa. "Papa is always working and you Mama are wrapped up in you charity work and art tours. I know you both love me, but things haven't been the same since Grandmother died. Not for me," Vanessa cried as Pandora licked her cheek. Vanessa calmed down the moment Pandora comforted her.

I told Paul I thought Pandora should be near Vanessa throughout the police investigation. Paul agreed with me. Only Pandora was able to calm Vanessa. He bent down to kiss my cheek and said, "Thank you love. I will insist on Pandora being present during all of the police proceedings."

Erika came into the bedroom. "Vanessa, I am going to ask you some questions now," she explained. "Detective Hoff is needed elsewhere, so he will be leaving."

"We would like to request my dog Pandora be present during all of the police inquiries," Paul said to Erika, "including any hearings or trial before a judge," he continued. "Vanessa and Pandora have a special relationship. We believe Pandora will help Vanessa get through this."

"I think that's a good idea," Erika answered. "I can't speak for the judge that will be appointed in this case should there be legal proceedings, but for now, I welcome Pandora at Vanessa's side."

"Vanessa," Erika said as she sat next to her on the bed, "how long have you known Finn?"

Vanessa thought for a moment. "About eight months," she offered. "But I can't tell you Finn's real name," she said as she stroked Pandora's fur.

"Why not?" Erika asked gently.

"Because, there may be a chance he still loves me. And he made me promise not to tell his real name. A promise is a promise. This is his blue sweater. He gave it to me. I need to keep it," Vanessa said, as she clutched the sweater she was wearing.

"Yes Vanessa, but he hurt you. I am going to examine you now. You can hold Pandora's paw while I do that. OK?" Erika asked.

"OK," whispered Vanessa.

"Rick and Paul, please wait in the living room. Rachel and Deena, please stay here as witnesses to the examination," said Erika.

Erika proceeded with the physical examination, as Vanessa clutched Pandora's paw. Erika looked over Vanessa's face, arms and chest area. She gently pushed Vanessa's clothes aside. She spoke into her cell phone. "Bruises on the victim's shoulders and arms." As she examined Vanessa further, she noted, "Severe bruising on the victim's upper thighs."

"I am going to take a sample from your private area with a cotton swab. Please close your eyes and hold Pandora," Erika said.

Before Vanessa could react, Erika was finished with the exam. She went into the living room, and I followed her, leaving Rachel to be with her daughter. "I want to complete things quickly here so Vanessa can rest," she said. "She does not want to reveal Finn's identity at the present time. Do you have any ideas?"

We all shook our heads sadly in the negative.

"Rick, why don't you keep your wife and daughter company in the bedroom." When Rick had left the living room, Erika said, "Please sit down. I want to know what you both heard and saw in De Wallen."

As we sat on the sofa and Erika on a chair, Paul said, "We were leaving my new club on the Vijzelstraat. We saw Vanessa and Finn across the street. He looked to be of medium build, about five feet ten inches. He wore a black baseball cap and sunglasses. Smart scum, that one. Knew to disguise himself."

Erika took notes as Paul spoke.

"Maybe I had better continue from here," I said. "I know this part will get Paul very angry."

"Go ahead then," Erika said.

"We followed Vanessa and Finn into a café," I said. "We sat a few tables from them. He told her she needed to have sex with more men. He said he needed the money. She kept saying she wanted no more of it. They then left the café and we followed them. Vanessa kept saying, 'I love you Finn. Please, I don't want to do this anymore.' She ran to the canal bridge, and started climbing on it. She would have jumped off the bridge if Pandora hadn't pulled her to safety."

Rick and Rachel joined us in the living room. "She is resting with Pandora," Rick said. "We will take her home with us after Erika has completed her inquiry."

"Vanessa will need to be helped by a psychologist who has experience counseling young crime victims," Erika advised them. "I am recommending you contact Dr. Belinda Boden. Here is her card with her phone numbers and email address. Please let her know I referred you. I would contact her as soon as possible. The fact that Vanessa is not giving you the boy's real name, just his street name Finn, means she is going to have greater difficulties psychologically. Here is my card also. We have nothing as yet to go on in terms of investigating who the perpetrator is. Only that one of his street names is Finn, and the blue sweater he gave Vanessa."

After a few minutes of digesting everything Erika told us, Paul said, "I have an idea as to how we could proceed with finding the scum that did this to Vanessa. Let me keep the sweater. My dog Pandora will be able to pick up his scent from the sweater, yes. Deena can meet Vanessa at school with Pandora every day and walk her home. Pandora may be able to zero in on the boy if he is a student at Vanessa's school, which we believe he is."

"I think that is a very good idea Paul," Erika said. "I will take the sweater overnight to the police station, and see if we can pick up some DNA samples, perhaps from strands of hair. Then I will return the sweater to you. In the meanwhile, call Dr. Boden as soon as you can. Once she has met with Vanessa and gains her trust, it is quite possible that Vanessa will reveal the boy's identity. It will go a long way towards her recovery.

"I must admit you are lucky I have been assigned to this case. Most police officers are overworked and would not take the time to follow up. Again, please call me with any news or any ideas, and I will do the same. I have a suspicion the boy will find another victim quite soon," Erika advised us. "Good bye for now. Vanessa is strong and she will eventually heal from this trauma."

After Erika left, I suggested Rick and Rachel meet with the school principal. "Good idea, Deena. I want Vanessa to begin her art classes again. She dropped out of them last year. She is very good with sketching and painting. I think her art work will help her to get back to herself," Rick said.

Chapter 32
Paul's Decision

"Deena, will Vanessa ever recover from this?" Paul asked me when Rick, Rachel and Vanessa had gone home. We were lying in bed together, holding each other under the covers for comfort and support.

"I know Paul, the picture appears pretty grim right now. But she is young, and with counseling from Dr. Boden, and lots of love from her family, she should be able to get back to a normal life," I said and kissed him gently on his lips.

He did not respond immediately to my kiss, which was unusual. He gazed up at the ceiling. I could almost hear the wheels turning in his mind.

I wasn't surprised when he finally said, "Deena, I have come to a decision about running for City Council. I am going to declare my candidacy with the PvdA party. If I am elected to City Council I can do something to make sure sex criminals like Finn get punished. I hope you will support me in my campaign."

"I will do everything I can to help you out. Just let me know what you need me to do for you, my love. I am so very proud of you. A political campaign opens your life to the public eye, so we both must be strong."

"Deena, I know you will be with me on this one hundred

percent, yes. But I have Claudia as my campaign manager. Vanessa needs you more than I do right now. Rick is brokenhearted, and so is Rachel. Rachel never could give Vanessa the warmth my mother did. Nessa needs someone to love and care for her now. Will you try to help her?"

"I would love if Vanessa got close to me, if she will have me. I think Pandora will be the bridge between us. We both love that big, affectionate dog," I said. I prayed I would be able to win my way into Vanessa's heart.

"I'll call Claudia now," Paul said as he reached for his cell phone. After a few minutes on the phone with Claudia, Paul said with a smile on his face, "That woman is acting like she won the million euro lottery! I will meet with her first thing tomorrow morning. She will have breakfast with us, all right, my love?" he asked me.

"Of course, Paul."

"Thank you Deena, I honestly don't know what lies ahead. I am a bit nervous about entering politics. But I know the families of this city deserve a safer life here than what they are getting now."

"I agree, I agree."

Next morning at nine o'clock we heard Claudia's loud knock. Paul opened the door for her, and she breezed in, coffee cup already in hand. "Paul, the party leaders are overjoyed you are running for City Council. They have waited a long time for someone as popular as you to enter the political arena. They think the best way to handle your announcement is on Amsterdam TV. How does the idea of a prime time interview with Elsbeth Stoker grab you?" Claudia asked Paul excitedly. "We won't have much time to prepare. I have already spoken to Elsbeth and Amsterdam News Network. Does tomorrow night at seven o'clock sound good to you?"

Paul hesitated for a moment and then said, "sure, Claudia, let's run with it, yes. Will it be live?"

"Yes live, more sincere, more believable that way. Elsbeth wants it to be in English," Claudia said.

"Why in English?" Paul said.

"Because we want your ideas to be conveyed to Americans, Brits and any other foreign tourists. The message is that our city will be a good place for people to raise their families…"

"Right. Prostitution will still be legal, but not when it involves minors or human trafficking, forced prostitution. My main idea to get across to the public is certain crimes, especially sex crimes, need to be punished, especially when minors are involved."

"There we go, Paul. You are off and running. As am I. Meet you at the Amsterdam News Network offices at four o'clock tomorrow afternoon, we can go over last minute details with Elsbeth. Oh, by the way, I hope you are on board with this, Deena," Claudia said to me as an afterthought.

"Of course, Claudia. I am so proud of Paul. I will leave it to the two of you to take charge. I am busy with my work and hopefully helping Vanessa now."

Chapter 33

Interview

Paul was busy the rest of the day, and all the next preparing for the interview. He said it was important for him to jot down all his thoughts on how he would change things in the city.

He left for the Amsterdam News Network studios at four o'clock. He asked me to come by the studio at about six. He wanted my moral support as he was nervous about a live interview. I knew Paul would be confident once the interview was underway.

When I arrived at the news studio promptly at six, Paul was having his hair and makeup done. He was his usual friendly self, and had the hair stylist and makeup artist enthralled with him. I came over and gave him a quick kiss on his cheek and wished him good luck. He kissed me on my lips and squeezed my hand tightly. I found a seat in the audience section of the studio and waited for the interview to begin.

A few minutes before seven, Elsbeth and Paul took their places on the set, which was designed to look like a comfortable living room, with two large chairs catty corner to each other. Elsbeth and Paul were seated, talking to each other.

Claudia walked past me with a curt nod and sat a few rows behind me.

I looked at Elsbeth closely. She was young, probably in her mid to late twenties and very pretty, with short blonde hair, light blue eyes, round face and prominent chin and chest. She was all business on the set, as she began the interview.

ELSBETH: Good evening, Elsbeth Stoker here at Amsterdam News Network. Our guest this evening is Paul Vermeer, an up and coming architect, living and working here in Amsterdam. Tell us, Paul, what brings you to Amsterdam News Network this evening?

PAUL: Good evening Elsbeth to you and your viewers. Thank you for the opportunity to share my ideas. I appreciate the fact that you have suggested our talk be conducted in English. You and I and your network want the many tourists, as well as the citizens of Amsterdam, to know about my announcement this evening and what that announcement implies. Yesterday, after careful consideration, I have made the decision to run for Amsterdam City Council on behalf of the PvdA Party. For those of you watching this evening that are unfamiliar with Netherlands government and politics, PvdA stands for Partij van de Arbeid, or The Labour Party. We are a social democratic party and our main concerns are to promote the employment of our citizens, maintain and expand social security and welfare and invest in education and health care. We are also proponents of the public safety of our citizens.

ELSBETH: Congratulations on your announcement Paul! I personally wish you good luck in your campaign, and if you are successful, in your role in the City Council. What will be one of the first things you will concentrate on if you are elected?

PAUL: Thank you for your good wishes Elsbeth. I hope your viewers feel the same way as you do. And I hope the public agrees with me about certain issues affecting their safety in this wonderful city of ours. We share our city with many tourists each and every day, 365 days a year. Tourists have made certain businesses in our city, prostitution and drug sales the most high profile of which, extremely profitable.

I am not advocating prostitution and certain drugs, such as cannabis, be made illegal. What I am advocating is if there are crimes committed here they be prosecuted according to the full extent of the law. Mayor Ruben and I both advocate an increased police presence in such areas as De Wallen to protect our citizens, as well as the prostitutes there from harm.

Besides the legal prostitutes there are many illegal ones as well. These illegals are often very young girls that have been lured into the trade or kidnapped by unscrupulous sex traffickers. What I am calling for is more stringent and comprehensive conduct on the part of law enforcement. It has come to my attention recently that there are not enough police officers to do the job properly.

The trafficking in underage prostitutes must be stopped. Many in our present government look the other way. Young girls are virtual sex slaves here in Amsterdam, especially those from our former colony, Indonesia. We owe it to that nation to have its children, and those of others countries as well, returned to their childhood.

ELSBETH: You are part Indonesian, aren't you Paul?

PAUL: (hesitates for a moment) Yes, my ancestors were nutmeg plantation owners in the Molucca Islands of Indonesia during the 1800s. At least one of my forefathers intermarried with the native population. I would guess many of our Dutch viewers this evening have Indonesian blood coursing through their veins. There is no such thing as a pure race or nationality, Elsbeth. You, for one, probably have a pretty German great grandmother from Cologne in your family history.

ELSBETH: (clears her throat) Thank you for bringing up a subject that is sometimes taboo here in Amsterdam. But you have no problem with legal prostitution in itself, Paul?

PAUL: No, I do not. If you compare Amsterdam with the

American city of New York, where prostitution is not legal but is widespread, you will find both the public and the sex workers are better protected here in Amsterdam.

ELSBETH: Paul, I hope you don't mind. I am going to ask you a personal question.

PAUL: OK, then Elsbeth, go ahead and ask me, yes.

ELSBETH: All right then. Have you ever been a client in the Red Light District, or as we refer to it in Amsterdam, De Wallen?

PAUL: I appreciate the fact that we are going to take all my skeletons out of the closet right now. Yes, in answer to your question, I have been a client in De Wallen.

ELSBETH: A frequent client?

PAUL: Let us just leave it at, yes, I have been a client in De Wallen in the past. I now have a wonderful girlfriend named Deena Green. She is an American businesswoman from New York. I have not looked at another woman since the day I met Deena.

ELSBETH: Well, Paul thank you. I understand you had some very difficult teenage years growing up here in Amsterdam.

PAUL: Yes, Elsbeth, they were difficult. There were some family problems that for a time went unresolved. I was lucky to have received the support I needed from family and friends both here and in America.

ELSBETH: So you have close ties to Americans then?

PAUL: Yes, I am fortunate to have business associates in New York, and now, Deena, my girlfriend Deena, who is American. We are very close!

ELSBETH: Thank you Paul for your time this evening. I know you are anxious to get your campaign off and running, and again I wish you good luck.

PAUL: Thank you Elsbeth for the opportunity to present my ideas. I understand your network is posting my email and twitter addresses after our interview on their website. I look forward to your viewers' comments, suggestions and criticisms, now, in the months leading up to the election and of course in the future as well.

ELSBETH: Good evening, Paul, and good luck.

PAUL: Thank you again Elsbeth for this opportunity to speak to our citizens.

They shake hands.

Chapter 34

After the Interview

As Paul and Elsbeth left the set after the interview, Paul said, "So who tipped you off to my Indo ancestry? Let me guess, it was Claudia."

"Yes, she thought your background would appeal to those voters of Indonesian, Turkish and other ethnicities. Although your good looks say Dutch to everyone, Indo gives an interesting edge to your profile," Elsbeth responded.

"Keeps you on your toes, Paul," Claudia added.

"Let's wait until Elsbeth is finished with the hourly news and head over to The Flying Fox, Paul," she suggested. "I think it went really well. Jan and Brian are preparing some food for us there, and we can talk further."

"Good idea, Claudia," Paul said. "I think Luke will be meeting us and Mayor Ruben will stop by as well."

We waited until the hourly news cast was over at eight. Like good Amsterdam citizens, everyone rode their bicycles to The Flying Fox in De Wallen. Paul and I had some time to ourselves for a few moments.

"Deena, tell me the truth. I know I can trust you and you alone. How did I come across? I want the people of Amsterdam to know I care about them, about their safety and the safety of their families.

"My love, you were remarkable. Sincere, concerned, honest, forthright. Everyone knows all there is to know about you. Even about your Indonesian ancestry. I am very intrigued by that. I'm always learning something new about you. If the election were held tomorrow, you would win hands down."

Paul's cell phone rang and he answered it. "That was Rick," he said after a few minutes of conversation in Dutch. "He was pleased with the way the interview went. He is happy……..Vanessa is eating a bit and getting stronger. Not ready to reveal who Finn is yet, but she has consented to seeing Dr. Boden on Thursday morning, yes. She is alright with you coming with her, as long as you bring Pandora."

"A big step for Vanessa. I am looking forward to helping her get through this crisis."

We went outside, got on the motorbike, and before long we were in De Wallen. The Red Light District was part of a world I did not yet understand. Prostitution, drug use, all felt like the underworld to me. But here I was once again, at The Flying Fox, celebrating Paul's announcement to enter Amsterdam politics.

Chapter 35

A Kiss in an Unexpected Place

Paul greeted me with a kiss and a cup of coffee the next morning. "Wake up, my love. I've got something special planned for us today. The Rijksmuseum is celebrating its reopening after a renovation project that has taken ten years to complete. City officials and hopefuls like me have been invited to view the exhibits and get together for wine and cheese in the newly renovated atrium. Are you in?"

"Sounds wonderful! Oooooh, what time is it, 9:30 already? I can be ready by 10:30. Is that OK?"

"Yes. And please run into the bathroom quickly, before I have to make love to you. Will you cover up those amazing sexy breasts?" he said.

"Go for a walk with Pandora, sweetheart. I'll be ready when you get back."

I showered and dressed in a black tank top, light pink skirt, and black high heeled sandals. I grabbed a pink floral sweater as Paul returned from his walk with Pandora.

"Let's go, my love," he said. "Five hundred years of art history await us."

It was a warm day and I enjoyed the walk to the Rijksmuseum. When we entered the massive, beautifully remodeled building, Paul was greeted by everyone we saw. "Congratulations, good luck with the City Council race! Your girlfriend is beautiful! Great interview on TV," and on and on went the comments.

"Deena, I want to try and hide from the crowd now. Let's hurry, I want to see *The Milkmaid* by Johannes Vermeer before everyone else does."

Paul seemed to know just where we could find the famous painting. "There, there she is Deena. We have her all to ourselves. Wonderful!"

He took my hand and held it tightly in his as we looked at the simplicity and beauty of the servant woman, pouring milk from a pitcher. "Her hands caress the milk jug. Who is she pouring the milk for so lovingly? Her master, or perhaps her lover?" he said. He brought my hand to his mouth and gently kissed it. "What do you think?" he asked, and kissed my hand again, this time licking it with his tongue.

"Her lover. She is bringing milk to her lover," I said. "As she is pouring the milk, she looks contentedly at what she is doing. She is happy. She will be with him soon."

"Her breasts are full. Perhaps she is breastfeeding a child," he said. He turned to face me, and kissed my lips with his. Softly. Then firmly. Then passionately.

"Now, my sweet, I need you now!"

"Now? Here?"

"Yes, here."

I was lost in his kisses, my tongue pleasing his tongue. Even in this public place, I wanted him. My tongue tasted his neck, then traveled to his chest, where his shirt was unbuttoned.

He held me tightly at my waist. "In here," he said as he pulled me into a darkened hallway. "I know of a room nearby."

It wasn't really a room, more like a closet, forgotten in the final plans of the renovation. He opened the door. We entered the darkness, groping for each other, not seeing, but feeling for the familiar places. He took off my tank top, unfastened my bra, and greedily sucked my full breasts.

"Give me your milk, my milkmaid, nurse me, take care of me," he said.

"Yes, Master Vermeer, yes. Take all you need from me. I am here for your pleasure," I said.

He put his hand up my skirt, and in an instant my panties were off. "You are so wet, Deena. Soaking wet. I'm here for your pleasure too, Miss Milkmaid," he said as his fingers stroked my pussy lips, parting them.

He pushed me against a wall. I heard him unzip his slacks, then felt his hard cock inside me. I opened my legs wide, the better to position myself to receive his manhood. I heard a soft murmuring sound. It was coming from Paul. I was coming with him, in strong bursts of pleasure, as he planted his desire deep inside me. His deep, never ending desire.

He found my panties, and a roll of paper towels, and cleaned both of us. "Come love, let's join the others for a glass of wine," he said.

We again entered the exhibit room where *The Milkmaid* resided. "Paul, where have you been?" said Claudia, with a scowl on her face. "I thought I'd find you here. What's wrong with you? You look sleepy. Wake up, your supporters are waiting for you in the atrium."

Chapter 36

First Session for Vanessa

On Thursday morning, Pandora and I picked up Vanessa at her home a few blocks from Spice Island, and accompanied her to the first counseling session with Dr. Belinda Boden.

We walked into a small office on one of the side streets off the Prinsengracht. There was a view of the canal and some lovely trees from the windows. It felt like an oasis, an escape from the hectic atmosphere of the city.

Dr. Boden greeted us as soon as we entered. "Hi, you must be Vanessa. Please call me Belinda," Dr. Boden said. She was petite, with short curly blonde hair, brown eyes and a friendly smile.

"Hello," said Vanessa.

"Well," continued Belinda, "why don't we all go into my office and get comfortable. Are you Aunt Deena? My goodness, your dog is a beauty!"

We all took seats in a room with a flowered loveseat, several comfortable upholstered chairs and many plants decorating the room. There was no desk or any other trappings of formality.

When we were all comfortable, Vanessa was the first one to say something. "She is not my aunt. Deena is my Uncle Jean-Paul's latest girlfriend," she said with no emotion in her voice.

"Well all right, hi Deena," Belinda said. "What a beautiful, friendly looking dog. What is her name?"

"Pandora. She is a Rottweiler. She is my uncle's dog," Vanessa continued in a cold, distant tone of voice.

"Do you like big dogs?" Belinda said.

"Yes," Vanessa said.

"I have a dog too. My Daisy is a black Labrador retriever. She is a bit crazy, but I love her," Belinda said.

"Pandora was wild as a puppy too. But I helped Uncle Jean-Paul train her," Vanessa replied, her voice growing just a little bit friendlier.

"Really, how did you do that? Maybe you can give me some suggestions for training Daisy. She is so friendly. She jumps up on everyone she sees to say hello," Belinda said with a big smile. I imagined Daisy's friendly ways mirrored the personality of her owner.

"Well, umm, Belinda," Vanessa said, warming to her subject, "keep a short leash and a good tight collar on Daisy at home. When someone comes to your door, make Daisy sit and stay and hold the leash firmly. Give her a dog treat as a reward for being good."

"Thank you so much for your advice, Vanessa. I hear you are a very good artist," Belinda said.

"I used to like art classes. I haven't painted or sketched in a long while though, not since my grandmother died. I just don't feel like it," Vanessa confessed.

"I'm sorry about your grandmother. When did she pass away?" Belinda asked.

"Two years ago, when I was fifteen. Her name was Sonya. She was very beautiful, and warm and loving and funny. Everyone used to say I looked just like her. We did everything together. She was a great artist. She painted in watercolors. We went to art classes at L'Ecole Des Artistes together. She died suddenly. Papa said she had a heart attack," Vanessa said.

Vanessa's eyes welled up with tears and she began sobbing. Pandora immediately put her huge head on Vanessa's lap, and she petted the big dog's ears.

Belinda put her hand on Vanessa's. "My mother died a few years ago Vanessa, so I know what you are going through. It is alright to cry and be sad. I can tell you what has helped me get through it," Belinda said.

"What helped you Belinda? I need to know how to do that," Vanessa said. "No one can give me any answers."

"My mother loved dogs," Belinda explained. "She loved helping people. I am training Daisy to be a therapy dog. Daisy and I will soon be able to visit a children's hospital. I think Daisy will make the sick children laugh. And I think my mother would have been proud of me."

"Grandmother would be proud of me if I went back to art classes. She would be happy if I started sketching and painting again. I think so. Deena, will you take me back to L'Ecole Des Artistes?" Vanessa said.

I was surprised and very pleased Vanessa would ask me to do that. "Of course Vanessa, of course. I'll call the school tomorrow and see when you can start classes there. And will you ask your art teacher in the high school if you can come back to her class too?"

"Yes, Aunt Deena, I will," Vanessa said.

"Vanessa, I think Pandora needs to take a walk," Belinda said. "Will you take her out while I arrange for your next session with Deena? Do you want to come back soon?"

"Oh yes," Vanessa said, and smiled. "I like you Belinda. I like you a lot." Vanessa took Pandora's leash and they walked outside together.

"Thank you Deena," Belinda said, "I am glad I have a few moments to talk to you before my next session. As you can see, we have made a lot of progress already. The first goal in therapy is to establish the trust of the client. And Vanessa is so wonderful and talented behind all that hurt, it was easy to find the pathways to her heart. Just as unfortunately the young psychopath who abused her did."

"Psychopath?" I said.

"Yes, in my experience these young men who take advantage of teenage girls are starting on the road to a lifetime of psychopathology. They are very charming and easily ensnare their victims. Then they hurt and intimidate to get what they want. These young psychopaths have no empathy for anyone, least of all their 'girlfriends,' and have not a stitch of guilt or conscience. I would bet this young man is looking for another victim as we speak," Belinda said.

"Thank you so much. Let's schedule another appointment for early nexr week. I am working on a factory renovation project and a residence in the Plantage. Do you think it would be all right if Vanessa helps me with some of it? I think she could help with color schemes," I asked Belinda, thinking out loud.

"Yes Deena, keep her very busy," Belinda said. "She will feel productive and start to gain confidence in herself. It will take time, but you will see. Each week will be better than the next. May I ask where Vanessa's mother is?"

"Rachel is very reclusive. She does attend various art and charity events, but otherwise seems to keep to herself. No wonder Vanessa was so close to her paternal grandmother. She needed love and affection," I said.

"Yes, well, I agree with you. Don't be surprised if Vanessa starts to transfer some of the love and attention she needs to you, Deena. Are you willing to accept that from her?" Belinda said.

"Yes I would be so happy if that happens. She is a charming girl under all that hurt and anguish. And I love her Uncle Jean-Paul. I would do anything to help someone he loves so much," I said.

"Well then, I am expecting my next patient shortly. See you on Monday, yes, same time?" Belinda said.

"Yes, see you then."

As I left Belinda's office, I was truly elated with the idea of getting close to Vanessa. I was expanding my love for Paul to his family. Nothing would make me happier than for me to be part of his family, too.

Chapter 37
Trouble

Paul's cell phone rang as we were finishing dinner on Friday night, the first week after discovering Vanessa's problem and Paul's announcement to run for City Council. We were hoping to hear from Rick that Vanessa had changed her mind and was finally willing to identify "Finn". From the phone conversation from Paul's end, I could tell it wasn't Rick.

"Yes," he said seriously. "Yes, Lorraine, if you think you have some more information for me, I will come to De Wallen tonight. Give me an hour and I will be there. OK, yes, I will be alone.

"That was Lorraine. She says she has information about the identity of Vanessa's loverboy. I am going to go to De Wallen to find out more from her."

"Why couldn't she tell you over the phone? Paul, do you really think you can trust her?" I was worried.

"She gave us fairly accurate information last time. I have to go see her and hear what she has to say, yes. Don't wait up for me, and don't worry."

He left about an hour later. I went out with Pandora for a long walk. I couldn't help but think Lorraine had used Paul's need to find out more about the loverboy as an excuse to lure him to her.

I was thankfully tired after our walk and went to sleep about ten o'clock, reassured by Paul's words that he would be back safe and sound.

I woke up at five o'clock to the sound of Pandora's snoring next to me. Paul wasn't home yet. I checked outside the houseboat, the bathroom, living room, everywhere. Spice Island was empty without him. He had never stayed out all night before.

He was still with her in De Wallen, at his so-called meeting with Lorraine.

So this is how it will end with him. He is in the arms of another women. His prostitute. He's never been able to break Tatiana's spell, her curse. Giselle was wrong. I have given Paul all my love, my heart and my soul. And though he says he loves me, at this very moment he is in the arms of another woman.

My cell phone was ringing. It was Paul! I answered it immediately.

"Deena, it's me. I'm in the emergency room at the hospital. I'm OK. I was attacked last night, actually early this morning, in De Wallen. My cousin Bram is driving over to pick you up right now and take you to the hospital."

"Oh Paul what happened?"

"Don't worry. I'll explain it all when you get here. Bram has a small dark blue Volkswagen. He's coming in five minutes."

"All right, love, all right," I said, more to reassure myself than him.

Of course De Wallen is the most dangerous neighborhood in Amsterdam. Maybe Paul was mugged, robbed. But what was he doing there all night long, into the early hours of the morning?

I threw on underwear, a tee shirt, sweatpants and sneakers. I heard a car horn honk. I quickly let Pandora outside to do her business, let her back in and filled her food dish. I locked up and ran out to the car, and jumped into the passenger seat.

"Hi, Deena, I'm Bram," he said. "I met you at The Flying Fox last weekend. You probably don't remember me. Sorry to see you under these circumstances. But is sounds like Paul will be OK."

"I do remember you Bram. You look a lot like Paul. Can't miss the family resemblance," I said. He was a shorter, huskier version of Paul, not quite as handsome, but with light blue eyes and thick dark hair.

We were quiet then, both worried about Paul and what had happened to him.

In another ten minutes we arrived at the hospital. Bram parked his car near the emergency room entrance, and we ran in. We found Paul in one of the treatment rooms. And he was not alone.

"There you are Deena!" Paul said happily.

"Paul, my sweetheart, what happened?" I said as I kissed him on his cheek.

"The doctor has just sewn up the wound. I was stabbed on the right side of my chest. Busy night here, she'll be back to check on me. You remember Lorraine," he said as he pointed to her, standing in a corner of the room.

The prostitute, what is she doing here? My man is stabbed and he calls Lorraine before he calls me. What the hell is going on?

"Sit down Deena. Please," he said. "This is what happened, as best as I can tell. Lorraine wanted me last night. As you suspected, she didn't have information about Vanessa and Finn. Yes, she wanted to have sex with me. I refused her. But she gave me some wine she laced with a date rape drug. My blood is being tested for that now.

"When it took effect, she forced herself on me," he continued. "Then I fell asleep. I woke up at about 3:00 AM and left her apartment. As I walked out of her building and onto the street, a man bumped into me and seemed to recognize me. 'It's you!' he shouted at me, and then pulled out a knife and stabbed me. I defended myself, punched him and tried to hold onto him, but he was able to get away. Lorraine was looking out her window, saw what happened, and called the police. The wound is superficial. It will heal quickly."

"Let me see it Paul," I asked softly.

He pulled back the right side of his hospital gown. The wound was about six inches long on the upper part of his chest. "The doctor is a plastic surgeon. She said the scarring will be minimal.

"The police have questioned Lorraine and me," he continued. "We tried to give them a good description of the attacker. Dark hair, dark skin, short, Hispanic or Arabic looking. Probably left handed. Like Tatiana's pimp, Eduardo. For all I know, it could have been him."

The doctor entered the treatment room. "Ah Paul, back to your old self. Always surrounded by women," she said.

"Dr. Yvonne, this is my girlfriend Deena. And my cousin Bram. By the way, Bram, sorry to wake you up at this ungodly hour."

"Don't mention it Paul," Bram said. "Happy to see you're doing well. But, my cousin, seems you have at least one enemy in DeWallen. Do the police think they can find the attacker?"

"Probably not," Dr. Yvonne said. "Fits the description of so many men here. Seems to me, Paul, you have angered people in De Wallen with your comments in your TV interview. Sounds like you mean to interfere with their lucrative businesses."

"I do, if they are in the sex slave or underage prostitution business," Paul said.

"Well let's look at my handiwork again. Nice small stitches. Will barely leave a scar. Come here next Monday and I'll remove the stitches. See how you are doing then. Don't get them wet."

"All right, thank you so much, Doctor."

"Don't mention it. Good luck with your campaign. You have enemies, Paul, as you know. I hope they don't aim for your handsome face next time. Be careful. Nice meeting you, Deena, Bram, Lorraine."

"Let's go Paul," Bram said. "I'll take you and Deena home. Here is some money for a taxi Lorraine," he said as he took out some euros from his wallet and put them in Lorraine's outstretched hand.

"So sorry Paul," Lorraine said. "I didn't mean for you to get hurt. I've missed you so much. I thought you'd be back to your regular visits to me by now. Sorry about the drugs. I was desperate for you. Take care of yourself, my lovely sexy man," she said as she ran out of the room.

"Aren't the police going to arrest her? She raped you Paul," I said angrily. I felt like I was in a strange world, a world in which I didn't understand any of the rules.

"No, they are not going to arrest her, Deena. I'm not going to press charges against Lorraine. Not that she's innocent. She lured me to her, she lied and she drugged me. But the police have enough trouble trying to control the violent criminals in this city."

Bram, Paul and I walked to Bram's car and got in. Bram drove us to Spice Island. I couldn't stop thinking about Paul and Lorraine, and how comfortable he was in her world. A world I could never enter, never get used to. I had made a mistake by getting so involved with Paul. I should have known better from the very beginning.

We all went inside the houseboat. Bram was very nice. He wanted to make certain Paul was all right.

Claudia was waiting for us in the living room. "I used my key Paul. Hope you don't mind. I heard what happened. You look fine. The attack will work to our advantage, that's for sure. Plays up the severity of crime in De Wallen."

"We'll put a positive spin on this. At the very least, it will get you a lot of press." Claudia said. She was looking for something good in a very bad situation.

I had heard enough. I felt Paul would never really be able to leave De Wallen and the prostitutes that were always waiting for him there. Just like his father.

I ran into the bedroom, grabbed a suitcase, and started packing my clothes.

"Deena, wait, wait come here please come back here," Paul begged me as he followed me into the bedroom. He took me by the arm and pulled me to him.

"Oh, Deena, what are you doing?" Claudia said as she came into the bedroom too. "Get over it. This is bigger than your relationship with Paul. It was only one night in De Wallen, anyway. You had better get used to the idea, Miss American Innocence, that every woman in Amsterdam wants to lure Paul Vermeer into their bed."

"Enough Claudia, enough already," Paul said. "Thank you for coming over here. Now go home to your husband, get some rest. I will call you later."

Claudia didn't say another word. Before she left though she looked at me as if to say, you will lose him, you will never have him.

After Claudia left, I continued packing. "Please Deena please this was a trick. Date rape drugs are very powerful. Deena, please, don't you see, I love you," Paul pleaded with me, and then sat down on the bed, covering his eyes.

"I am going Paul. I can not take the pain of all of this. I love you, but I can't trust you anymore. I need some time away from you, to think things through."

"Where will you go?" he said resignedly.

"To the hotel I guess."

"No, don't. Bram has a room to let in his house. It's still available. You will be safe there with him and his wife Irena, yes," he offered as he stood up and stroked my cheek.

"Don't touch me. Don't. I feel like heading back to New York, but I'm still in the middle of overseeing the renovations. And I can't leave Vanessa now. She has become very attached to me. She is helping me with the designs. Belinda thinks it's therapeutic for her. When you can, take Pandora to Vanessa's school. She seemed to be on the verge of finding Finn's scent in one of the classrooms the last time we were there. I think Vanessa will identify Finn soon. He will be found I'm sure," my voice trailed off as I threw some more things into the suitcase.

"Yes, Paul, the room is still available," Bram offered sadly.

"Yes yes all right. I'll pay you though for the rent, not Paul," I said.

" Will you call me Deena, let me know you are OK? Please, I beg you," Paul said.

"Nessa will let you know about me. Bram too. That's enough. Good luck with your campaign. Sounds like your spin doctor Claudia can handle things very well for you. I'll wait outside for Bram. Please don't follow me."

I was in shock, which was a blessing. If I could feel something, anything at that point, it would have felt like a knife being plunged into my heart.

Bram came out soon after. As he put my things in the car, he said, "don't worry, Irena and I will take good care of you. Give you a chance to recover some and then go back to Paul."

Chapter 38
In Limbo

The first month at Bram and Irena's seemed like a bad dream. They were very nice to me, too nice. They always included me in their dinner and weekend plans, but most of the time I refused. My days were busy with the renovations on the factory and designing the residences in the Plantage. Late afternoons I picked up Vanessa, and either took her to art class or to the Plantage building to help with the design. We continued meeting with Belinda twice a week. I waited for the day when I would start thinking things through about Paul, waited for the time when I would start to heal. The time had not arrived as yet.

Each night, alone in bed, it was only then I admitted to myself I still loved Paul. My heart just would not or could not stop holding onto the wonderfully crazy love we had experienced together. And in my soul I knew I wanted to find a way back to him, but I was too afraid to face him, too afraid to deal with the humiliation of his night in De Wallen.

Chris called and wanted to have lunch with me. He said he was curious about how the renovations were going in the factory and the Plantage building. But I knew what he really wanted was to find out if I was back with Paul.

We met at the factory. His long sensual hello kiss told me he had only one thing on his mind. I showed him around and he was very impressed with how all the details in the workspaces were progressing. "You should be very proud, Deena," he complimented me. "All your hard work is paying off. Very soon, this will be up and running, all thanks to you."

"No, Chris, thanks to you. Without your assistance with the government approvals, we wouldn't be standing here right now admiring this place."

"By the way, have you spoken to Paul recently? The hype is his campaign is still on track." Chris was venturing into territory I did not want to discuss.

"No Chris, I don't want to talk to Paul yet. I may never be ready to," I answered him, sadly.

"Deena, I have a new girlfriend but I would leave her for you. Just say the word and I am yours," Chris said hopefully.

"No, Chris, no, I couldn't," I demurred as I walked him to the factory's front door. "After the project is completed, I'll go back to New York and start over there. I hope you understand, though, I am eternally grateful to you. I think I'll get back to work now, Chris, it makes me feel better." I reached up to kiss him on his cheek, and he turned his face so my kiss found his mouth.

"I love you Deena. Please remember that. Always," he said as he left me on the factory floor, alone.

In the evening I decided to visit with Bram. I knew Irena was at her mother's out of town. It was the end of August and the rent had come due for the second month on the flat. I was feeling lonely and very much in need of companionship. Without thinking about it, I dressed in a low cut black sweater, tight jeans and black boots. After a quick dinner I went downstairs to their first floor apartment.

I rang the bell. Bram answered the door and said, "Hi Deena. How are you? You look very pretty this evening. Are you seeing

Paul?"

"No Bram. I'm not ready yet. I have the rent money for you. Mind if I come in for a few minutes?"

"Of course Deena, please come in. I just opened a bottle of wine. I'm kind of lonely. Irena is visiting her mother in Friesland for a week."

"I would love some wine," I said as I sat down on the sofa. Bram filled a glass and sat next to me. "Thank you, Bram, mmm, white wine, with some sweetness to it, my favorite." I relished the taste of it. I was starting to feel like my old self.

As we sipped the wine, I told Bram the work on both the factory and Plantage residences was going forward better than expected. Bram informed me that Paul was not doing well. He never slept, and roamed the streets of De Wallen with Pandora most every night, searching for the attacker.

"I'm sure Paul is managing just fine without me. By the way," I said as I moved closer to him, "you look great tonight. How about just one kiss?" Without waiting for an answer, I kissed him on his lips, and then licked his mouth with my tongue.

"Nice Deena, but save it for Paul. Are you sure you want to stay here for another month? Paul needs you desperately."

"But I want you tonight Bram. You look so sexy and lonely," I said as I sat on his lap and pressed my tongue deep into his mouth.

"What are you doing Deena? I'm happily married! Stop it! Trying to seduce me? It won't work."

"It already has Bram. I can feel you are hard for me." I wiggled my ass on his lap.

"Enough, enough already," Bram shouted and pushed me away. "Can't you see? You are trying to rape me Deena. I bet you thought it's not possible, a woman raping a man. What if you drugged me, like Lorraine drugged Paul? It has been confirmed, you know. Paul tested positive for the date rape drug."

"He did?" I asked in disbelief.

"Yes, oh I forgot you don't read the Amsterdam newspapers. You are American through and through Deena, despite what you say about your love for things European. Just another spoiled, sheltered American girl. Paul made one mistake in visiting De Wallen for information concerning his beloved niece. And he got attacked in the bargain. You turned your back on him when he needed you most."

It was as if Bram had slapped me in the face. I felt like I was waking up from a nightmare.

"Maybe you have a point," I conceded.

"The point, Deena, is I am evicting you," he said. "Take the rent money. I don't want it. Now go back to Paul and make things right with him. Make this part of his life whole again. He hasn't had it easy. I will forget the whole seduction scene. I won't discuss any of this with Paul. Just go to him now. I will give you a ride on my motorbike."

I sighed deeply. I knew Bram was right. I had been acting like a spoiled child, thinking only of myself.

"OK Bram, let's go to Paul now." I had my doubts Paul would even want to see me. Suddenly I remembered an old Jewish proverb my father would say to me whenever I felt troubled. "What can be broken, can be fixed." I hoped the wisdom of the saying held some truth for me tonight.

Bram and I got on the motorbike and he quickly drove me to Spice Island. It was about eleven o'clock. There was a light shining through the living room window. I could see Paul's handsome profile. I didn't hesitate. I knocked on the door. Bram had already sped off on his way home.

Paul flung open the door, Pandora right behind him. He looked out, not seeing me at first. But then he looked down at Pandora, who was already approaching me, her tail wagging excitedly.

"My lovely Deena? Are you really here? Have you come back to me?" he said.

"Yes Paul! Please please forgive me, I acted like a frightened child."

I couldn't say anything more, nor did I want to. His kisses stopped me, his lips covering mine as he held me on my hips and pressed me tightly to him.

"You, woman, will never ever leave me again. Never!" Paul carried me inside the houseboat. He sat me down next to him on the sofa, holding me.

"Deena, my only love, I have had plenty of time to think this last month," he said as he held both my hands. "I have been haunted by all the things I did to hurt you. I knew if you came back to me it would be because you truly loved me. Your true love is stronger than the curses of my father or the spell of a sorceress."

"I am so sorry, Paul," I said as I kissed both of his hands. "I thought only of myself. Maybe Claudia was right about me. The innocent American. I should have stuck by you. How foolish I was."

"You have a right to your innocence, to your sweetness, to be able to trust me every moment of every day. You were frightened by my connection to Lorraine, and by the attacker. I'll withdraw from the campaign, yes, so we can start to get back to the way things should be between us. I will call Claudia in the morning…."

"No, no, don't do that! You can't!" My eyes filled with tears. "Don't give your enemies what they want. You must continue to stand up for what you believe in."

"OK, OK, you're right Deena. Please don't cry."

"Yes, Paul, I'm still so in love with you. I'll help you in any way I can. I'll do anything for you my love, anything."

"I know Vanessa with be very happy you are back here with me. Let's invite her for breakfast to celebrate tomorrow, it's Saturday. I hope she will identify Finn soon. Rick has told me there is now another girl in Vanessa's school who is the victim of a loverboy. We have to stop Finn."

"We'll call her in the morning. Bram will bring over my things then. Now let's go to bed, my love, you are so tired," I said as we stood up and walked together to the bedroom. Pandora followed us, happily wagging her tail, and laid on the floor near the entrance to the room, as if to protect us from harm.

"I've missed you so much, my love," he said soothingly. "Your laugh, your beautiful green eyes. Missed your warm body next to mine. Next to me all the time."

We took off our clothes and lay on the bed together. I stroked his thick hair and rubbed his neck. He felt comforted in my arms. His breathing slowed and he fell asleep. I relaxed on the pillows, still holding him gently against me.

I fell asleep too, but was awakened by Paul's voice loudly calling out words in a language I did not understand. *"Verdomde niksnut klootzak, mietje, flicker!"* he shouted. Before I could wake him up, he said some things I did understand. "Damned useless asshole, pussy, faggot! You with your big cock. You are thirteen already. When are you going to go to De Wallen and get yourself a prostitute for your own like me. I want you to be just like me! A different whore every night!" He stopped shouting and started to weep.

"Paul, wake up, wake up!! What is it? What are you talking about?" I shook him until he woke up.

"Oh what did I say? Oh no, it was the nightmare! It started again when you left me. It is the voice of my father coming back from the grave to curse me in Bargoens, the language of the Amsterdam underworld. Every night from the time I was thirteen until he brought me to De Wallen when I was seventeen, he would tell me I was no good, not a man. The only way for me to be a man was to have a different prostitute every night, like him."

"How awful!" I said to Paul, holding him in my arms, rocking him, comforting him.

"My mother was powerless to stop him," he continued. "It was probably better when he brought me to De Wallen. It was better for me there than being home with him."

"But now you are here with me Paul. No need to feel alone like a frightened boy any longer. I'm here and I will never leave you again," I said as I kissed his cheek gently.

"Thank you, my love. Thank you for being here with me."

"This is where I belong. Now go back to sleep."

"Impossible to sleep with your sweet naked breasts near my lips. I have to taste them," he said and began licking my breasts, slowly, so achingly slowly.

I wanted him to hurry, to lick and suck them. I cupped my breasts in my hands, and pushed my nipples in his mouth. He began sucking them harder as he grabbed my ass and pulled me on top of him.

"Now you have what you want. I am yours," he said.

I slid down his body and began licking his large erection. He groaned and said, "Come here lover. I need you to kiss me."

I obeyed him then. I kissed his mouth and straddled his hips, covering his large moistened manhood with my pussy, holding him and guiding him deep within me. He was more erect and larger than ever before. I made love to him with each movement of my body, each downward stroke of my hips. We came together, my climax the most intense I had ever experienced.

Chapter 39

Enlightenment

Paul woke up before me the next morning and called Rick and Rachel to tell them I had returned. He asked if he could speak to Vanessa, who happily agreed to bring fresh croissants over for breakfast. His second call was to Bram, who said he would bring my clothes over soon.

After Paul let Pandora out and fed her, he crawled back into bed and hugged me to him, gently kissing my hair and my lips before falling back to sleep.

Bram knocked on the door and brought my suitcases into the bedroom, observing Paul still fast asleep. "Sshh, he's fine now Bram. Thank you so much for showing me how wrong I was."

"It is OK Deena, just be good to my cousin. He loves you," Bram said and was gone.

Paul woke up soon after Bram had left and we showered together. We dressed in jeans and tee shirts. I brewed some coffee as we waited for Vanessa to arrive. Soon, Vanessa knocked on the door. Pandora was the first one to greet her, with not only her tail but her whole body shaking with happiness. Pandora wasn't the only happy creature – Vanessa gave me a big hug. "I am so glad, Aunt Deena, so glad you are back here with Uncle Jean-Paul. He was so sad without you!"

"I know, Nessa, I know. I'm happy to be back. I see you have brought croissants from my favorite bakery. Let's have breakfast." I truly was happy!

We ate leisurely, talking about the factory and the Plantage building and how much Vanessa was enjoying her art classes.

Paul cleaned up the breakfast dishes as I said to Vanessa, "Come with me into the bedroom and help me do my hair. It's such a mess."

I soon found my brush and some hair ties and we sat on the bed together. I quickly did my hair as Vanessa watched me. She said to me, "Aunt Deena, could you do my hair, too?" "Of course," I said and began brushing Nessa's beautiful long black tresses. "Shall I braid your hair? I think it would look beautiful ."

"Yes, Aunt Deena, please do." Vanessa was relaxed and trusting. I heard her breathe deeply as I continued brushing her hair and then wound the long locks in a thick braid.

Paul had set up an easel and chair in the entrance to the room, and was sketching. Vanessa and I were soon lost in conversation, about dogs and all the other animals we shared our love and concern for.

"Uncle, I haven't seen you draw in a long time. What is it? Can we see?"

Vanessa got up from the bed.

"Not as yet, sweet Nessa. Continue your talk with your Aunt. You will soon see it. I am drawing perfection," he said and went back to his work.

A while later, Paul said, "Come here my beauties, see what I have done so far." We went to look at the easel as Paul stood up and moved the chair away. It was a drawing of Vanessa and me, as I braided her hair. It had a familiar look to it.

Vanessa was the first to say what was evident to both of us. "It is in the style of our famous ancestor, the painter Johannes Vermeer."

"That's right, Vanessa. Now I understand what Johannes was telling us in his paintings. The simple moments in life are the most pure, the most rewarding, the most wonderful. I feel like a fog has been lifted from my head and my heart. I love you both so much," he said as he put an arm around each of us and kissed us on our cheeks.

Chapter 40

No Longer a Secret

"Uncle Jean-Paul, Aunt Deena, I love you both so much," Vanessa spoke softly to us, barely above a whisper. "I am sorry, Aunt Deena, sorry for the way I treated you in the beginning.

"It was Sander. Sander Smit," she said. "He was the one who raped me, abused me." Paul and I listened carefully, standing still with our arms around her shoulders.

"At first, we were boyfriend and girlfriend. He was in my classes in school. We went on dates together, movies, dances, silly high school things. At the beginning, we just kissed. Then Sander wanted to go further, touch my breasts, my body. I loved him and loved his touching me. I wasn't ready though for what he wanted next. One night, he forced himself in me. He said I would learn to like it. He didn't care that I was afraid.

"But I loved him, I was so lonely, I needed his love. We smoked marijuana and hashish. Strong stuff. Made me forget who I was. When I was drugged up, he had his friends have sex with me. They paid him to have sex with me.

"Then," Vanessa continued after taking a deep breath, "Sander said he needed more money. His parents refused to give him money.

"He took me to De Wallen. Dressed me in revealing clothes, my breasts popping out, short skirts. Said I looked so beautiful to him that way. He wanted me to make even more money for him. He forced me to have sex with many men. That went on for about two months. Then I couldn't take it…" Vanessa cried, hiding her face in Paul's chest.

"Please forgive me Uncle, please," she said.

"Of course I forgive you, Nessa. You were lonely. And you trusted Sander. Sander Smit? Is his father's name Stefan Smit?" Paul asked.

"Yes, I, I think so," Vanessa said through her tears.

"Stefan Smit. I knew it, yes. Something so wrong about him," Paul said as he wrinkled his nose. "Deena, Stefan Smit is Deputy Mayor of Amsterdam! The man that is against efforts to clean up crime in De Wallen! His law partner is Niels Niemands, my main opponent in the City Council election."

Vanessa continued as if she didn't hear Paul. "He made me call him Finn. Said it was a cute, sexy nickname. Uncle Jean-Paul, is Sander in trouble now?"

"Yes, Nessa, we have to stop him. We have to protect other girls he will hurt."

"OK, Uncle," she sighed. "Call Erika, the police officer. I am ready to talk to her about Sander."

Chapter 41

Continuing Investigation

Paul called Erika right away. Within an hour, she was at our home accompanied by Henry Hoff.

"Hi Vanessa," Erika said. "It took a lot of courage to identify Finn."

"Why don't we all sit down and get comfortable," Paul suggested. "Vanessa, call Pandora to you. She will keep you calm if you get nervous, yes."

Vanessa sat on the sofa, with Paul on one side and Erika on the other side of her. Detective Hoff and I sat in chairs close by. Pandora lay at Vanessa's feet.

"Thank you Paul," Detective Hoff said. "Erika, start recording. Vanessa, tell us about your relationship with Finn."

"Sander, Sander Smit," Vanessa corrected him.

"Right, Sander Smit," Detective Hoff said. "After our talk today, we will bring this information to the prosecuting attorney's office. Then a juvenile court judge will be designated. You and Sander will appear before the judge, and he will determine whether or not Sander is guilty."

"He raped me, Detective. Sander forced me to have sex with him. We were boyfriend and girlfriend, but he made me have sex with him, and then with his friends. They paid him."

"Let me get this straight. Sander's friends paid him to have sex with you," Detective Hoff said, as both he and Erika made notes even though the conversation was being recorded.

"Yes. And then he made me have sex with men in De Wallen. Sander needed money, he said. He threatened me. He said he would beat me if I didn't do what he wanted me to." Vanessa's eyes welled up with tears.

"We know, Vanessa. This is very hard for you," said Erika. "We took note previously of the physical signs of assault on your body. We will be taking Sander in for questioning. We will test his DNA samples, and compare them to the samples we took from you. There will be a trial before a judge."

Pandora leaned against Vanessa gently, as she stroked the dog's head and neck. "Will Sander go to jail?" Vanessa asked.

"Usually in cases like this when the perpetrator is a minor, he would only have to do a year of community service, and be seen by a counselor," Detective Hoff explained.

Paul reacted to this information just as I thought he would, with anger. "That is what is wrong with the criminal justice system here in Amsterdam, yes!" he said. "A slap on the wrist for this scum who raped and forced my niece into prostitution! Isn't there some way he can be tried as an adult?"

"Listen to what they have to say, Paul, listen," I said as I tried to calm him.

"Well," said Erika, "depending on the prosecuting attorney and the judge who is involved in the case, we may be able to have Sander tried as an adult. Then he would be facing a three year jail sentence."

We were all quiet for a few moments, except for Vanessa, who was weeping. Paul wrapped her in his arms, and held her tight.

"It will be all right, my love. It will be all right," I kept repeating to her.

Detective Hoff and Erika realized Vanessa had enough for one day. "We will get in touch with you soon," Erika said as they left.

"Paul," I said, "I think you should take Vanessa home now. She can come back here tomorrow if she'd like to."

"Nessa, how about a ride on my motorbike? We need the fresh air, yes!"

Paul took Vanessa home, and he came back in about an hour. "It was too much for her. Rick and Rachel are so happy it will all be over soon. But why did you want her to go home?"

"I have a feeling Paul, a feeling about tonight. Something will happen here tonight," I told him.

"Don't worry, my love. Nothing is going to happen. Vanessa is safe now," Paul reassured me.

Chapter 42

In the Jordaan

To calm down from all that had happened, I suggested we take Pandora for a long walk. The heat wave had subsided in Amsterdam and throughout The Netherlands as well.

Paul and I put on our running shoes, and got Pandora ready. We took some bottled water for her with us and set off. The afternoon breeze coming from the canal cooled us as we made our way towards the Jordaan neighborhood. We followed the Prinsengracht there, the canal street Spice Island was moored on.

We passed the Anne Frank House with its long lines of visitors waiting to honor the memory of the brave girl hidden there with her family, and then taken away by the Nazis during World War II.

The lovely weather had brought out both the tourists and residents of Amsterdam to the Jordaan neighborhood. Saturday was outdoor street market day. Paul wanted to introduce me to the vendors he knew would be there.

We soon were in the street market, located in a large plaza area. Brightly colored canopies covered each of the many stalls. "Paul, hi good luck on your campaign," shouted one elderly man, selling old glassware and china. "How are you feeling? Well I hope!"

"Paul, introduce me to your girlfriend! She is beautiful!" called a pretty woman displaying her handcrafted jewelry.

"Good luck Paul, we are definitely going to vote for you," an older woman said to Paul, as she gave Pandora a dog treat. "Be brave, my friend, be brave." She had hand knit sweaters, scarves and hats for sale.

Pandora and I accompanied Paul as he mingled with people in the marketplace and in the many art shops, bookstores and cafes that lined the streets of the Jordaan.

"The Jordaan was originally a working class neighborhood that has undergone a transformation," he explained to me. "Successful artists and professionals now live here. But the neighborhood is still filled with so much charm, don't you think? I love the inner courtyards, let me show you what I mean," he said as he led Pandora and me through a winding street. "How about a drink, my love? Let's sit here and order some wine," he suggested, pointing to an outdoor café.

We ordered a bottle of white wine and a sandwich to share. Pandora lay submissively at Paul's feet.

When the wine was served, Paul held my hands, and looked deep into my green eyes with his striking blue ones. "So, Deena, welcome to my life. I am very well known, I guess you could say very popular in my city. And judging from the recent opinion polls, I will probably be voted onto the City Council. Maybe I am too confident. Can you see yourself being a part of this life with me, my love?

"Your love and something else too has broken the witch's spell cast on me. I have a sense you are more powerful than you will admit to me," he said.

"You want to know so much," I replied. "The most important thing is yes, I love you. I want to be a part of your life. I love you and I love Amsterdam. Sometimes I think I have a sixth sense, I can foresee something that will happen. Now, I can sense you want to kiss me," I said seductively, as I moved my chair closer to his.

He did. He kissed my lips long and hard, and then licked my

tongue with his tongue. The cafe was filled with people, but neither of us took notice. We were too busy tasting each other. We sipped the wine and feasted on each other for the rest of the afternoon.

We strolled back along the Prinsengracht towards the houseboat, stopping to eat dinner at a canal side café. We shared our food with the grateful Pandora, who then drifted off to sleep as we had more wine and more delicious kissing.

Paul and I were intoxicated by then on wine and each other.

We finally arrived at Spice Island. We collapsed on the bed. Every kiss he gave me made me laugh – every place he touched me, licked me, caressed me, lit a fire. I closed my hands around his manhood, and bent down so I could rub it hard on my nipples. His sexual prowess never ever wavered. He was ready to please me, his erection found where it needed to be. He was on top of me, thrusting himself in me, deeper and harder, and harder still. "More, more," I screamed at him, until he brought me to climax and I brought him.

We laughed and fell asleep holding each other.

Chapter 43

Confrontation

A crashing noise woke us. What time was it? The clock said 11:30 PM. Someone was banging on our door.

"Vermeer. Open up. You scum. Coward. Open up!" a male voice yelled.

Before I could stop him, Paul ran to the door. His naked body still glistened with sweat from our lovemaking.

"Who is it?" Paul demanded.

"Vermeer, it's me. Smit. Did you think I would let your niece lie about my son without confronting you?"

Paul opened the door and said, "you are the coward!" I had grabbed a robe and stood right behind Paul, holding his arm.

"So here you are Vermeer. With another prostitute, this time a short red headed one. I though you like them tall, thin, dark haired," accused Smit.

"So Smit, happy about my troubles in De Wallen, are you? Well don't worry, I will still win a seat on the City Council."

"No you won't. My son is innocent. We will prove it, and show that you, your niece and your red headed whore are all liars!"

Up until that point, Paul had his anger under control. Now he let out a growl and put his hands on his hips, his legs spread apart, his chest thrust out. He was my knight in his strong skin made of armor.

"You leave now Smit. I am warning you, I could kill you with my bare hands," he said as he held up his palms to Smit's face. "Pandora and I will destroy you, YES." Pandora was snapping at Smit's crotch, waiting for Paul to command her to attack him.

Smit shrank from Paul and Pandora's fury. "Don't ever come near us again!" Paul shouted at him. "Go home and teach your son to respect women, respect our people, or you may be visiting him in jail for a long time to come."

Smit got on his motorbike, and sped away quickly into the night.

Paul was sweating and steaming with anger. "Are you OK Deena?" he said, turning towards me with concern, as we walked inside.

"Yes I'm fine. Paul, I have never seen you like this. Almost superhuman."

"I have to make sure you and Vanessa are safe. We will win in court. I am calling Erika to tell her about Smit. I will protect you. Always. Forever," he said, taking my robe off.

Chapter 44

Questions and Answers

Paul embraced me, his body still hot and damp. He lifted me up so I straddled his hips. My legs tightened to hold on to him.

"I will hold you. Care for you. Love you passionately forever Deena. Say yes!"

"Yes. Yes to what?" I laughed and licked his mouth with my tongue.

He licked me in return and said, "Yes to spending the rest of your life entwined in my life. Love me only. Marry me. Now!"

"Yes, yes, yes!" I couldn't stop saying it. Yes to his kisses. Yes to his passion. Yes to my desire for him. Yes to loving him. Yes to love and sex and wanting him every moment. And to Paul loving and wanting me too.

He showed me all night long what love coupled with passion felt like. Yes yes yes!!!

Paul woke me in the morning with a steaming cup of coffee in his hand, and a warm smile on his face. I couldn't get enough of his smile that creased his cheeks with laugh lines.

"So, my wife, let us plan our wedding today. I have already talked to Erika this morning. She is going to try and get Sander's trial before a judge scheduled by September 15. How does September 30 sound to you as our wedding date? It is a Sunday. Hans and Giselle are already ecstatic. We will be married in their castle, yes!"

"You have been very busy this morning my husband! Let me check my calendar and see if I am free September 30," I joked with him. "Can we really plan a wedding in one month?"

"It's all been planned already, sleepy head! Hans and Giselle will come to Amsterdam tomorrow, and help with everything, yes!" he said.

I called my parents as soon as it was nine o'clock in the morning in New York. "Mom and Dad, Paul and I are going to be married. We are so happy! We hope we have your blessing."

Before they could respond, Paul took the phone from me and put it on speaker phone. "Mr. Green, Mrs. Green, your daughter and I have promised to love and care for each other for the rest of our lives!"

"We are so happy for the two of you! We can not wait to meet you Paul," said my mother happily.

"When is the wedding already?" my father asked.

Paul laughed and said, "The wedding is very soon, Mr. Green, Sunday, September 30. I know you have heard about Hans and Giselle, my dear friends from Rheinberg, Germany. They have offered to host our wedding at their castle. Everyone will be staying at the castle for the weekend. There is plenty of room, yes."

"Congratulations, mazel tov y'all! We are going to make our plane reservations now," my mother said as my father echoed her "mazel tov!"

Next, I called Uncle Alan to give him the good news. The phone was on speaker so Paul heard every word. "At first, Paul, I didn't trust you with my favorite girl. I am so glad you are going to be married. I will be at the wedding for sure. September 30, I look forward to it, and to meeting you," Uncle Alan said.

"I look forward to meeting you too, Mr. Rosen," Paul said. "It is because of your idea, your diamond artisans idea for Amsterdam, that I am standing here now, holding Deena's hand and inviting you to our wedding."

"Mazel tov to you love birds, and see you in one month!" Uncle Alan said happily.

The day was a lazy one, with Paul and I in bed together for most of it. After dinner, Paul said, "I am going to check on things at the club tonight in De Wallen. I'll take Pandora with me."

"I'm going too, Paul," I said.

"No Deena. Almost every night since you left me, I've walked the streets of De Wallen. Just Pandora and me," he said. "I have been baiting the attacker. I want him to try again. Next time I'll be ready for him."

"Either I go with you tonight, or I'm leaving again. You need me Paul, and I need you."

"All right, all right, you win. But Pandora will stay next to you. She'll protect you."

Paul, Pandora and I walked together to De Wallen at about nine that night. We stopped in at The Flying Fox. Brian had prepared some pasta for us. We weren't hungry. I looked closely at Paul's face. He had gotten thinner in the last month. The stress of the attack and my leaving him had caught up with him.

"Please Paul, eat something. Here, have my pasta. You must eat, you look too thin," I said.

"You too love, we both are. Here, taste the bread, it's delicious," he said. I did, and then gave some bread to him too. He ate it ravenously. "I've been so hungry for you, hungrier than I've ever felt in my life. Are you really here with me?"

"Yes, I'm here. It's me. I promise I'll never leave."

We ate and drank for hours, listening to the club's music.

"Deena, it's time for Pandora and me to search for him. Please stay here. Please," he begged me.

"No, I won't. I can't."

I followed him out the door with Pandora by my side. We went from the safety of The Flying Fox to the dangers of De Wallen. It was another busy night in the District. We could barely make our way through the narrow streets. The usual crowds of men were gathered at the windows, hungering for sex with the women displayed there.

I lost track of time. Had an hour gone by, or was it two or three? Finally Paul said, "Let's head home, love. Even Pandora seems tired." I glanced in back of me to check on Pandora's whereabouts. I noticed a short man standing behind Paul. I saw the glint of a knife blade as the man brought his left hand near Paul's left shoulder.

"Paul, it's him WATCH OUT!" I screamed.

But before the knife found its mark Pandora jumped up on the attacker, and pushed him to the ground. The knife was knocked out of his hand and skidded across the pavement.

Pandora growled fiercely at the now frightened man, who was curled up in a fetal position.

I let out a sigh of relief, as Paul called the police. In about ten minutes two officers on foot patrol appeared.

"Paul, is this him?" the younger of the two policemen asked.

"Yes, it's him, Jager. Left handed, short, dark hair and skin. Check his left arm or shoulder. I'll bet he has a tattoo that says *Tatiana*."

The police officers brought the attacker to his feet. Jager rolled up the attacker's left sleeve and checked his arm.

"Yes, there's a tattoo with the letters T A T I A N A on his left upper arm. What's all this about, Paul?" Jager asked.

"You made a mistake, Eduardo, by chasing me, attacking me, after all these years," Paul said. "I loved Tatiana. I was just a kid back then."

"You were no innocent, Vermeer. You knew just what you were doing. You took my prettiest, best prostitute out of my bed, out of my control. Away from me. I loved her too," Eduardo said, "and after all these years, I still want to kill you."

"Jager, Henk, if you check the police records from the first attack on me about a month ago, I think you'll find Eduardo's knife was the weapon used," Paul explained to them.

"OK Paul, we will be taking him with us now," the young officer said.

When the police had left with Eduardo in custody, Paul and I collapsed in each other's arms. We left De Wallen with Pandora, that part of Paul's past now safely behind us.

Chapter 45
Monday Morning on Amsterdam News Network

ELSBETH: This morning on Amsterdam News Network we have a late breaking story for you. The alleged attacker of City Council hopeful Paul Vermeer has been arrested late last night and will be brought to justice. Mr. Vermeer has been combing the streets of De Wallen for the past month, using himself as bait to lure the attacker out in the open.

Last night his efforts paid off. The man tried again. This time Vermeer's Rottweiler Pandora held the attacker at paw point until the police arrived. It was a canine citizen's arrest by the German born, Netherlands trained dog. We thank you, Mr. Vermeer and Pandora, for your brave and successful efforts to make Amsterdam a safer city. We can only hope the city government and its police force will follow your example.

Chapter 46
Plans

The next two weeks were a whirlwind of visits to Karime, my Spanish friend, who was designing my wedding gown, and discussions with Giselle about what foods to serve at the wedding reception. Ali wanted to come to Amsterdam as soon as she heard about the wedding. I convinced her to wait until a few days before, when I would need her to help me with last minute details and calm me before the big day.

We met with Erika, who was putting together the case against Sander. Because of the severity of the charges, rape and assault, he was in custody in the juvenile detention center. Erika informed us Sander could be charged with human trafficking or sexual-enslavement as well.

It was Tuesday evening, September 3. Paul and I had just finished having a late, delicious dinner. I explained to him about the holiday of Rosh Hashanah, the Jewish New Year, which began the next evening. "On Rosh Hashanah, we pray to be inscribed by G-d in the Book of Life for a good year. And then ten days later, we pray and fast on Yom Kippur for forgiveness for our sins against G-d and all the people in our lives."

"Only one day a year to ask forgiveness for our sins," Paul said.

"I think it would take me a whole year to ask forgiveness from you."

"No, not a whole year, but a lifetime together, my love. I will give you a lifetime to ask my forgiveness."

"By the way, have I told you I love you this evening?" Paul said, rubbing my shoulders as I did the dishes.

"No you haven't my sweetheart, please do…."

There was a knock at the door. Paul and I looked at one another. We weren't expecting anyone. Paul went to the door and opened it.

I heard a very familiar, very American southern female voice saying, "Paul it is you, finally, we have finally met you!!!" I couldn't believe it, and I ran to the door……it was my mother and father, surprising us!!!

My parents and I hugged one another and kissed and cried and hugged some more. "Paul, meet my mother and father! I can't believe you are here with us!! You didn't tell me you were coming!" I said.

"Well, of course not, my sweet girl," my mother said. "That would have ruined the surprise for y'all!!! We couldn't wait to meet Paul, and thought it best to get here before all the wedding excitement started. And, Dad and I wanted to spend Rosh Hashanah with you."

"So wonderful to meet you Mr. and Mrs. Green. Your Deena has changed my life, given me true love and magic in my world. How can I ever thank you for raising such a wonderful daughter?" Paul said with emotion in his voice.

"You can thank us, Paul, by calling us Mom and Dad. We loved you from the moment Deena told us about you and your love for each other. Now that we have met you we love you even more. You are our son, just as Deena is our daughter," Momma said and reached up and hugged Paul to her.

Paul hugged her back and said, "Thank you Mom." In his voice

I heard the longing and sadness for the loss of his own mother, and the greater loss of never really having the father he needed and deserved.

"Have you eaten something, Dad?" Paul asked my father.

Dad replied, "Yes they fed us like royalty on the plane. We flew business class. I wanted to start off my retirement in style. After Rosh Hashanah we will travel to Berlin and stay with some cousins there. Then we will meet you in Rheinberg for the wedding weekend celebrations."

"Then drinks are in order! Now I know why I bought this old bottle of cognac the other day. Deena, please get us some glasses, yes!" Paul said.

I got some glasses out of the cabinet. Mom was busy cooing over Pandora saying "sweet, pretty dog," as if Pandora was a little bit of a thing and not the imposing canine she was.

We drank and laughed together for the rest of the night with my parents. Paul, Pandora and I walked them to the cozy bed and breakfast nearby where they had booked a room.

The next day was spent showing my parents the beautiful city of Amsterdam that was now my home. They loved the canal boat ride Paul's friend Jaap took us on, and the beautiful old buildings. We were all invited to Rick and Rachel's for dinner in the evening, so my parents could meet Paul's family and we could begin our celebration of Rosh Hashanah together.

Rachel had arranged to have some of our special holiday foods, such as challah, a sweet braided bread made from lots of eggs, and apples dipped in honey, to usher in a sweet year.

After dinner, Vanessa took my mother and me into her studio to show us her paintings. Some were hanging on the walls, as they were completed. Others were on easels, waiting for the devoted and talented attention of Vanessa.

"These paintings are wonderful!" my mother said to Vanessa. "Look Deena, look at the beautiful scenes of parks. The colors, the serenity, the people all relaxing with their families! And the ponds, I love them the best."

"So do I," said Vanessa. "Do you see in each painting I have a pair of beautiful white swans? Swans mate for life, did you know that Aunt Deena? I want you to choose one of these paintings for you and Uncle Jean-Paul as a wedding gift from me. And Grandmother, please choose one for you and Grandfather to take back to Baltimore with you."

My mother and I looked at each other for a few moments. Our hands touched and we could read each other's minds. We shared the same thoughts, and those were of love for Vanessa, who needed me and now needed my mother and father as her new grandparents. We knew the swans represented Paul and me, and our relationship which started out as one of sex and desire, and grew into one of true love.

Vanessa wanted to join Paul and me and my parents when we went to synagogue the next morning to worship for Rosh Hashanah. I think Vanessa would have taken any opportunity to spend more time with my mother. We arranged to meet in front of the houseboat the next morning at ten o'clock.

Rosh Hashanah morning was warm and beautiful, just as it so often was in New York. Pandora accompanied my parents, Vanessa, Paul and me as we walked along the canals and streets of Amsterdam. My parents' first view of the old Portuguese synagogue overwhelmed them.

My father took me aside, held my hand, and said to me, "Deena, I can now see why you love this old city so much. So much Jewish history here, and so much you have contributed to this city already. You have reinvented an old Jewish artistry here in Amsterdam. And soon, you will start a family here. I love you my daughter, I do!"

Before my parents left for Berlin on Sunday, my father wanted to have a man to man talk with Paul, so they took a walk along the Prinsengracht together. Momma was very excited to show me something as soon as the men had left. She took an envelope from her purse.

"Here Deena, look at this," she said as she opened the envelope. "It's a picture dated June 14, 1865. I can't believe it has survived in the attic all these years. We've been cleaning out the old house in Fell's Point, thinking we might move to a condo nearby."

"Who are those people, Momma?" I said as I looked at the picture. "The woman is very beautiful, and the man is so handsome. They made a great couple, didn't they?"

"The woman is your great great great great grandmother Delilah," she said. "I don't know who the man is though. It says on the back simply *Daniel and Delilah, June 14, 1865.*"

I looked more closely at the photo. The man had an uncanny resemblance to Paul. Daniel's skin looked darker than Paul's. Otherwise, minus the scar, it could have been Paul himself. And I looked very much like my distant grandmother.

"Can I have the picture Momma?" I asked her.

"Of course sweetheart of course. What are you thinking, my love? I know y'all are thinkin' bout something," she said.

"Yes I am. Paul said something unusual when we first met on the plane. He told me I looked very familiar to him. I thought at the time it was just a good pick up line. Now I'm thinking there was more to it, there's more to Paul and me. Much more, Momma, so much more."

Chapter 47
The Trial

After saying our goodbyes to my parents at the airport, Paul drove back to Spice Island. I thought about Vanessa and my mother. I was grateful Vanessa was able to establish such a warm and loving relationship with her. She would need all the love and comfort to strengthen her in dealing with the days culminating in the trial.

The trial was scheduled for Tuesday, September 17. Erika visited with Vanessa several times to let her know what type of questions to expect from the prosecuting attorney, Sander's attorney and the Judge. Judge Talitha Appelman had been appointed to the case. Erika said Judge Appelman was very familiar with juvenile sex offender cases. The problem was Her Honor made varied decisions, based on the merits of each case. There was no way to know how she would rule in this one.

We all arrived at the courthouse promptly at nine o'clock on Tuesday - Rick, Rachel and Vanessa, Paul and me, and Pandora. It was a typical rainy Amsterdam day. Erika had arranged previously with the prosecuting attorney, Frans Van Dyck, and Judge Appelman for Pandora to accompany Vanessa to the trial and be with her at all times.

Soon after we arrived, Sander Smit, his father Stefan and Sander's attorney Niels Niemands arrived. Stefan Smit approached

Paul as we were seated in the courtroom. He said to Paul loudly enough so he could be heard by everyone, "Sander is pleading not guilty. And we will win this case. You will look like a fool, and you will lose in the City Council election."

Paul ignored Smit. I was grateful he did, as we had a long day ahead of us, and we all needed our strength to lend support to Vanessa.

Judge Appelman arrived and the courtroom was quiet with respect for her. She was in her early 40s, tall, slim and pretty, with blond hair cut short and bright intelligent blue eyes. Paul had explained to me that in The Netherlands there were no jury trials. The judge made the legal determination in each case.

Mr. Van Dyck was the first person to speak. He explained the details of the case, how Sander had initially manipulated Vanessa into trusting him as a boyfriend and then with threats, coercion and drugs, forced her to act as a prostitute over a two month period of time.

Mr. Van Dyck called Sander to the witness stand. Pandora growled as Sander walked to the front of the room. Paul quickly told her to be quiet in Dutch and pulled on her leash. Judge Appelman said sternly, "I am sure you are aware, Mr. Vermeer, we can not have a disturbance like that again in this courtroom."

"Yes, your Honor, I apologize," Paul said, with a slight smile on his face. Judge Appelman returned the smile. Paul leaned over to me and whispered, "We are in luck, Deena. Judge Appelman is known to be an animal lover. She has two German shepherds of her own, former guide dogs."

"Proceed with your questioning of the accused, Mr. Van Dyck," Judge Appelman prompted him.

Mr. Van Dyck: Yes, thank you, Your Honor. Please state your name.

Sander: My name is Sander Smit.

Mr. Van Dyck: How old are you, Sander?

Sander: I am seventeen.

Mr. Van Dyck: Are you acquainted with Vanessa Vermeer?

Sander: She is a classmate of mine at my high school.

Mr. Van Dyck: And you have no other knowledge of her?

Sander: No.

Mr. Van Dyck: She has never been your girlfriend?

Sander: No.

Vanessa began to cry softly. She reached for Pandora's neck and put her arms around her.

Mr. Van Dyck: And you have never been in De Wallen with Ms. Vermeer?

Sander: No.

Mr. Van Dyck: You have never forced her to be a prostitute? You have never acted as her pimp?

Vanessa was crying louder, as she reached to hug Pandora again. But Pandora was not near Vanessa any longer. She had slowly walked up to Sander, and leaned aggressively towards him, growling loudly.

"Please, Mr. Vermeer, one more time and you must take your dog out of the courtroom," the Judge demanded. "Let's take a short recess. Mr. Van Dyck, have you completed your questioning of Mr. Smit?"

"Yes, Your Honor," Mr. Van Dyck replied.

After the fifteen minute recess, Mr. Van Dyck called his next witness.

"I call David Coen as my next witness," Mr. Van Dyck said.

Vanessa and Sander both gasped at the same moment. "I can't believe it," Vanessa said. "I never thought David would be brave enough to do this."

Mr. Van Dyck: State your name please.

David: My name is David Coen.

Mr. Van Dyck: How old are you, David?

David: I'm seventeen.

Mr. Van Dyck: Do you know the defendant, Sander Smit?

David: Yes he is, mmm was, my friend.

Mr. Van Dyck: Please tell us what you know about Vanessa and Sander.

David: Sander and Vanessa were boyfriend and girlfriend. Sander would brag about how he could get Vanessa to do anything he wanted her to do. Our friends didn't believe him. One night, Sander said he would prove it to us. We went to his house when his parents were out. He told Vanessa she had to have sex with all four of us, plus Sander.

Mr. Van Dyck: What happened next?

David: I tried to tell Sander that was not the right way to treat Vanessa, if he loved her like he said he did. He told me to leave, but I didn't. I wanted to try and protect Vanessa somehow. She was high on something. He said she had to do each of us, to prove she loved him.

One of the guys wanted to be first. When Vanessa realized what was going to happen, she started screaming, No, no, Finn, no please, don't make me do this.

The first guy forced her to have sex with him. She cried and screamed the whole time. By the second and third time, she was so tired she just let it happen. When my turn came, I told her to come outside with me on the porch. I didn't make her do anything. I just held her, and let her cry.

Sander threatened us all. He said if we told anyone about this, he would hurt us or someone in our family. He turned really mean that night. I stopped being friends with him after that.

Mr. Van Dyck: Thank you David. You may step down now.

As David made his way towards Vanessa, Sander began shouting at him. "You're a liar, you dirty Jew! You'll pay for this!"

"That is enough, young man! This is a court of law. And I have heard all the testimony I need to make a decision in this case. The police reports and Vanessa's statements to the officers will guide me as well. We will reconvene at three o'clock this afternoon," the Judge said.

We knew Judge Appelman would find Sander guilty, but were totally in the dark as to how she would sentence him.

When we came back at three o'clock, the Judge didn't hesitate as she spoke.

"I find the defendant Sander Smit guilty as charged - rape, assault and battery and forcing a minor to act as prostitute, human trafficking. I am sentencing Sander as a minor. I have consulted with two psychiatrists by telephone during the recess, who are experts in juvenile psychopathology, and they have helped me to make the following decision. Sander will be remanded to a residential juvenile psychiatric facility for a period of one year. His case will be reviewed after one year, will a possible extension of the mandatory stay in the facility for up to a period of three years total. When he is released from the residential facility, he will have mandatory counseling for a period of two years, and be on probation.

"This is an unusual case in The Netherland because so-called loverboys, boys who take advantage of their girlfriends in such a deviant way, have up until now for the most part been foreign born Dutch citizens or residents. As this may be the beginning of a new trend in juvenile social deviancy, I am calling for an education program in the high schools to teach male students how to treat young woman properly. The message should be that not every young woman in Amsterdam is a potential prostitute. I am asking our elected officials, and those to be newly elected, to follow up on my recommendation. Is that clear, Mr. Vermeer?"

"Yes, Judge Appelman," Paul said as he stood up and

approached the bench. "I understand your recommendation, and thank you on behalf of Vanessa and her family for your learned decision."

"Isn't this a lenient sentence, your honor?" I couldn't help but comment.

"Well, as an American, Ms. Green, you may be unfamiliar with criminal justice here in The Netherlands," Judge Appelman said. "Compared to the average sentence of five months detention for juvenile rapists in this country, this is a very severe sentence, indeed. Two thirds of all juvenile rapists are not sentenced to detention at all. My decision will be noted as groundbreaking in legal circles as well as by the general population.

"Thank you for your patience in this case. And now, Sander Smit, please accompany the court officer. He will take you to the psychiatric facility. You are young and can learn quickly to change your ways, if you apply yourself. The court is adjourned," she concluded.

Before we left the courthouse, Vanessa reached down and hugged Pandora to her with all her might. "You saved me. You are so brave, Dora. You saved me," Vanessa said.

We all looked at one another and silently agreed.

Chapter 48
Wedding Day

I was consumed with last minute preparations the week before the wedding. Paul was busy with work, he said, so I could concentrate on the final fittings of my wedding dress and other last minute details.

My dress was made for a fairy tale princess. Giselle, Karime and I had designed it together. It was ivory in color, with a low, rounded neckline, thin gauze sleeves and a lace train. There were pale pink and green flowers around the tight waist and trimming the train.

With the trial behind her, Vanessa was free to use her artistic talents to design the floral arrangements. They were all in wondrous shades of pink. Vanessa was to be my maid of honor and her dress was the palest of pinks.

Paul was keeping two secrets from me – what his wedding suit looked like, and where we were going on our honeymoon. When I pressed him for details, he said only, "be patient my princess, you'll not have long to wait."

Our wedding rings were hand crafted by the first Jewish artisans to arrive in Amsterdam from New York. They were simple thick gold bands, with a thin line of small diamonds in the middle of each ring.

Finally our wedding day arrived! The weather was sunny and beautiful, temperature in the low 70s in Rheinberg.

My friends were getting me ready in Gisselle's room. I didn't know where Paul was dressing. Hans, who was a local magistrate, would be officiating at the wedding.

The large lawn in back of the castle was where the wedding ceremony would be held. We were expecting about fifty guests, and there were as many chairs divided on two sides of a center aisle on the lawn. Bouquets of flowers in all colors adorned the aisle on either side.

The wedding band began playing and everyone was quiet, anticipating our entrance. First Vanessa walked down the aisle, serene and beautiful with her dark hair flowing down her back. Rachel and Rick followed her, finally both looking happy and relieved. Then it was Paul's turn. I saw him as I waited with my parents, and couldn't believe how striking he looked. He was dressed in a dark brown silk suit jacket and very slim brown silk pants, tucked into brown leather boots that came to his mid calf. His shirt was of ivory linen, with a Mandarin banded collar, buttoned at the neck. Walking next to him down the aisle was the regal Pandora, with a garland of pink flowers around her neck.

Paul looked so handsome to me, so royal. He was my prince and I couldn't wait for the ceremony to begin.

All the guests stood as Paul and Pandora walked past them. They waited for me half way down the aisle.

It was my turn next. With a thin veil covering my face, my father and mother led me down the aisle to meet Paul. I heard oo's and ah's as everyone looked at me, but I only wanted to know how Paul felt about seeing me in my wedding dress.

His blue eyes were ablaze with love and passion as he took my right hand from my father, and slowly raised it to his lips, kissing each finger just as he did on our first night together at Tempo Doeloe. I took his hand and kissed each of his fingers gently. We were ready for our two lives to become one.

For most of the ceremony, I could concentrate only on Paul, on how he was looking at me with the promise of love and passion.

When it was his turn to speak, he got down on one knee, took my right hand, kissed it and said to me, "Deena, my one and only love, my magical princess, our hearts and our souls have been together forever, and will continue to be together in this world. Will you marry me, yes? I promise to love you, to honor you, to respect you and cherish you, from this day forward, and forevermore."

I answered Paul, saying, "yes, I will marry you, Jean-Paul, my dearest prince. I promise to love you, to honor you, to respect you and cherish you, from this day forward, and forevermore."

Hans declared, "I now pronounce you man and wife! You may now kiss the bride!"

Paul stood up, embraced me and we kissed - long, hot, wet. Time stood still. I felt we were blessed for all eternity with our love for each other.

Soon, the explosion of happiness everyone felt for us reached us, and we were brought back to reality, to the castle garden once more. We walked to the great hall of the castle, where the reception was held.

The band played all types of music. My parents and I were especially thrilled with the band's klezmer style rendition of Jewish music. We held hands and danced in circles. Paul and I were lifted up on chairs and carried in celebration. The older guests ate and relaxed, content to watch us and our friends dance to the latest songs, especially our favorite, "Where Have You Been All My Life."

Our guests made a large circle around us, as Paul held me in his arms, our hips swaying together in time to the music. We both were hot and sweaty. Paul had taken off his jacket earlier. He now slowly unbuttoned his shirt. Everyone was encouraging him, but Paul saw and heard only me.

"We will be leaving on our honeymoon now, but first there is something I must show you," he said to me, as he took off his shirt and displayed his right shoulder. There in large dark blue letters in an ornate script was a tattoo that said D E E N A, with a heart on either side.

"Thank you all for celebrating our wedding with us! Bye, we love you all!" Paul shouted happily.

Chapter 49

Honeymoon and More

We waved goodbye. Then Paul took my hand and led me to the front door of the castle. There waiting for us was a magnificent black stallion. His reins were held by Worster, one of the stable hands at the castle. "Here is our transportation to our honeymoon hideaway, my love! His name is Passion Pete, or Pete for short!" Paul said.

"But where are we going? And what about suitcases, clothes?" I wanted to know.

"Don't worry, my sweetheart, I've arranged for every detail, yes. Now, let me assist you, Madame, in mounting your stallion," he said as he gave my rear a hard squeeze, picked me up at the waist and placed me on a bareback pad on Passion Pete. Paul positioned himself on the stallion in front of me.

"I thought you were my stallion," I said in Paul's ear. "Haven't I been good at mounting you?" I held on tight as Paul turned Passion Pete around, squeezed his calf muscles against the horse's girth, as we galloped away from the castle.

"Pete and I are both in a hurry to arrive at our honeymoon cabin!" Paul called to me.

After my initial panic at Passion Pete's pace, Paul slowed the horse down to a trot. I relaxed and enjoyed the scenery. We were traveling through a thickly wooded area Pete seemed very familiar with. After about an hour, Paul dismounted and helped me down from the stallion, who gratefully drank water and ate some food waiting for him. Paul tied Pete's reins to a tree.

"Welcome to our home for this week, Mrs. Vermeer," Paul said proudly to me, as he put his arm tightly around my waist and led me to the entrance. "This is an old hunting lodge Hans let me refurbish just for us, yes. I hope you like it."

Paul opened the door, picked me up under my arms and rear, and carried me over the threshold. Pete whinnied and went back to eating his dinner.

"What do you think, lover?" Paul asked. I looked around at the interior of the cabin, which was one very large room. The walls were made of wood logs. A huge fireplace dominated one wall of the room, with a small table and four chairs in front of it. Another wall had an old cooking stove and some wooden kitchen cabinets. But the focal point of the room was a king sized bed. It was in the center of the room. Its headboard and footboard were carved from dark old wood. Against the headboard were several white pillows trimmed in lace. The blanket was made of white fur, lined with white satin. There were candlesticks on the table near the fireplace and on the night tables next to the bed. Two armoires held clothes for Paul and me. In my armoire were jeans, short fur jackets, walking boots and shoes, and sexy nightgowns and underwear.

"I love it! So romantic, so other world," I said, kissing him on his lips.

"Yes, old world. No phones, no email. The only concession I made to this world is a modern toilette. We will live here for the week, with our passion and the fireplace to keep us warm! Worster will provide us with all of our meals.

"Let me help you take off your dress. We both smell like stallion. I asked Worster to prepare a hot bath for us."

In one corner of the room was a large white antique tub, filled with hot water.

"Come with me wife. Let me bathe you." Paul took off my dress and underwear and coaxed me into the hot water. He then quickly stripped his clothes off and joined me, facing me in the tub. I moved close to him so I could inhale his smells and taste him.

"Not yet, sweetheart. First our bath. Then I have another treat in store for you, yes."

He turned me around and began washing my back with soap that smelled like sandalwood. He continued washing me everywhere, my face, my breasts, my neck, underarms and in between my legs.

From a separate basin of water he wet my hair and then washed it too.

He got out of the tub, grabbed some towels nearby, and helped me out, drying every part of me.

He lay fresh towels on the fur blanket and commanded me to lie on my stomach, with my back and rear exposed to him. The next thing I felt was his strong hands rubbing warm oil on my neck, my back, my ass, my legs. I closed my eyes, for how long I don't really know. Paul woke me with kisses on my cheeks, my rounded rear.

"You are rested? You are ready for me, yes?" he said.

He turned me over gently and I looked into his eyes. The passion was there in the dark blue color they turned during our lovemaking. His thick black hair was the same, and so was his familiar crooked grin with its devilish look. His body – yes – his chest was outlined in the same deep dark chest hair. My hand found his erection easily. The room was lit only by candles.

Something though was different about him. I looked at his face again, and the scar on his cheek had disappeared! Without thinking I reached to touch the place where it had been.

"Don't question, Deena," Paul warned, his voice deep with a dangerous tone to it.

"Let's just experience each other this week, yes. We have always been together. And always will be," he said as he kissed my lips softly, teasingly.

We wanted our first night together as husband and wife to last forever. Paul was more gentle than he had ever been to me. He lingered over each kiss, each lick of his tongue on mine, each sweet suckling of my breasts. When I reached down to stroke his manhood, he pushed my hand aside. "Not yet, my sweet. Not yet," he said. "Let me first show you how much I love each and every part of you."

And he did. His wet hot lips and his luscious tongue caressed me. He brought me to a sexual crescendo that was achingly beautiful. More wonderful than any music was the sound of his voice saying "Deena, Deena, DEENA!" as we reached an orgasmic ending to the first part of our honeymoon symphony.

The week was a blur of passion and desire. I could not get enough of him, and he needed me every waking moment. I caught a glimpse of myself in a pond during one of our walks through the forest. The color of my hair had turned redder, as if it was on fire, just like it was on our first night together in the Indonesian restaurant.

Was our honeymoon a dream, a fantasy, a fairy tale? It all seemed magical but he was only too real to me. Our mornings were spent lovemaking, and eating the food Worster silently left for us. Our afternoons were spent walking in the woods, watching the wonderful changing color of leaves from green to reds, yellows and oranges. Evenings and nights were spent eating dinner in front of the fireplace, and making love again and again and again.

At the end of the week, riding back to Rheinberg on Passion Pete, Paul stopped for a moment so the stallion could take a drink from a stream. He looked back at me, and I saw the scar had returned to his face. I took a lock of my hair in my hand, and saw it was once again its original reddish blonde color.

"Don't worry, we will return to our honeymoon hideaway, yes my love, we will," he reassured me. I hugged Paul tightly, leaning my head on him for the rest of the ride back to the castle.

I now knew that Paul was mine. I would never question his love and devotion to me again.

Once upon a time, was he mine as well?

ABOUT THE AUTHOR

Cassandra Dallas has lived her entire life on Long Island, New York, in close proximity to John F. Kennedy International Airport. The location has made for noisy backyard barbeques, but has afforded her the opportunity to travel to Amsterdam at a moment's notice.

Besides being infatuated with that Dutch city, Cassandra is obsessed with large dogs and handsome men, or is it handsome dogs and large men?

Cassandra is hopeful you will enjoy her first novel. She is currently working on her second book - PG 13 - and a third one - R tending towards X-rated.

Terminal 1
Counter 1 A